Lucky Ride

A Novel

LUCKY RIDE
Copyright©2021 TERRY TIERNEY
All Rights Reserved
Published by Unsolicited Press
Printed in the United States of America.
First Edition Printed in 2021.
This is a work of fiction. Names, characters, places, and incidents are products of the author's imagination or are used fictitiously and are not to be construed as real. Any resemblance to actual events, locales, or persons living or dead is entirely coincidental.
All rights reserved. Printed in the United States of America. No part of this book may be used or reproduced in any manner whatsoever without written permission except in the case of brief quotations embodied in critical articles or reviews.

Attention schools and businesses: for discounted copies on large orders, please contact the publisher directly.

For information contact:
Unsolicited Press
Portland, Oregon
www.unsolicitedpress.com
orders@unsolicitedpress.com
619-354-8005

Cover Design: Kathryn Gerhardt
Editor: S.R. Stewart
ISBN: 978-1-950730-93-3

Lucky Ride

A Novel

By Terry Tierney

The author would like to thank members of his writing groups, particularly The Berkeley Writing Circle, for their community and feedback, his editor Dorothy Wall, and Michaelyn Burnette for her literary mentorship.

Chapter 1

NO SOONER DID I decide to hitchhike to California than I got a surprise call from Rick Gardiner, one of my buddies from the Navy. He had just delivered a load of Mexican marijuana to Boston, and he would swing through Binghamton in a few days. Did he want company on his drive back to Fort Worth? You bet. Hanging up the phone, I was already gone, off on my first lucky ride, a thousand miles of interstate from my wife Ronnie's affair with her boss.

Rick pulled up in front of our apartment, the top floor of a rundown triplex, on a Wednesday evening. The family of Jesus freaks who lived below us was already asleep, but I saw Grandma Roller peeking through her bedroom curtains when I went to help him unload. There wasn't much to witness that night: just Rick in his blue jeans, unbuttoned white shirt, three empty Coke cans in one hand, and his wild blonde hair flopping over his John Lennon glasses and scruffy beard. He leaned over the trunk and dragged out his Navy issue duffel bag stuffed with marijuana and dirty laundry.

The hood of his old '64 Ford steamed under the streetlamp, its red paint flaked off from the heat, revealing the gray primer underneath as if it had driven through licks of fire. I listened to faint cracks of metal and escaping air as the huge machine began to cool. With hot forged steel, thick joints and beams, the car was built to drive all night long. Rick could tell I was ready to leave right then, but he wanted a bed and a smoke. We were quiet, not to wake the neighbors, but we shook hands and hugged like brothers, spilling his Coke cans onto the soggy lawn. One of the things that always impressed me about Rick was how he could chug a Coke with one gulp and ask for another, his one bigger-than-life Texas habit.

"Hey Flash, good to see you out of the suck," he said.

My friends called me Flash because of my uncanny good luck and because I was often slow to make decisions. I liked to check all the angles as if my life were plotted on one vast astronomy chart. Rick glanced up at the porch.

"Ronnie's working late, but she'll be home soon."

Rick and I retreated to the rusty kitchen table, eating ginger snap cookies, and drinking a pot of deep black coffee brewed in the electric percolator, our only luxury and purchased at a discount from my dad's company store. I retrieved a jar of Tang from the cupboard.

"Remember all that Tang we drank when we were stoned?" Rick asked, helping himself and recalling the time we were stationed together on Adak in the remote Aleutian Islands.

"The official beverage of astronauts." I stirred a heaping spoonful into a jelly glass and downed it, smacking my lips.

Clearing space on the table, I lined up baggies in front of my chemist's scale while Rick retrieved my pound of Mexican from his duffle bag.

"How about $105?" he asked. "My Seabee discount."

"The best GI benefit," I nodded, calculating how I could sell ounces for twenty and finance my trip with the proceeds.

We dumped the pound out of a large freezer bag and admired the brick's silver rectangular shape, a loaf of dope wound in duct tape. I tore off the tape. The weed had an earthy smell, one tangled dark mass with flecks of mold. We broke up the clumps and threw away the big sticks – some of them as thick as pencils – and most of the seeds. We made sure each ounce was equal and a good count. The pound weighed out 15 1/2 ounces. Not bad for a Mafia score.

"I'll make up the difference," Rick said. "It's not like I'm short of dope."

"Nah, we'll probably smoke the difference before we hit Texas."

Rick rolled a joint from his private stash of well over a pound of sifted marijuana packed in a plastic bag like the one we just emptied, large enough to store a turkey. We assessed the character of Rick's weed like Ivy Leaguers tasting Daddy's wine.

"Smokes dry," Rick said. "Has a nutty taste."

"Good quality," I squeaked in my high hit-holding voice.

"No distinctive bouquet."

"Table dope."

When Rick headed for the shower, I took the dog outside. I had liked Bobo better when he was a puppy before Ronnie countermanded all my attempts to train him. She claimed he was a free spirit with all the inherent rights of existence, and it was not our place to discipline him; he should answer to his own being, not what we wanted him to be. He was his own dog.

And ever true to his sense of purpose, he raced for the neighbor's garbage can as soon as I let him loose. Bobo gathered his momentum and launched himself like a canine Evel Kneival, a small white and black stunt dog, hurling himself over the rim, expertly catching the edge, and tipping the can. Before I caught him, he had torn a hole in the plastic garbage bag and pulled out a chicken carcass that smelled worse than anything I could imagine. He growled and shook it back and forth. I managed to grab his collar and drag him back to the clothesline while I collected the remains of his feast.

I stood up from the pail of garbage and scanned the overcast sky beyond the streetlights, trying to catch a fresh breeze to chase the putrid odor of rotting potatoes, sour coffee grounds, and blackened hamburger packages. Spring was oozing down the hillside, and the wind smelled of dead leaves and wet mud, a mildewed smell. Under the thickest stands of spruce, the dirt was still frozen in an icy crust, though it was the first week of May. The sky never brightened, but it seldom rained, just a dreary intermittent mist changing to snow if the temperature dropped. Only a few buds had cracked on the trees, and the pale, gray branches merged into the gray canopy of sky. I wondered if the trees and flowers would ever bloom.

For our converted triplex, ugly in any season, it was the worst time of year. Without the seasonal blankets of snow or leaves, the old house revealed its poor upkeep. A large farmhouse successively remodeled by generations of handy men, it sprawled up and back from the street like the abandoned shells of a colony of mussels. Green shingles of varying shades from moss to canned spinach covered the roof. Looking over the old farmhouse apartments and the gray sky made me want to leave even more and head south, where it was sure to be warmer and brighter. And then west to the sparkling Pacific.

While I had waited for orders to Alaska, Ronnie and I had lived on the beach in Ventura, where my friend Jack now lived. We spent most nights on the warm sand, watching plankton erupt in neon tubes of blue light and spread across the breakers, only to fade like an idea you can't quite articulate. The blue would ignite again and spread across the wave and the next like a strange, ethereal presence.

Spying my neighbor's light, I decided David would be my first sale. I found him lying back in the Lazy Boy recliner he had salvaged from Volunteers. David was about my height and just as thin with a sharply chiseled face and rough complexion. His hands were wide and strong with calluses and blackened scratches from his night job fixing cars. He carried himself with an air of mystery, which had to do with his tour in Vietnam, but he only mentioned it late at night when he might recall the hot mud or the superior smoke. The skinny joints he rolled were holdovers from Southeast Asia, but given the quality of the Mexican marijuana we usually scored in Binghamton, each one was only about as intoxicating as a Camel.

I rolled a thick joint. After a few tokes, David's expression turned serious. "Ronnie told Janey she's not happy about your trip."

I took a hit and held it, shrugging my shoulders. Ronnie and David's wife Janey were fast friends, closer than David and me.

"She says you're leaving her with no money."

"She can take care of herself." I waved the joint, trying to read David's blank expression to see how much he knew about Ronnie and her boss Mr. Bardeen skipping lunch most days to rock and roll in the backseat of Bardeen's family Buick. "So, what about the smoke?"

David was a tough sell, but I knew he would bend. He bought a quarter pound for $60. I rolled another joint to seal the bargain, a thin one this time.

"Seriously, Flash. If Ronnie needs anything, all she has to do is ask. She'll be up there by herself."

I paused at the door. "You could help her sell some weed if I don't sell it all."

We agreed he could have an ounce in payment if he sold three for Ronnie, and if our old Plymouth broke down, he'd fix it for free.

Back in our apartment, Rick and I finished off the pot of coffee, waiting for Ronnie. About eleven, she appeared, clutching a bag of Mother's Ginger Snaps, my favorite, replenishing our supply. She wore the black cape she had worn since college, which always made her look sexy, hanging down to her thin waist and emphasizing her full breasts and long legs. The tips of her straight, black hair rested on her shoulders, and her bangs had grown long and untrimmed, framing her brown eyes. Tilting her head in the questioning smile she often used, she held out her hand to Rick. Although she appeared athletic, her manner was careless and unpracticed as if she might slip at any moment.

Rick reflexively leaned in her direction as I often did.

My pulse clicked up a beat. This was the old Ronnie, the one I thought of as Ronnie the Rebel, the carefree woman I fell in love with, not the woman who now worried about our impending lack of money once the GI checks ran out. We had one more check coming for the semester, and I would have plenty of time to find a summer job when I came back from California. If I decided to come back.

Ronnie gave Rick's hand a quick shake. "How much weed did you run to Boston?" she asked.

"About 130 pounds."

"Wow, such an outlaw." She pulled off her cape and threw it across a spare chair. Her T-shirt rode up her firm stomach.

"Sold it all too," Rich stammered, his cheeks reddening.

"Except for your personal stash," I added.

Ronnie sat side saddle on her chair. "Every man needs a personal stash." She reached for the pile of weed on yesterday's sports section and commenced rolling a ceremonial number.

Sitting at the kitchen table with Ronnie and Rick, my memories flowed and mixed. On Adak, Rick and I had spent a series of weekends in the kitchen of an abandoned mess hall, barely standing from World War II, playing our guitars with Jack Ferro and Phil Briones, high on grass and LSD. I remembered how much I had wanted Ronnie with us as we sang our lonely songs, sounding almost perfect like Crosby, Stills, Nash, and Young. Now, in our apartment, my dreams should have been answered with Ronnie's soft voice probing our memories. She waved her hands over the table when she talked as if she were directing my emotions, and I felt mesmerized by her presence despite the hundreds of evenings we had shared.

We left the kitchen for the floor pillows around our wire spool, where Rick and I took turns playing my guitar with Ronnie joining now and again with her electric piano turned low. Grandma Roller didn't seem to mind our music, and if she did, it served her right for inviting me to sing at their Spirit coffee house, which I never did, and sending up a stream of teenaged Jesus freaks to pray for my soul. If we played for our souls that night none of us played very well, and we soon tired. Ronnie fixed a bed of blankets and sleeping bags on the living room floor for Rick.

When she came to bed, she opened the window. Wisps of her dark hair blew across her brow and back over her head. Her eyes gleamed in the dim halo of the reading lamp.

"You finally met Rick." I watched her undress.

"He's the blondest man ever." She rolled down her pantyhose. "I love his accent. Not twangy like a redneck."

"Too much time around us Yankees."

"He reminds me of the Sundance Kid."

I laughed. "You're attracted to him."

"You're so paranoid."

I laid back and stared at the stained ceiling.

"You need to work on redirecting your feelings," Ronnie continued. She was a psychology major before she dropped out of college, and this was her usual diagnosis. During our fights, she said the same thing about my feelings toward Bardeen. She thought I made too much of him, insisting she just felt sorry for him. I never understood how she could pity him and still sleep with him. I didn't feel sorry for him in the least. I wondered how long I could repress all the phobias Ronnie had identified, and how long I could keep myself from grabbing him by the throat. I was sick with jealousy and the risk of losing her.

I sat up and reached across the bed, but she slid away, promising a more prolonged hug in a few minutes. She stripped and raced toward the shower, draped only in a tattered beach towel, a remnant of our trip to California after I was released from boot camp. On her way through the living room, she stepped over Rick, who was already asleep, curled up in my Boy Scout sleeping bag.

I traced her footsteps through the apartment, listening to the bathroom door open and close. I heard the shower gush and imagined her stepping lightly over the lip of the tub and swinging her hair back over her sleek shoulders. Something in her artless manner made her irresistible and easy to forgive. This would be our last night together, maybe forever, and my desire for her surged. The nerves beneath my skin tingled for her touch.

She strode into our bedroom, moist and dripping, unwrapped her towel and leapt under the covers. She squirmed close to absorb my body heat. I twisted my arm around her wet hair and shoulders.

"Wow, you're really going to truck off. I'm jealous." She sounded like it was the first time she had known my plans.

I shifted my position, so we were lying side by side, facing one another. Her eyes focused in a distant stare as if there were someone else in the room. I glanced around and listened for Bardeen's middle-aged wheeze. I would never ask if she was thinking about Bardeen, but I knew she was. His presence passed over us like a cold breath.

She said, "Please don't go, Flash. You belong here with me. I love you."

"I love you too," I said automatically. But it was the truth. I still loved her enough that I would have changed my mind about leaving right then if I thought it would make a difference.

"I promised Jack I'd visit him," I added. It was a hollow excuse, and she knew it.

"I can't believe you're going back to Ventura without me," she said. "Remember how we sat on the beach at night and watched the waves break? Holding each other all night long, wrapped in that scratchy, wool blanket you stole from the barracks? That night we made love so long we were sore, and we could hardly walk back to the apartment? Those two months in Ventura seem like a dream."

I nodded, wondering how our marriage might have progressed if I had not been ordered to Adak. If I could rerun our marriage, I would keep it there in a warm stasis of ocean, sand, and unquestioned love.

"I think we should have a baby," she continued as if parenthood was just another detail of her California vision.

"I don't think we're ready to have a baby."

She looked at me. "You'd rather hitchhike to California."

I shook my head.

She waited for an answer.

"What about Bardeen?" His name shocked her since we seldom said it aloud.

"You're obsessed with him," she shot back. "He has nothing to do with this."

I glanced toward the living room, hoping our voices would not wake Rick. When Ronnie didn't answer, I added, "Grandma saw his car the night I took my astronomy exam."

"That old bitch."

"So, he was here." I shook my head, remembering how she had tried to end their relationship several times or at least she said so. Bardeen seemed like the runaway dog on her doorstep, tired and muddy from his ordeal. Bobo in a cheap polyester suit. Ronnie always let him in, and I always let her in. The only way I could break the dizzy cycle was to leave.

"It's not like you think." Ronnie forced her voice lower. "He's just a friend. He understands how I feel about wanting to have a family and wanting to have a real life. He's someone I can talk to. Whenever I try to talk to you, you think I'm pressuring you to drop out of college and get a job."

I turned away from her.

"You don't want to have a real marriage," she said. "You want us to live like hippies forever."

"I never said that. I think we should both finish college before we worry about buying a house or having a family. That's what we always planned."

"How can we afford tuition for both of us?"

"We'll make it." I stroked her cheek. "Hey, I'm lucky, remember? Just like Rick showing up with a ride and a pound of weed to finance my trip. My luck will pull us through."

"I think you like living like this," she continued in the same tone.

"Well, I don't hate it as much as you do. You used to say you didn't care how we lived as long as we were together."

"We're not together. You're going to California."

"Why don't you come with me?"

"You know I can't just pick up and leave." She sat up as if she knew what I was going to say. But I would not bring up Bardeen again, even if he was more important to her than her minimum wage job. She faced me. Our tense expressions filled the space of his unspoken name. "If you don't want to settle down, what's the point of being married?"

I held her eyes, biting back my anger.

"You should stay in California," she hissed and flopped back down, pressing her face to the pillow. She started to cry.

"I never said I was coming back." I was unsure if she heard me.

For a long moment, I lay there thinking I should say something. I touched the back of her head, but she shook me off. I twisted away and lay back down, staring at the ceiling, its paint chips and mold stains appearing like shadows in the dim light of our bed lamp. I wished they were stars, something I could see more clearly, that they might form constellations and help me navigate.

When I finally reached across the blankets to comfort her, unable to resist her crying for long, she accepted my touch, and our bodies wound together like nuclei of the same cell, thin membranes of skin merging. Ronnie clutched my back like she'd never let go, and I pressed her to me. Our hearts beat with the same pulse, blood of the same flesh, squeezing out the cold draft from the open window.

As our sweat began to cool, Ronnie drifted off to sleep, her breasts pressed to my chest and her legs intertwined with mine. She whispered into my neck. "Please don't go."

I reached over and tucked the blanket more firmly around her, unwilling to get up and close the window.

"We fit together." Her voice was weak, dreamlike.

I softly stroked her shoulder as she began to snore. "Like a puzzle."

I lay awake and watched her sleep, wishing I were two men, one who remained by her side and one who tore himself away, heading for warmer climates and an earlier spring.

Chapter 2

RICK AND I took off the next afternoon and sped down through Scranton, cruising at seventy on I-81, a nonstop drive to Fort Worth. Twenty-four hours if the weather held. His old Ford barreled past school buses and commuters, oblivious to the dreary staccato rain and overcast sky. Inside, we traveled in comfort, just enough heat, our last New York joint snubbed out, leaving a healthy roach for our pre-dinner cocktail. The local rock station blasted The Beatles. We crooned over the radio, singing along with "Get Back."

Flash left his home in Binghamton, New York, for some California grass...

We yelled back and forth like auctioneers, our blood surging, carburetor sucking hard, Rick's foot to the floor. The Pennsylvania hills and forest greens blurred past our windows.

Before we left, we each dropped two white crosses. David had traded us twenty whites for a fat ounce, and now we were getting off on the Dexedrine, joking about speed traps.

The whites reminded me of our year in Alaska: how I would set my alarm one hour early, grope for a couple of whites, go back to sleep, and wake up rushing. Quick shower, no breakfast. Strutting like John Wayne in "The Fighting Seabees," ready to defend the country.

The lifers praised our ambition as we ran from one shit job to the next. Dig that trench, weld that pipe. Rick was a champion plumber and so was Jack Ferro. I could survey a day's circuit in three hours. We spent our afternoons relaxing, our work finished. The Seabee Can Do spirit, just like the posters proclaimed all over the base.

By Friday, our moods declined, and our nerves were fried. After taking two whites on Monday, we took three to wake up on Tuesday and a handful by Friday. Tempers flared. A good morning greeting could tick us off. But a weekend of partying and sleeping set us straight for another dull workweek.

Rick and I laughed and chewed gum to keep our jaws loose. We knew better now how to keep the edge without getting strung out. We reminisced about the old times, chatting over the warm rumble of the V8 and rolling with the soft wheeze of the tired suspension. Rick said he was glad to meet Ronnie after hearing me talk about her every day in Alaska. "She does look like the photo taped inside your locker," he grinned.

I had taken the photo on the beach in Ventura with my Instamatic. Ronnie wore her red flowered bikini, her skin honey brown, and her head thrown back in her fuck you pose, usually reserved for authority figures. Her sassy expression greeted me every morning and evening those twelve months.

"She begged me to send you home after we get to Fort Worth." He winked.

I fumbled in my pocket for a fresh stick of gum, thinking he'd turn around and hitchhike back to Ronnie if he were in my place. I stretched my arms and shook out the kinks. "Remember Sue Knapp, the Executive Officer's daughter?"

Rick hooted and banged his head against the steering wheel.

Sue was one of a dozen eligible women stranded with us on the island, most of them ranging in age from fourteen to seventeen, daughters of officers and lifers who could bring their families to the island. The lifers called it "good duty" because they could live in suburban style three-bedroom ranch houses. Not so for us grunts crammed into the barracks on the hill with large open rooms divided only by banks of six-foot lockers, one locker and one bed to a man.

When I first saw Sue, Pam Wilson and two of their friends prance into the base snack bar, I thought I was trapped in a Star Trek alternate world where pubescent maidens tempt the stranded spacemen to join them and preserve their species. Sue wore tight low-slung jeans and a loose halter-top that barely veiled her firm, pointed breasts. The top two buttons of Pam's blouse were left open, and her creamy white cleavage quivered for her male audience who studied her every movement. The girls strutted like movie starlets, transforming the snack bar into a Marilyn Monroe movie with a crowd of buffoons crashing into one another as they offered the girls their chairs. I couldn't believe what I saw. I mocked Rick and the other Seabees, but within two weeks, deprived of Ronnie's touch and most other healthy diversions, I joined the fan club. My loyalty to Ronnie kept me from risking jail, but few of my friends had such reservations. Every day, the Navy mess hall hummed with plots against the girls' virtue, and at night, the snack bar filled up for the show.

Our fantasies took a peculiar twist during my second month when Jack Ferro arrived. Like the other men in the barracks, Rick and I hated him at first. He was cocky, and he had reason to be: well built, tan, and blonde, with arresting blue eyes. He had a way of looking you straight in the eyes, his hypnotic gaze hard to release. When he began to crack a smile, you smiled too. After a while, it was impossible to dislike him. He put us to the test though, moving into our cube and proceeding to ball Sue Knapp the next weekend. They carried on like they were trying to preserve the race all by themselves. If Rick could forgive him that he could forgive him anything, and Jack was careful about Rick's feelings once he understood the situation. Like a star athlete, Jack avoided talking about his successes, reluctant to claim too much credit and even embarrassed by it all. Besides, he knew we would kill him if he acted any other way.

"I got a letter from Sue a couple of weeks ago," Rick shouted over the blare of a fading gospel station. We had lost all the civilized rock and roll stations.

"Any chance you'll get to see her?"

"Shee-it no. She's married to a seaman, which must have freaked out her father, the Annapolis grad. Her husband was transferred to Hawaii last year, and now she has a little baby boy. Sent me a picture. She says he looks like me, but there's no chance of that, and she knows it." He shook his head.

"Maybe she'll dump the seaman and come out to Texas."

"No way." He paused. "She still asked about Jack in her last letter."

With that, Rick pulled off at a rest stop near Hazleton so we could roll a number and change drivers. Our drive had become difficult and slow. The fog rolled in as thick as it had in the Aleutians. I eased the Ford back onto the highway, pulling in behind a big semi with bright running lights, content to cruise at fifty if I could see.

Rick said if Sue showed up now, she would just mess things up anyway, and he began telling me about Angela, his girlfriend in Fort Worth, who he'd met playing foosball at a local bar. Normally, anyone who challenged Rick at foosball bought him drinks all night long. He was the Roger Staubach of foosball, humbling most of our friends and me with one hand. Angela played meekly at first, losing a couple of games, but then she ran the ante up to double or nothing for a night's bar tab and rocked him good.

Rick knew her from high school, and he had worshiped her from a distance, thinking she was too fine for him and off limits, a cheerleader with a string of jocks on her leash. Now, she had a toddler boy and a German Shepherd, and her husband Bobby was off in Kansas. He took a job on a wildcat rig after she told him she wanted a divorce. Rick knew Bobby from high school, a halfback with a growling temper that grew worse with Army service. He got drunk and went out on her when they had fights.

"That doesn't give him an excuse to treat her like that." I stared ahead at the semi's running lights, thinking my leaving Ronnie wasn't the same. I wasn't a drunk for one.

"He ain't that bad usually," Rick said. "Everyone wants them to get back together, except her sister. And me, of course. But her sister doesn't approve of Angela seeing me either. A strict Baptist. Kind of reminds me of your neighbors."

"Maybe, but Bobby still sounds like an asshole."

Rick winced at my comment, though he passed it off with a grin.

I felt edgy from the speed, and I had no desire to argue with him. He fumbled in the ashtray until he pulled out a roach big enough to light, clipping it in his hemostats and roasting it over a match before passing it to me. Staring ahead into a blowing veil of fog, I lost the lane lines for a brief second and eased back on the pedal.

Rick crawled into the backseat for a nap. I didn't mind driving all the way to Texas if he wanted me to; I was just glad to be out of New York. I thought about the miles ahead. Rick's description of Angela reminded me of Diane Killian, a woman I had met on Adak. She and her mother owned a head shop in Hollywood, and I thought about stopping to see her. My map of America was marked with friends I planned to visit. After Fort Worth, I'd stop in Arizona to see Donna Felton, a friend Ronnie and I had met in California, and then maybe I would visit Diane on my way to Jack's place in Ventura. Phil Briones, another Seabee, had moved back to Las Vegas, so I could swing by and see him. My friends might help me make sense of my unraveling marriage, how my dreams of returning home from Adak to Ronnie had gone awry, and how I might move ahead, rebuild the dream, or fashion a new one.

North of Harrisburg, coming into the Appalachian ridges, the hills rose higher, and the curves bent more sharply. The fog grew so thick I could barely see. The highway was deserted. If I had enough money for a motel, I might have stopped for the night, but I only had twenty dollars to get me to California and back. The trucks now sped by too fast for me to tuck behind and follow. I stared at the white edge line and tried to stay close, away from the tractor-trailers.

The damp chill reached through my skin, the car wrapped in deep fog and darkness, but my jacket was stashed in the trunk. I flipped on some heat. The radio blared with static, all stations lost, not even country or gospel, like we were cruising in a void. I turned it off and stared into the gray mass lit only by our headlights. The roadside reflectors flared hypnotically, coming on too slow, too far apart.

A station wagon loomed out of the fog, parked on the narrow apron with hazard lights flashing. It aroused my fear of being flattened by a semi, so I braked hard and pulled over on the side shoulder just past it. A man hardly visible except for his yellow rain gear stood by the driver's door and yelled his thanks as I walked up. He said they were only changing drivers, but it was nice to know someone would stop to help on a night like this. We shook hands, sharing a brief camaraderie of souls on the road in the middle of nowhere. His wife and two small children were bundled in blankets in the back, and his son slid over to drive. I figured he wanted to take a leak because he kept standing there, waiting for me to leave, so I headed back to the Ford.

Another car had pulled off and parked right behind us, a light blue Falcon with dark blue Pennsylvania plates shining with bright yellow letters in the station wagon headlights. A short man with a flat top haircut and black horn-rimmed glasses stood in my way. Another fellow traveler. "Would you like to stop up the road a ways?" he asked.

His offer seemed weird, but I needed a break. My nerves were jangled from the fog and the waning white crosses. Before I could say anything, the guy waved and pointed up the highway, then he jumped into his car and swung around me, pulling back onto the road.

Rick sat up to see what was going on, and I told him some dude wanted to buy us coffee. "Strange, but I'll take a free cup of coffee." He lay back down. I began to wish I had refused the guy's offer, though I needed some caffeine. There had been nowhere to stop for miles.

The Falcon pulled over up ahead of us, waiting with his motor running. He accelerated on to the highway in front of me as I pulled out. I figured he must be lonely. While hitchhiking, I had often met lonely people on the road: people who had nowhere to go and only wanted to talk. I had listened, watching the miles tick by. The Falcon slowed down when I did for the thick banks of fog. He must have been watching me in his mirror.

He turned on to the gravel shoulder, signaling me with his hand out the window to pull over. We were far from any exit. He might have wanted to tell me where we were going, but I didn't want to stop again on the narrow shoulder. I was too spooked by all the big rigs flying by, sucking the damp air behind them like B-52s. I drove past him.

Within seconds, he started up again and passed me on the highway, waving like something was wrong. I rolled down the window and waved him off as he went by. His coffee was hardly worth the risk of his dangerous driving. He pulled in front of us again, and after a hundred yards or so, he signaled and pulled off the pavement.

Uneasy, I accelerated as fast as I dared and left his headlights deep in fog, but he caught me again, cutting me off sharply enough that I had to brake. He pulled off the road again. Persistent. But along with the fog and my Dexedrine nerves, I had had enough. He flew past and cut me off even closer. His license plate number, just feet ahead of me, burned into my memory. 405 IAB.

Stepping on the gas, I passed and tried to lose him, but the Falcon burst through the grayness, steaming over sixty, a reckless velocity in the fog. I yelled for Rick to wake up, to tell me I was not hallucinating, but he was already staring out the back window. The Falcon matched our speed and swerved toward us from the left lane. His inside lights were on so I could see him trying to say something, still signaling us to pull over.

"What's the matter with him?" Rick called up to me.

"He wants to buy us coffee." My edgy voice conveyed what I really meant.

"We don't want none of his coffee."

I slammed on the brakes, hoping there were no semis behind us. He breezed ahead and waited for us on the shoulder like before and pulled out to resume our game of tag.

"He's a sicko. Get away from him!" Rick blurted out.

I was too intent on escaping to say anything.

"Do you think he's got a gun?" Rick wondered.

Just then a green exit sign appeared above us like a message from heaven. I let the Falcon pass me again before I broke hard, swerved, and tore off the Interstate. None of the businesses near the ramp were open, so I turned into a dark gas station and switched off the car.

Rick patted my shoulder and whispered, "Good idea."

Soon the Falcon sped past, racing down the two-lane highway toward a motel with a dim yellow sign on the edge of our vision. I started the car, but Rick told me to wait, so I turned it back off. Sure enough, here came the Falcon, speeding the other way. We waited several seconds. Now.

I peeled out of the gravel lot and headed back to I-81, Rick and I hooted and congratulated one another. But there on the entrance ramp sat the Falcon, waiting until we went by and then pulling in behind us. We saw him too late to go back.

The coffee man shook his fist when he passed, looking straight at me. He turned on his inside lights and rolled down his window to call out to me, but I ignored him.

The owl-like taillights kept jumping out at me from the fog and flashing at me to stop. Each time he veered closer, and I even considered pulling over just to get it over with. There were two of us. We could handle him unless he had a gun.

At the next exit, we tried our ploy again. This time, after he sped past our hiding place behind a rack of tires, we beat our path back to the ramp before him. But as we turned onto the highway, our headlights caught the bearded face of a hitchhiker stranded in the foggy hills. I saw myself in his predicament, miles from anywhere.

"We should stop and pick him up." I slowed and the hitchhiker reached for his bags.

"No way," Rick shouted. He was about to climb over the seat and hit the pedal himself if I didn't stomp on it. "Besides, one hitchhiker's enough."

I caught his meaning. The hitchhiker might be our salvation. I punched the gas, urging Rick's old Ford into the foggy void while I watched for the coffee man in the rearview mirror.

Before we reached the end of the ramp, the blue Falcon swung in behind us and abruptly swerved to a stop for the hitchhiker. Soon enough, their images in the mirror were erased by the fog.

I shot Rick's Ford blindly up the highway, stretching the miles between the Falcon and us until we began to breathe easier.

A few exits up, we found a 76 Truck Stop for a real coffee break. I turned off the engine, and we sat in the car a few minutes to regain our equilibrium. Rick clapped me on the back and credited me for our escape. "You really are lucky. No telling what would have happened without that hitchhiker." He lit up a celebration roach before we went inside.

In truth, I hoped my luck extended to my brother hitchhiker up on the ramp. Staring into my coffee and watching the cream boil and mix, I felt as alone as he was, far away from Ronnie and our shabby apartment. After Fort Worth, I would be traveling by myself, and the Falcon reminded me of the dangers on the road. A trucker wearing a Pittsburgh Pirates cap at the counter asked me if I was sick. He noticed my hands shaking.

I expected him to question our haircuts and accuse us of using drugs, but when Rick and I told him our story, slipping in that we were vets, the trucker pursed his lips.

"I think I know that guy." He called over one of his buddies.

"Yeah, sounds like a guy who comes in here sometimes," the second trucker said. "Likes to talk to the truckers. Must be some kind of a fag."

"Might be he works a night job some place. He seemed harmless," the trucker with the Pirates hat said. He looked us over. "You guys should call it a night. They have rooms upstairs reserved for truckers, but I could talk to the manager."

"Thanks," I said, "but we need to keep going." I glanced at Rick, who stared at the truckers with disbelief. It was hard for either of us to imagine that the coffee man might be harmless.

"That guy tried to kill us." Rick was adamant.

"Well, someone should talk to him. You should give his license plate number to the highway patrol," the trucker shrugged.

"He needs more than a talking to," the second trucker sneered.

After the they left us alone, I wondered aloud if sending them out was the right thing to do. "I'd hate to have those guys and their big rigs after me."

"Are you nuts?" Rick blurted.

Staring into Rick's speed mapped eyes, I realized how frayed we were from the night of driving. I knew Rick well enough to know when to back off. He was right in a way. The road carried more dangerous threats than diesel vigilantes, the coffee man for one, and I'd be living on the road for the next several weeks. "Better them than the coffee man," I finally said.

Chapter 3

RICK AND I drove through the night. By the time the fog burned off in the late morning, we were deep in the Shenandoah Valley, and my pale arms began to bake luxuriously. To my sunlight-deprived body, the rays descended like an instant spring, and the bright blue sky improved our moods. We cruised down past the edge of the Smokies in the afternoon and passed through Little Rock during the late Friday sunset, just hours before date time. Good ol' boys in jacked-up pickups roared past us. Their customized red and yellow running lights gleamed like costume jewelry.

We pulled into the carport of Rick's apartment that night after dinner at a Texas steakhouse where Rick almost earned a free meal, nearly finishing the dare-you-can-eat-it Porterhouse. Despite my thousand-mile hunger, I held myself to a small T-bone, conserving my road funds.

Furnished with sculpted, synthetic carpets, thinly stuffed chairs, cheap wooden end tables, and pastel paintings, Rick's place resembled the parlor display on Ronnie's floor at Dick's Furniture Store back in Binghamton. Rick let me crash on a waterbed I could drown in while he headed over to Angela's. My joints felt so loose, and my backbone so soft I thought I might melt with the least vibration. My body settled like hairy jelly, and I recalled floating in the ocean on the drugstore air mattress Ronnie and I had bought in Ventura.

I thought about calling her, but our last fight was too fresh. I wanted to drift further away, and I knew she might be warming Bardeen the way we warmed each other before I left. I began to want similar comfort, an impulse I had suppressed even in the bleakest moments, not wanting to sneak around like her and sanction her affair, but my reluctance weakened with distance. Tomorrow, I would be on my way to Donna's place in Sedona, and it would stretch even thinner.

Just after dawn, I rolled out of the waterbed with its sloshes and waves reminding me of the surf three days away, depending on my luck. I scribbled Rick a thank you note on a lined page torn from my notebook and lugged my things toward the entrance ramp a quarter mile from the apartment. From what I had seen of Fort Worth, there was always a freeway close by, and this one led due west with a swing south through El Paso.

With no money for an aluminum frame backpack, I made do with my old Boy Scout knapsack, khaki washed out to a dull shade of gray, held together with black cotton thread and safety pins. I carried my small, blue hard-shell suitcase, also a veteran of hitchhiking trips. My sleeping bag was too floppy to tie to the knapsack, so I carried it rolled up with nylon rope. Deep inside was an ounce of reefer Rick had given me as a present to Jack, and I promised myself not to touch it until I reached Ventura. We had burned my own small ration of dope on the way to Fort Worth, but my friend Donna was sure to have weed. I had left a message at her mother's house last night, since I didn't have her new number.

I trudged out of the apartment parking lot, whistling "Mr. Tambourine Man." My prospects for the day were good: bright sky, steady traffic, and plenty of room for cars to stop on the long suburban entrance ramp. One or two lucky rides, and I might see Donna that night. I recalled the gargoyle faces she had made when we were stoned during the several months

Ronnie and I had spent with her and her husband, Walt, in California, waiting for my eventual orders to Adak. She would look through my eyes, forcing deep laughter, and often causing me to cough up a hit. Three years ago, none of us imagined either couple would be separated.

She loved Ronnie from the moment she had met her, but she was unsure of me at first because of my boot camp haircut, even if Walt had one just like it. Now, as I stood alongside a Texas highway with my beard and my hair tied back in a rubber band, I more closely resembled a man she might like.

Still singing and walking backwards, I started down the shoulder of the entrance ramp toward the interstate. I might have a long wait in conservative Fort Worth, but once I got to the city limits, I should have less difficulty thumbing rides.

A Texas Ranger pulled up in front of me in his black and white squad car, and I stopped singing mid-measure.

He waved me over to his car with a circular motion like he was directing a roundup. His squinting eyes followed me as I approached. With his shaved head, he looked like a gung-ho Marine, a type I tried to avoid.

When I lowered my face to the open passenger window, he pointed a shotgun at my teeth, about two inches away, his finger tight on the trigger.

I froze, afraid to move a muscle. No one would blame him for shooting a longhaired hitchhiker. I was big game in season.

"You got some ID?"

I carefully retrieved my wallet and my driver's license.

"You Patrick McCarthy?" he asked, and I nodded. He called in the number. "That's right, New York," he said. Then he barked at me, "Throw your bags in the backseat."

I stared down the barrel of his shotgun, trying to figure out what he planned to do with me. He held the gun firmly in his right hand while his left hand worked the radio. He reported our position and a code something, and then he squinted at me. "You deaf? Throw your bags in the car. Move it."

He had the voice of a drill sergeant, and I reflexively wanted to hop to, but I remembered the parting gift from Rick, the baggie of Mexican weed, rolled deep in my sleeping bag, and I paused. This wasn't the first time I'd been hassled for hitchhiking. Usually, the trooper called in my ID to make sure I was not an escaped convict, threatened to arrest me if he saw me again, and threw me off the highway. Then I would wait until he was out of sight and walk back up to the road. But now I was in Texas. Twenty years to life for one joint.

I tried to think. I was already busted for hitchhiking, and I assumed he was hauling me in. I studied his short sleeve uniform, and the tattoo of a snake coiled and poised to strike on his trigger arm. I was good at talking my way out of trouble if I could stay calm enough.

"I think I'll leave my stuff here," I said. Then I felt myself blush, realizing it was the worst thing I could have said.

"What?" He sounded suspicious.

"I might as well leave my bags here. We're coming back, aren't we?" I forced my winning smile.

"You ain't coming back." He pointed his shotgun at my pile of baggage. "Put your damn bags in the car."

Walking deliberately while keeping my hands in view, I went back to retrieve my belongings, which suddenly seemed more valuable, representing my fragile freedom. I grabbed the suitcase and the knapsack and threw them in the backseat. His dark barrel followed me like radar. Thick, wire mesh separated the backseat from the front. I started to climb in.

"You sit up front," he said. I closed the back door and reached for the front handle. He waved his gun, and I stopped dead. "You going to leave your sleeping bag?"

Hanging up his radio, he lowered his head and shook it in frustration. I remembered that gesture, common among lifers in the Navy whenever they tried to get us to do something we didn't want to do. They would shake their heads and tell us we were dumber than cows. "Go pick it up," the ranger ordered.

I did as I was told and sat up front. I buckled my seat belt, even though he wasn't wearing one. He powered up the windows and locked the doors, still holding the shotgun between us, pointed at the dash, and he kept his grip on it even after he pulled onto the highway. He drove with his left hand on the top rim of the steering wheel.

I tried to ignore the gun; I was still trying to think of a way to convince him to let me go. I wondered if having me sit up front was a good sign. I was on the right side of the wire mesh, but I was also closer to his shotgun, where he could watch me better and blast me quicker.

I wanted the ride to go slow, so I had time to think. But the ranger promptly buried the speedometer needle. We were going as fast as the car could go, and I glanced down to see his cowboy boot pressing the accelerator to the floor. He wanted more speed.

"Straighten up, boy," he drawled when he caught me looking at his boot. He tapped my knee with the shotgun muzzle. I turned my eyes back to the windshield and made sure my hands were visible on my lap. I looked at him sideways. He stared at me full on, paying little mind to the road, and he slowly squeezed his right eye like he was taking aim. "You better straighten up."

"Where we headed?" I asked. My eyes faced forward again.

He didn't answer.

"I'm only hitchhiking because I don't have enough money to take a bus," I said, trying to probe his human side. "I'm going out to California to look for work. Hard to find work these days, especially if you're a veteran. Are you a veteran?"

"Marine Corps, Da Nang, '68," he announced like he was signing in at an alumni reunion.

I seldom mentioned my service record to anyone since I was not proud of enlisting in the Navy to avoid the draft, but my situation was desperate. I figured he must be about my age or a few years older.

"I was a Seabee. Being a Marine, you know Seabees. How they build bases and airstrips for Marines. Most people don't know that." I glanced over, but he didn't respond. "I just got out last summer, and I'm going back to school on the GI Bill. I need work to support my wife, but we haven't been getting along. If I can get a job in California, I might stay out there and go to school. Maybe she'll come out and join me. It's cheap to go to college in California if you're a resident."

The cop stared at the road, passing the commuters like they were parked cars. We seemed to be the only vehicle moving.

"I feel better knowing you're a veteran," I babbled on. "We had so many things happen to us that other people don't understand. You had to experience it. We have a special brotherhood beyond the American Legion or any of those old veteran groups. The guys I served with are like my brothers. I just visited a Seabee buddy of mine in Fort Worth, and I'm going out to see another buddy in California. We veterans have to stick together."

I paused to let my argument sink in. I hoped it would work even if some of it was bullshit, especially the part about brotherhood among all veterans, extending beyond my own friends. But Marines often served as military police on Navy bases, and they usually left the Seabees alone. They came to us for favors since we controlled the motor pool and tool shop. We also had more dope than they did. On several occasions, I blew a joint with a Marine while giving him a ride somewhere.

"Shit," he finally responded. "Two-thirds of the people we put in jail in this here county are veterans." He squeezed his aiming eye again. I could tell by his tight grin that he thought he had made a joke, or he was just enjoying himself.

I tried to smile, thinking it was better to try and share the joke, even if I was the butt of it.

"What are you smiling at?" he asked. He glanced forward in time to brake for a commuter who was driving ahead of us in the left lane. He let go of his shotgun to grab the wheel with both hands. I fell forward, against the shoulder harness, and when I swayed back, I felt the gun behind me, pinned between my ass and the seat. I watched the commuter swerve into the right lane. As the ranger accelerated again, he jerked his gun loose, gripping the barrel and pointing it at me.

"Shit," he hissed, eyeing me like I was responsible for making him slow down. I eyed him sideways. My face still showed the shock of our near accident. His grin widened.

"Not all veterans are criminals," I said, trying to control the quaver in my voice. When he didn't answer, I went on. "There's no need to point that gun at me."

"How do I know that, sailor?" When I didn't say anything, he erased his grin and glared at me. He lowered the gun and turned back to the highway.

I should have shut up sooner, but I was never good at knowing when to stop talking. Even in boot camp, my talking back earned me extra punishment, dozens of pushups, forced marches, and midnight shaving parties outside under security lights, scraping my face until it was pocked with bloody cuts. The ranger reminded me of boot camp and the lifer drill instructors, but none of them ever pointed a gun at me. Some guys who experienced both jail and boot camp said boot camp was worse. I never believed them. I knew a Texas prison would be worse than anything I could imagine.

I peeked at the ranger, recalling my own bristle haircut. His face bore the chapped look of frequent shaving. He might have been a drill sergeant himself, scraping his face raw as an example to the recruits and an excuse to force them to do the same. Or he could have been a guard in the brig with even more power over his captive subjects. Or just one of those guys who claimed to love the war.

"What the fuck are you looking at?" he asked in a measured cadence. He quickly glimpsed between me and the road.

I pointed my face forward again and the barrel of the shotgun pressed against my thigh. I forced myself to remain still.

"You don't like guns, do you?" he asked.

"Not when they're pointed at me."

"I don't even have my finger on the trigger." He shook his head. "You're kind of a wise guy hippie, ain't you? When did you get your last haircut?"

"Before I got out."

"I figured as much. You sailors always look like damned hippies anyway." He waited for me to say something. He raised his shotgun and pointed the muzzle at my ponytail like he might blow it off. When I didn't respond, he shifted his eyes back to the road and relaxed his grip on the gun, lowering it into the seat.

Now I was convinced he was enjoying himself, despite his grim expression. I recalled how the Marine guards had treated a prisoner on Adak. The grunt lived in the brig by himself, and I'd see him marching twelve miles with a full pack followed by two armed Marines in a pickup. The truck sped up and backed off to make him accelerate to double time. Some days, I saw him doing endless pushups on the snow encrusted tundra, always with two guards. I sympathized with him, regardless of his crime, and now I imagined a similar life for myself.

"Your wife like your hair like that?" the ranger asked.

His question surprised me, but I stammered, "Yeah, I guess so."

"What did she think of your haircut after boot camp? Did she like it then?"

"No. She went out and bought me a wig."

"She made you wear a wig?" He smirked.

"Only once. Made me look like Liza Minnelli."

"My wife hated my haircut too. Bitch wrote me a Dear John letter in country. So, I reupped for another tour."

I shook my head, thinking about Ronnie and her complaints about my lack of maturity, and how Bardeen with his steady job and fatherly manner had become a role model, at least in her eyes. "Yeah, my wife thinks I should settle down. But I've only been out since August."

"What's she think about your hitchhiking across the country?"

"She doesn't like it."

He nodded like he understood. He let go of the shotgun and stretched out his arm, twisting his wrist like he was trying to loosen up. The cruiser started to slow down.

Gripping the wheel with both hands, he jerked it hard over, and we bounced off the interstate and skidded to a stop on the gravel shoulder. He popped up the door locks and turned toward me. "Get out." He was back to business.

I leaned toward the door, moving slowly at first. His sudden halt stunned me, and I tried to figure out why he wanted me to get out. I had no idea where we were, but I knew we were still on the interstate.

"I said get out," he repeated louder, raising his shotgun for emphasis. He still clasped it by the muzzle.

I crawled out of the car, wondering if he planned to shake me down before bringing me in. Or give me a haircut. But why would he do it here in front of all the commuters? A deserted back road would be better.

"Hey, sailor," he said, waving his gun toward the backseat. "Take your shit with you."

I jerked open the back door and saw the double barrel pointed at my face through the steel mesh. I pulled out my sleeping bag first and threw it behind me. Then the suitcase, which I set down next to the car. My hands shook again, despite my efforts to control them.

I had to reach in farther for my knapsack. As I leaned over my suitcase, I lost my balance and sprawled across the backseat.

The ranger looked back at me and said, "Fuckin' sailor." He laughed and called in something on his radio. It was the first time I heard him laugh, a high-pitched tone, sounding oddly boyish.

I scrambled out of the backseat with my knapsack and heard him chuckle again. I stood there, waiting for him to get out of the car, every muscle tense, my attention focused, like I was preparing for a fight. If he wanted to fuck with me, I was ready. I had nothing to lose.

He stared at me for several seconds, still clutching the handset and grinning like he was trying to decide what to do with me. Finally, he hung up his radio and scribbled a note on a clipboard he kept under his seat. He peeled out and swung a U-turn across the median strip, waving a peace sign back at me like he was throwing away a cigarette.

I watched him merge onto the highway and disappear. My first thought was that I must have gained his sympathy somehow. He had to know I was carrying drugs. He must have decided to give me a break. Then I noticed the city limits sign on the other side of the interstate. He had just escorted me out of town.

I stood dazed, my ears ringing, and I had no sensation in my toes or fingers. As the fact of my escape began to sink in, I felt stupid standing there with my fists clenched. I angered at the thought of how he played with me, and I was mad at myself for letting him. I imagined him telling his ranger buddies how he scared the shit out of me. The threat of jail was bad enough, but he also reawakened my nightmare of being sucked back into the Navy.

With a deep breath, I realized I was free once more, and nothing else mattered as much. I recalled the day I was discharged and how I carried my papers straight to the main gate, leaving my uniforms hanging in my locker in the barracks. Now I left it all behind again and turned west.

A car honked on the roadside up ahead. Two guys in a maroon Chevy with bent Tennessee plates were offering me a ride. They backed up, their old car stirring up a cloud of sand and oil rich exhaust.

One of them jumped out and threw open the back door and trunk for me like I was a celebrity. I lifted my baggage into the dented trunk, and my host tied the lid back down with a strand of rope, which looped through a hole in the lid where the lock had been. I glanced back toward Fort Worth, thinking the troopers would send another car to make sure I left town.

"How'd you get that ranger to let you go?" he asked. "We pulled over when we saw him drop you off." He had a loose-jawed grin, reminding me of the younger guys I met in college, the ones too young for the draft who always wanted to know what it was like to be a veteran. I never had much to tell them.

"Let's just get out of here," I murmured, still half stunned, but I shook his extended hand, catching the stale scent of beer on his breath. "Let's get the hell out of Texas."

"Yahoo! Let's get the hell out of Texas!" he shouted.

Chapter 4

I SETTLED INTO the backseat, straddling a huge hole in the once plush upholstery, revealing seat springs and the rusted inner body of the old Chevy. Judging from the dark road dirt, the hole went through to the highway.

"Fang, my Great Dane, dug that tunnel!" Al, the driver, called. "Don't you sit too close to that hole now."

Larry joined him in laughter and erupted into a rebel yell.

I yelled with them. I was free, no twenty years to life staring me in the face, no Texas prison. Larry told me to help myself to a can of Lonestar beer out of the cooler next to me. He passed me an opener.

They prompted me for the story of my brush with the trooper, hollering over the blast of four open windows and the buzz of road noise from Fang's den. They detected the kernel of my story, though I never told them about Rick's gift. Their logic was pure: a hitchhiker with a ponytail is a hippie, and all hippies smoke dope. So, where's the dope, man?

"Come on, Flash. Turn us on," Larry called.

"You got me crying, man. *Please*. Please roll one of your joints." Al pointed at an imaginary tear rolling down his cheek past his drooping gunfighter moustache.

"I'm not dumb enough to carry weed in Texas!" I replied.

"So, you had some." Al called and slapped the dash. "Can you get us some?"

"You want to go back to Fort Worth?"

Larry rapped Al's shoulder. "We ain't going back."

I snickered. "Where are we going?"

"Yuma. Through El Paso and Tucson." Larry rested his chin on the back of his seat.

"The fucking desert!" Al roared. "Bones of cows and hitchhikers who refuse to turn on their rides!"

Shaking his head, Larry flipped a thumb toward Al and grinned over the headrest. "I met a guy building condominiums in Yuma. Said he'd give us both a job."

"Shit, you dreamer," Al said. "We don't even have his phone number. Might not be anything but sand and retired widows."

"Deep purses, tight pussies, and heavy breasts," Larry yelled back, cupping his hands below his pectorals, and lifting them to make his point.

Any foreman would hire Larry. His arm, thick as a ham, reached back to poke me, so I knew when to laugh. I laughed, eyeing his bruises and scars, particularly one jagged discolored bead on his forearm.

"Got that when a bronco threw me into a barbed wire fence on the rodeo circuit. That was it for me."

"Why are you off to Yuma?"

Larry jerked his head toward Al.

I glanced at Al who studied me in the mirror. "That a wedding ring?" he asked, holding up his hand to show me his ring.

I nodded. The groove in my finger still felt funny without it. "I'm taking a solitary vacation this year."

Larry winked and lifted his beer can. "We won't be solitary for long if we can help it."

Al shook his head. "I ain't ready to find a new woman yet." He turned toward Larry. "Shit, I don't even remember a lot of what happened back there."

"By the time we left town, you couldn't stand. You were swelled up with beer like a water balloon. Would've killed most men." He swung around to address me. His beer sloshed on the back of the front seat.

The speedometer wavered around eighty.

"Al goes out for lunch, see, and he nurses his attitude with some cold ones. He gets back to work and tells his boss to go fuck himself. You have to know his boss, Roscoe. An old shop teacher who swung a mean wooden paddle, bigger than a tennis racket. I had the welts to prove it. Al leaves before Roscoe kills him and goes over to his wife's lawyer. Al tells him to take a big dick the hard way, and after a few more beers, he goes home and fights with Louise. Then he packs his jeans in his old cardboard suitcase."

"I didn't fight with her. I told you. She told me not to leave, and if I did, I should keep right on walking. So, I said, 'Leave me be, bitch.'"

"You called her a bitch?" Larry asked, suddenly serious.

"Hell, no. I was kidding." Al grinned. "You'd kill me if I did."

Larry nodded. "Then he goes down to Scratchy's Lounge and calls me. By the time I got there, Scratchy was about to toss him out on his ass, and we've known Scratchy since we needed booster seats to sit at the bar." Leaning out the window, Larry let fly a hawker the size of a small bird. I ducked as the wad whizzed past the open rear window.

"Shit, Larry," Al groaned. "I shouldn't have done Scratchy that way, but sometimes a man has to take a stand." He leaned back and crooned, "I told him we should shoot all the lawyers. And all them other motherfuckers. Yeah, man. Shoot all those motherfuckers." He looked to Larry and me for support. Larry pumped his fists and starred back at me.

I smiled. No time to split hairs over which motherfuckers deserved bullets.

"We blew that fucking town." Al hooted a few times to punctuate his anger. "We blew that fucking town." He repeated his observation, emphasizing different words each time, first "town," then "fucking," and finally, "We *blew* that fucking town."

Larry chuckled. "We stopped at my mom's house to pick up some underwear and sandwiches. You probably don't remember," he said to Al. "You were near passed out by then. By the time you woke up, we were in Texas. If we hadn't left Tennessee, you'd be in jail by now. Maybe Roscoe, Louise, and her lawyer will cool off enough for you to go back. In a few years." Larry gazed at Al. "Good thing I was already planning to take off for Yuma."

"I'm through taking shit. Fuck Roscoe. Fuck that lawyer. Fuck marriage. Fuck *all* them motherfuckers!"

I stared out the window at the rocks and sage brush flying by, thinking about the trap Al saw springing around him. He and Louise had parted like shrapnel. Ronnie and I parted as if our separation were just another one of many. This one might be final, but I couldn't believe it yet. The grenade was still ticking.

Al reached back and poked me, taking his eye off the road. Larry grabbed the wheel and kept control. Facing forward, Al addressed me in the rearview mirror. "I carry a gun under the seat. Just so's you know. You can never tell who you might pick up on the highway even if you look harmless enough."

I nodded and watched the road ahead.

"You shouldn't have brought that gun to Stevens' office. He'll swear a complaint. Billy Stevens is Louise's lawyer." Larry twisted toward me.

"Should've blown his fucking toupee off." Al took a deep breath. "Louise won't let him send me to jail."

"She'll protect you, though I can't say you deserve it."

"Remember when I wrecked my car? She borrowed money from her folks and her savings account and paid off the insurance company so they wouldn't sue me."

"You're lucky you were fucked up that night too, or you would've been killed." Larry winked at me. "Don't worry, Flash. He's not nearly as drunk now as he was then. But it's early yet."

"Hand me a beer from that cooler back there and grab one for yourself," Al called back. "I don't intend to stay sober today. It's too fucking hot already."

I opened a beer and passed it up to Al and fished one out for Larry, who noticed I didn't take another one for myself.

"See, hippies don't like to drink beer." Larry rapped Al on the shoulder.

I grimaced and squinted ahead at the bleached sky, feeling the road hum and wind pushing hot dry air. The rising heat gathered into reflecting pools of imaginary water, evaporating as we sped by and drawing us toward their cool promise. I finally popped a beer to wet my throat.

Al pressed the pedal harder, still talking about the world he left behind. How he met Louise in high school, about two years ago. I ignored him and traced my own thoughts.

Ronnie and I had met one afternoon at the Boar's Head, a bar near college. Each of us sat at our own round wooden table and pretended to study. She wore a shiny red barrette, holding her hair back over her ears with bangs falling over her forehead and high cheeks tinted with rouge. Her profile recalled a Medici countess and her thick, sensuous mouth softened the angles of her face. She brushed her lips with light pink lipstick. She looked at me with soft brown eyes and long lashes. I held her glance until she looked away.

She wore a short, black wraparound skirt clipped together with a big silver pin and bunched up over her thighs. She pulled at her hem and crossed her long legs. My cheeks burned. She downed her beer, and I followed her toward the door. As she pushed against the wind, she lost her balance. I grabbed the door, and we stumbled outside, clasping hands for support.

After that moment, we stayed within sight of one another, within touch, swept along by our emerging love and the sense of impending change all around us, the Vietnam War always in the background. Our talk might start on collective farms and leap to civil rights, free love, and The Beatles' "Revolution #9," through the long night over coffee and No-Doz. Our albums blared with scratches – Bob Dylan, Byrds, Buffalo Springfield, and Jefferson Airplane – stacked again and again on Ronnie's portable stereo after I sneaked into her dorm room.

The war became personal when two of my high school friends were killed, one in the Army and one in the Marines. It became more personal when I received my low lottery number after I dropped out of college for lack of money. Ronnie said I should deny the existence of the government and ignore the draft. Ronnie the Rebel was easy to love and sometimes impractical. Never forgiving my decision to enlist in the Seabees to avoid the infantry or the Marines, she continued to see me as the college student she met, even when I wore a uniform. I wondered if our marriage and the war would finally end at the same time.

Larry erupted with a rebel yell and threw two empty beer cans into the backseat, one just missing my head and the other bouncing off my chest. "Where you at, man?" he called. "We need more beers up here."

I grabbed a full can out of the cooler, drawing my arm back for a fastball.

"Whoa," Larry said. "Sorry, I didn't mean to hit you."

I fished out another beer from the dwindling supply and passed them both underhand.

Al began describing his fantasy woman, who looked like Tuesday Weld with the physique of Rachel Welch. Larry yelled out bits of color and anatomy: how she looked and talked, what she ate, what she thought about, and how she made love. I joined in.

The temperature kept rising, and the beer flowing, our words fragmented like grits of sand, breaking into dry howls, hounds of Hell racing through the baked prairie and lifeless rocks. Heat waves distorted the highway, the cars we passed, and the mountains. Inside the shell of the Chevy, the heat squeezed and inflated our faces like circus reflections. Al floored the accelerator to get max air. Our beer sweat flowed and congealed on our skin like sticky oil, embalming insects and road dirt. The rubber band around my ponytail cracked and broke from heat stress like an old tire. My hair was blown and tangled. Al wore a red bandanna and Larry a Cat hat with his T-shirt sleeves ripped off and biceps bulging. We hooted like outlaws.

We coasted into El Paso about lunchtime, looking for an air-conditioned bar. The adobe brick and stucco buildings resembled pottery in a kiln, bright glaze dripping in the ambient glare. Larry spotted a dull sign shaped like a polar bear, the name bent and chipped to rusted steel.

Inside, the air chilled our sweaty skin. We stood in the doorway and waited for our eyes to adjust. Farmers and ranchers emerged from the darkness, sitting at round unfinished tables. The bare wooden floor was heaped with sawdust and peanut shells. Country music blared from the jukebox. We groped our way toward the high, varnished bar, stained dark mahogany and lit by plastic Tiffany lamps, each advertising a different beer. On a shelf behind the bar near the cash register, stood a two-foot tall hula doll, and in front of her, a large glass ashtray filled with nickels. Two men tossed coins at her well-worn belly to make her dance. She rocked back and forth whenever a nickel clanged against her body. She was the only woman in the room.

Several pairs of eyes followed us to the bar, locked onto my knotted hair and untrimmed beard. I sat between Al and

Larry, who propped his thick arms on the bar, flexing his muscles like he was leaning on an exercise bench.

One of the guys pitching nickels, with a leathery pocked face and a burr haircut reminiscent of the Texas Ranger, yelled to Larry, "Is your friend there a boy or a girl?"

Larry swiveled around. The tables near us grew quiet. Al stared at his hands like a boxer preparing for a bout.

The burrhead's friend, a meaty guy with a red drinker's face, looked around the room as if summoning support and said to me, "Yeah, you a boy or a girl?"

"I'm a Martian." I stared down the bar and flashed a smile.

The burrhead and his friend gawked at me, but they finally turned and nodded their heads into their beer glasses. My confession brought a few grudging laughs from the unsympathetic crowd. We ordered our Lonestar drafts.

The burrhead's friend kept checking on me. He had a wide, flat face and thin lips with decayed teeth that looked like sharpened fangs. His brown baseball cap pressed down on his large ears.

We sat and watched the hula girl as our parched bodies cooled.

After Al and Larry started their fifth round, Al pointed at the burrhead's friend. "Look at those *lizard* lips. That guy's got lizard *lips*."

Larry waved his hand up and down to try and shush him.

"Shit, all these guys look like *lizards*, but he's the worst."

I tried to distract him. "My wife's boss might be a lizard. Small brain."

Al nodded his head. "Just *look* at that guy with his sunburn and zits. I know he's one of them, and so's Louise's lawyer. That old snake." He laughed, shooting a spray of beer out his nostrils. He grabbed a napkin to blow his nose.

"You're real cool, man." Larry turned to me. "You shouldn't egg him on."

"How can he drink beer with those *lips*? We should pour some beer in a bowl so he can lap it up. I bet he eats *flies* with his tongue."

The lizard man laughed at Al's slurs, but his smile grew rigid. He yelled down the bar, "Why ain't you boys in Vietnam?"

I cleared my throat, ready to recite my veteran speech, but I didn't get the chance.

"We're too fuckin' smart. Too fuckin' *smart*," Al yelled back. "Not like you!" He snorted into his beer.

Larry shook his head and whispered, "They wouldn't take us because of his DUI and my knee."

"We were lucky then," Al said, raising his voice. "But we're too *smart* now. Smarter than the stupid *lizards* under this fuckin' rock."

"You boys think we're stupid for defending our country?" the lizard yelled at us. "Me and Lucas here both fought in Nam."

The lizard swigged his beer and stood up from his stool, swinging his gut around to gain momentum. The burrhead, who had left the bar for a table in the corner, came back with another red-faced buddy.

The lizard took a linebacker stance behind Larry's shoulder. All four of them glared at us. Larry raised his eyes and winked at me.

"The war's almost over," Al blurted. "We better hurry up and ship all the dumb *lizards* over there. We're going to miss our chance. Our *big chance* to get rid of all the fucking *lizards*."

Two of the men moved closer. The tattoo of a devil on Larry's left biceps swelled. He studied the red face from the corner of his eye.

The bartender appeared in front of us, sweeping our empty glasses out of the way. "You guys better leave."

"You fuckin' *lizards* want something?" Al slurred. "I got some nice *flies* in my pocket. Or maybe some *worms*. Hey, I got one great big *worm* right here," he yelled, holding his crotch.

"Stand up, you little shit," the lizard said.

At that, Larry swung his stool around and stood up between the locals and Al. Larry was taller and stronger than any of them. He could handle a few of them alone. But the faces in the bar said he would not get such good odds.

"Get out of the way, Larry. This *fat, juicy lizard* is all mine." Al stood and swayed by his stool. He and Larry squared off in front of the two nearest locals. I stood close to Larry, the safest spot in the bar. The burrhead and his buddy hovered behind the lizard and his second. I wondered how I ended up in this fight. Neither side looked like my friends, but my side was clear.

Pretending to glance away, the burrhead lunged toward me, grabbing at my shoulder. I leaned back with his weight and parried his thrust with my forearm. I used his momentum to push him toward Larry, who flung him back against one of the tables like a sack of cement. He jumped up, brushed the peanuts shells off his white T-shirt along the curve of his belly, and strode back for more, pausing when he met Larry's stare. Other locals gathered behind him.

The lizard and Al faced off, their fists raised, feinting lefts and rights. Neither found room for a blow. Al hissed at him and stuck out his tongue.

Lowering his head like he was going to butt the lizard, Al leaned over but did not move. Instead, he started retching, throwing up his beers and hundreds of miles of junk food.

All eyes watched the pool expand. Al was careful not to get any on him. The lizard backed away. The bartender came around the bar and grabbed Al by his collar and pulled him toward the door. Al was too sick to protest, but he pushed the bartender's hand away and started walking out. Larry and I backed out after them, watching the room like gunfighters.

Someone started to laugh.

Pausing at the entryway, the bartender pushed Al over to Larry and said he'd call the cops if we came back in. He said we were lucky he didn't make us clean up the mess.

We fell through the door into the white-hot sunlight.

Inside, the lizard yelled, "That little shit sure showed me his stuff!"

"Yeah, but he was right about your face, Smitty."

Larry fished some mouthwash out of Al's suitcase and poured it down his throat until he gagged and spit it back up.

I was glad to get out of there. I eyed the road back to the interstate, anxious to log more miles before sundown and hoping the dry air would purify the lingering stench of Al's

Lonestar breakfast. Might be better to say my farewell and thumb another ride, but I doubted many cars took the forsaken side road with dead weeds waving from the asphalt cracks.

"You drive," Larry said to me with a deep belch. He shoved Al into the backseat where he curled up around Fang's burrow. Larry crawled into the front seat and leaned against the passenger door. Both boys were snoring before we reached the city limits.

I punched the throttle up to eighty and surveyed the bleached landscape, sweat trickling down my neck. Pushing against the wall of heat, I missed the cold and damp of the Northeast, where fights with local reptiles were less common than arguments about how to end the war. But the lizard bar reminded me of the American Legion where my dad took me when I was on leave from Adak. After years of arguments about the war and my resistance, he expressed pride that I had enlisted, and he wanted to show me off. More sparsely decorated than the lizard bar, the legion had cement block walls with chipped beige paint hung with a few combat crests and a long bar occupying one side under a large, faded American flag nailed to the wall. More flags on poles rose from a large bronze shell case in the corner. Wooden tables with fold up chairs were erected in rows across a checkerboard floor of brown and white tiles. They held dances on Saturday nights with colored lights disguising the drab military décor. I had visited many joints like it during my time in the Navy.

My dad told his Legion buddies about my pending deployment to Cam Rahn Bay when we took our stools at the bar. Most of the men were heavier than me and all were older, about my dad's age. They seemed happy I was getting an opportunity to defend the country as they shared their memories of World War II and Korea. A high voice down the bar called, "Bet you're still eating our leftovers."

"They made enough rations during the world war to feed several armies," my dad confided, but I knew that story already. "K-rations stacked everywhere."

"No one will trade for ham and eggs," I replied, trying to sound like one of the guys.

"They still make you eat that shit?" my dad asked. He was the only one wearing a suit and tie, along with a American flag pin in his lapel, having picked me up from home after work. "I smoked my cigarettes first to kill the taste."

The same guy who started the discussion about K-rations waddled over to my stool. He stood with bowed legs supporting a squat torpedo frame with salt and pepper hair shaved in a flat top. He held his thick arms bent at his side like a wrestler ready to rumble. Not a man to mess with.

"We won our war," he said, swaying slightly and ending with a burp.

"Westie," my dad chuckled. "You're too old to reenlist."

"You're all pussies," he spat at me. "You should have kicked their slanty little asses by now."

"Take it easy," my dad said.

Westie never took his eyes off me. He grunted, "Allya are losers."

Something snapped, and I jumped off my stool, returning his stare. I hated the war, and I hated myself for enlisting. I hated what the war had done to my life and my marriage. I never thought it was my war but that didn't make me a loser, nor anyone else caught up in it. My dad appeared at my side, ready to back me up. Eyeing him, I finally shook my head and stayed silent, not wanting to drive a spike between my dad and his buddies.

An older man slid to Westie's side and threw an arm over his shoulder. "This kid's going into harm's way," he said. "We should buy him a beer, not yell at him."

"Yeah, I'll spring," someone else called, and the tension diffused.

A firm squeeze on my upper arm jolted me back to the present. Larry tightened his grip and rubbed my biceps against the bone. I yelled with pain, waking Al, as my hand went numb on the wheel.

"When are you going to break out your pot?" Larry asked. "I could use something for my head."

"Yeah, Flash. Put out." Al cuffed the back of my neck.

"You want us to crash?" I swerved the car across the line and jerked it back before we hit the median, still pushing eighty in the old Chevy with its bald tires and weak suspension.

Larry's shoulder smacked against the door, and Al nearly fell into Fang's den. They backed off, too tired and drunk to push the issue.

I looked in the mirror. Al pissed through the hole in the floor, and Larry crawled back to do the same. Soon, they were sleeping again, curled up like puppies, Larry in the back and Al up front.

I pushed the old Chevy up past ninety as if I was trying to escape the draft again, burning through the parched desert like a Bonneville test run until I saw the Yuma turnoff emerge from the heat waves up ahead. Easing the brakes, I swung off the pavement and skidded to a stop, waking Al and Larry.

I threw open the door and jumped onto the burning gravel, retrieving my suitcase, sleeping bag, and knapsack from the trunk and retying the lid. With one last rebel yell serving as a goodbye, Larry peeled back onto the concrete roadway, blowing sand like the apocalypse.

Chapter 5

I STILL HOPED to see Donna before dark, but I had several hours to go, measuring the distance by walking my thumb along my roadmap. I-10 to Phoenix and then North on highway 87 to Sedona. The heat was unrelenting, over a hundred degrees with no shade or wind. If I failed to get a ride soon, I would be dried meat, pemmican.

The cars on the branch of I-10 and I-8 whipped by so fast I felt like a broken flipper in a pinball machine, never quick enough to catch one. The drivers had little time to see me and stop. I counted over two hundred cars, nineteen semis, and thirteen RVs before a dark green Chevy pickup with New Mexico plates pulled over about fifty yards up the road.

I sprinted to the cab and slid my sweaty frame onto the plastic covered seat, cracked and split at the seams. The driver was about Bardeen's age, but that was where the similarity ended. He had a waxed handlebar moustache, short curly hair, and wore a light blue work shirt. An overlarge coffee cup sat on the dash, and behind him rested a rifle on a rack made from antlers. Antelope, he informed me with a proud smile when he caught me looking. My legs straddled a cardboard box heaped with 8-track tapes of Nashville stars, but I had plenty of room. Compared to Larry's car, the pickup rode like a Lincoln.

With my limp T-shirt and hot face, I looked like I belonged in a pickup, except for my hair, which I tamed into a ponytail and secured with a fresh rubber band. I fished out my crumpled Yankee baseball cap and stuffed my hair underneath it. The rubber band and hat strategy had served me well in the Navy, where I often avoided haircuts for months.

"I'm Raul." He held out a thick hand. "I'm headed to Phoenix to pick up a new Doberman puppy."

"Flash. Just split from my wife and headed to California to find a job."

Raul nodded like he understood.

I had shared my plans without thinking, but I enjoyed naming my escape for what it was.

"She has champion bloodlines. I'll mate her with Klaus," he said. "He's a certified champion, best of three shows, and only four years old. I can't show him because he got his ear nipped in a fight with a mutt." Raul laughed. "They said I could pay for her later. I'm already a month behind in kennel fees, but I don't care because when I call my dogs, they come."

I remembered the times I came home after a double shift, and Bobo ran up and peed on my leg.

"I was married. Still am. I got a wife in Florida and a wife in Ohio. Love them both." He dropped into a more serious tone. "I'll go back to Florida this fall, and maybe I'll go up to Ohio. I haven't been to Ohio in a while. Do you have kids?"

"Just a dog."

"I have two kids in Florida and one back in Santa Fe. My boy in Florida – he must be fifteen now – looks just like me. My wife, Allie, won't come back to New Mexico because her mom's in Orlando with cancer. I can't get work there. Allie always says, 'Stay here with me. I don't care if you work.' But it's too hot for the dogs."

I shook my head. "Nixon's recession."

Raul furrowed his eyebrows. "My dogs are in jail. The kennel won't let them out until I pay the back fees. Might go there one night and break them out." He laughed. "All I'd have to do is call Klaus. I'd like to see the kennel owner try to stop him from coming to me."

He asked me to put in a tape. I rummaged through his box of country and western tunes, digging out "American Beauty." Raul vetoed that selection, saying his wife left it there; he didn't say which one. We finally agreed on Creedence Clearwater Revival, the only other name I recognized.

I injected the tape and leaned back on the hot upholstery. My ears slushed with sweat, and my eyes glazed from the incessant light.

"I have this dream." Raul raised his voice over John Fogarty. "A big kennel with big dogs, all of them champions. I go to shows in my black van, lowered, with lots of chrome, and my sign painted on the side in yellow letters: Doggone Kennel. I had a friend draw it up. She's an artist."

"I'd take the van." I yelled back.

"My dogs win all the top medals. My dogs get in movies. I get on talk shows. Johnny Carson says to me, 'Raul, you're the most famous dog trainer in the world. But why would you name your enterprise Doggone Kennel?' I say, 'Johnny, I call it Doggone Kennel because this country's gone to the dogs. Something's wrong with a country that shoots kids in college, makes war on little countries, and votes for mongrels like Nixon and Agnew.'"

"That would end the interview."

"You don't understand me, man. I'm one rich dude with expensive suits. Rich people can do anything they want."

"Thousand-dollar suits covered with dog hair."

Raul looked at me uncertainly, but he finally laughed. "Yeah, you bet. Big suits, big dogs, and lots of dog hair."

He went on about his dream kennel while we sweated, squinted, and bounced in his pickup like popcorn in a hot oiled pan. He turned up the volume for "Down on the Corner" and sat back with a satisfied gleam on his face.

The sun began to set, though you could hardly tell by the temperature, and Donna's place in Sedona was still a few hours away. My mind skipped back to the week Ronnie and I had spent with Donna and Walt at his parents' condo in Pacific Palisades.

We had packed what we could in the few days after I flew home from boot camp, and we raced across the country in four days, pushing our old Plymouth and arriving wide-eyed on Walt's doorstep. Ronnie and I were sticky with road sweat, afraid at first to sit on the leather furniture, so we perched at the long dining room table with its expansive view of the Pacific Ocean and white surf. I stared out a side window overlooking the building next door, which had slid partway down the cliff and leaned precariously over a row of palm trees.

Walt followed my eyes and said, "Don't worry, man. My dad has insurance."

I shrugged and leaned back from the window. "Let's roll a joint." I pulled out our scant baggie of leftover shake. Ronnie and I had been smoking the dregs of sticks and seeds since no new dope had been available in New York.

Walt took one look at my sad stash. "We can't smoke that stuff." He produced a quarter pound of Colombian buds, rolling one number after another.

Dancing through the condo that week, Donna trailed the scent of patchouli oil, wearing a halter-top, a roach clip necklace, and an impish grin. Ronnie wore her red flowered bikini most days. The massive stereo pumped rock and roll: Janis Joplin – Donna's favorite – Joe Cocker, The Beatles, Jimi Hendrix, and The Doors. The condo felt like a rest area before military training and our impending orders to Vietnam.

Wild and horny, primed by the two-month separation of boot camp, we tried to cram an idyllic life into a one-week hiatus. Late one night as we sprawled on the thick carpet with the ashtray piled high with roaches, we stumbled on the idea of switching partners and reached a self-conscious impasse. Our conversation was indirect like we were discussing a movie. Our voices were sleepy despite the sexual currents, sounding detached by the endless weed, so we hardly knew who was speaking. Leaning against the couch, Walt wore a smirk on his face. His heavy eyes watched the rise and fall of Ronnie's breasts as she lay across my legs.

Donna popped up from her prone position on the floor, her eyes wide with inspiration. "How about we take turns revealing some dark inner secret?" She paused. "It's not a secret how much I love Walt. But sitting in a circle with people I love makes me feel one with him."

Walt nodded. "I love you deeply. I feel close to all of you. I love you all." He held a roach clip over the thick white candle until an ember glowed on the tip of the joint. He took a deep hit, passing it to Donna.

Ronnie eyed the candle. "Sharing moments like this is the essence of being human, and our ability to share distinguishes us from the mass of humanity who are unable to feel."

"Just like Lennon," Walt said.

Walt and Ronnie stared at one another, mystified.

Before long, they were all looking at me. I heard the swish and click of the turntable as The Rolling Stones launched into "Sympathy for the Devil." I tapped my finger on the coffee table through the first few measures. "I always admired The Rolling Stones because they never climbed the mountain to see the Maharishi." The others stared at me with blank faces. "It's like the company chaplain blessing the Marines before they go on patrol. The real meaning of God and universal love is lost in platitudes."

"This isn't about the war, man," Walt replied. The war was effectively over for him since his father planned to buy off a bureaucrat, a family friend, for his discharge.

Donna grimaced like I had just farted.

"Flash has difficulty revealing his feelings," Ronnie explained to Donna. "He was taught to hide his emotions."

"Many men think they have to hide their feelings, and that's why I'm so proud of Walter."

Walt took a deep hit and exhaled. "Don't be afraid, Flash. We love you."

I almost told Walt to spare me his love, but I bit back the words. I did not want to appear uncool.

We continued to smoke and expound on forms of love from Lennon and Gandhi to Romeo and Juliet, all vaguely similar. We slumped against the floor pillows and furniture as the stereo cycled through the stack of records, and the volume pulsed. I still resisted the communal moment, unable to reconcile the meaning of love with my pending orders to

Vietnam. I understood personal love well enough, but the existence of universal love hovered beyond my grasp. Maybe Donna felt disconnected also, eventually leaving the room while Ronnie and Walt bent their heads together in an extended dialogue about their fathers. I gave up trying to listen to them, losing interest and dozing off on the couch.

I couldn't have slept for long. I awoke to the droning voice of a disk jockey predicting warm, clear weather for tomorrow. Next up, Elton John. I arose slowly, stiff from lying with my head propped up on the arm of the couch. The air was heavy with late night ocean air, sleep smells, and lingering cannabis. I turned toward the center of the room where Ronnie was pinned beneath Walt on the blue Persian carpet. Walt was much heavier than me, and I wondered how Ronnie bore his weight. They kissed languorously, like sleepwalkers.

I wanted to shake them awake, my blood rising.

But I heard Donna rustling in the kitchen. I tiptoed past the mass of Walt and Ronnie toward a flickering yellow light, and I found Donna sitting at the breakfast table, staring at a thick red and orange candle and sipping herb tea. I poured myself a cup. Chamomile.

"Hey, man. Where you want to get off?" Raul yelled at me, popping out the tape at the same time.

"You know Phoenix better than me. Where's the best place to catch a ride up Highway 87 toward Flagstaff?"

Raul dumped me on a ramp that resembled a bobsled shoot. Cars honked as we yelled goodbye, their drivers angered by Raul's abrupt stop. There was no safe place to stand, let alone set down my suitcase and sleeping bag.

An older man in a Chrysler stopped out of pity and dropped me off at the next exit. Three hours and eight rides later, I had progressed only as far as the intersection with Highway 87, a freeway running parallel to a wide business route lined with a shopping center and several fast food restaurants. Between 87 and the business route ran a two-lane service road, connected to the freeway by an entrance ramp. I hiked a half mile up the service road and parked myself at the mouth of the ramp. The traffic had slowed to a trickle.

A patrolman in a black and white Phoenix squad car stopped behind me, flashing every light. The still air around us burst in red flashes as his spotlight focused on me.

I sat behind the chicken wire in his patrol car, waiting while he called my numbers into the sluggish FBI. While he waited, he set a McDonald's bag on his lap and ate two cheeseburgers and a bag of French fries, savoring each one with a drip of catsup. He was messing with me. He had the power, and he enjoyed every ounce of it. If he wanted to haul me in, he would have done so already. My anger began to churn, my cheeks glowing warmer than his soggy fries, despite the fatigue of my long day in the sun and my Lonestar breakfast, but I knew I couldn't say anything. I watched the sky beyond our canopy of flashing lights darken to pure night.

"I'm not going to arrest you this time," he said after well more than an hour. "But you're a road hazard standing here after dark. You'll have to stand over there." He pointed toward the business route, on the far side, in front of the dark shopping center. My chances of getting a ride had fallen like a stock crash while he stuffed his face.

Less than a dozen cars drove past in the next hour. One car filled with drunken young cowboys honked and hooted at me, tossing a beer can that landed with a loud clang about a hundred feet up the street. I watched the pickup's taillights squeeze together with distance. Soon the same carload careened past with two cans ringing on the curb a few feet from me. I wanted to throw them back on their next pass, but I didn't want to prolong my stay.

I headed back to the ramp to take my chances. My legs quivered from fatigue, and I had lost the feeling in my fingers and toes. There was nowhere to sleep in that concrete desert if I was so inclined. My anger at the cop and the locals was the only thing keeping me awake. I needed a ride out of there.

Before I extended my thumb, a green Ford pickup with red and yellow running lights pulled over. My new driver wore a cowboy hat and didn't say much, reminding me of *Shane,* the classic movie cowboy, with his weathered face and strong demeanor. He carried me safely out of town. He said his name was Harold, and he was on his way to Flagstaff, so I would be getting out before he reached his destination.

I dozed off, something my road adrenaline normally prevented. But Harold seemed safe enough, and I was too tired to care.

Chapter 6

WHEN I AWOKE, the brown National Monument sign for Montezuma Castle flashed in the headlights before whizzing past my window. Ronnie and I had stopped at the ancient Indian city on our way to California and Walt's parents' condominium. The sandstone and adobe structures were so well preserved they could be lived in today, except the rooms were small and the ceilings low. The doorways resembled a skeleton keyhole, so visitors had to crouch to pass inside, making it easy for the residents to club unwanted guests on the head. Pre-condominium security.

Although little remained of the tribe aside from their timeless construction and a few artifacts, Ronnie and I had sensed their presence as we walked through the rooms. Their footfalls had worn pathways in the solid rock, and we could almost hear them shuffling around us, the souls of the past. We left our footprints in the same ancient dirt. We breathed the same air. I even thought I heard their voices inviting us into a sense of oneness with the ancient society in a way we had seldom felt in our own country. The war had thrown up thick adobe walls between people, isolating us from other souls and generations.

But despite the empathy we shared with the spirits of Montezuma Castle, I crept like a trespasser in someone else's home, trying to reconcile my emotions, not unlike my discomfort the night Donna and I shared cups of tea in the condo while our spouses embraced on the living room carpet.

She had brewed chamomile tea because she intended to stay awake.

"Did you see what's going on out there?" she hissed when I poured myself a cup of tea.

I still fumed at the sight, wishing I had kicked them awake. Maybe joining Donna in the kitchen was a mistake.

In an exasperated whisper, she said, "Your wife and my husband are fucking in the living room."

I grimaced, unsure what to say.

"I came in here because I didn't want to watch. I guess I don't really care. I hope Walter's having a good time."

"We allowed it to happen."

"We sure did." She talked into her tea as if it were a periscope through the textured plaster wall into the living room. Her head jerked up. "What do you mean by that?"

"All the talk about freeing our emotions and our inner selves. Anyone could see Walt and Ronnie were attracted."

"And you fell asleep."

"Not on purpose."

"How could you?"

"I tried to listen to them, but I got bored. I didn't think they'd go that far." It was a poor excuse, and we both knew it.

"It's really your fault." She sounded like a therapist. "You never reveal what you feel inside."

I shrugged my shoulders. "The game was fun, but I thought it was kind of silly."

"It was silly." Donna shook her head. "You're avoiding the issue. Walt wanted to ball Ronnie ever since he met her, and he wasn't sure if she felt the same way. Ronnie is one of the most beautiful chicks I've ever met, and I'd ball her too if I was a man. So, I told him it was okay with me." She paused and grimaced. "God, how I could be so gullible? Walter was worried about how you would react. Now he knows. You fell asleep."

I clipped a roach to Donna's hemostat and fired it up, careful to avoid the leather thong and turquoise beads. I inhaled the smoke and shook my head. "You let it happen as much as I did."

She ignored my accusation. She took a hit and squeaked on in a high, tiny voice, holding her breath, "No, the game was just a game." She paused and sucked in another ribbon of smoke, pursing her lips, and moving the hot coal safely away from her mouth. "The game was a medium like a gypsy reading tarot cards."

Her high hit-holding voice sounded like Minnie Mouse. We exhaled at the same time and coughed, which brought on a mutual giggle followed by sips of tea to cool our throats. When we recovered, she looked to me for concurrence. "Why didn't you stop it? You could have."

I noticed a glint of conspiracy in her eyes. I wondered what she was thinking. I glanced out the kitchen window, just past Donna's shoulder. I saw the dark edges of the building next door, part of which had slid twenty feet down the cliff, where it rested against a retaining wall built to protect the next row of condos. The condos were not secure in their cliff any more than we were. I knew our moments were temporary.

Donna waited for my reply, her wide eyes bright in the candlelight, holding her teacup in front of her full lips. I imagined sliding down the cliff and landing on her soft flesh.

I leaned closer to Donna's edge of the table. "I could stop them now. I almost did. But you and I would wonder when it might happen."

Her glazed eyes locked mine in a mutual stare.

"Or Ronnie and I could just pack up and leave."

"That would be too radical." She looked down and raised her cup. Her robe fell open as she moved.

I studied her cleavage in the periphery of my vision, resisting the impulse to turn my head for a better view.

"Too bad we're not attracted to one another."

"I wouldn't say that." I picked through the ashtray for a roach large enough to light. Donna was certainly attractive. She had a voluptuous figure that fit her infectious, bawdy manner. She was also subdued at times as she was that night, self-consciously sexy, projecting herself as an earth mother, a woman for long nights in the wilderness.

"It would be so much easier if we just balled each other," she said.

I fixed another roach on her clip, lit it, and passed it to her.

She inhaled. "Easier for all of us, especially for them."

"Maybe they just fell asleep."

Donna squinted at me, and we broke out laughing. We tried to suppress our laughs into whispers, which sounded more ridiculous and made us laugh all the harder. We talked about making love, whether it would sanction what Ronnie and Walt were doing or give us a measure of revenge, until we grew so weary that our elbows no longer supported our chins. The candle melted and sank into a yellow puddle on its paper plate.

Donna's head slipped back and tapped the kitchen wall. She stood up, announcing she was going to bed. We kissed good night like cousins, and she strode away without looking back.

I smoked another roach, a small oily one, before extinguishing the incense and candle stub and following her out of the kitchen. The rising sun already bathed the condo in red, filtered light.

The living room was empty of extramarital lovers, and I didn't find Ronnie in our bedroom. I stole back down the hallway to the master bedroom, where the door was ajar. I saw Donna asleep on the bed, still wearing the robe she wore during our tea ceremony. I leaned against the doorframe and thought about entering her room. I reran our conversation. I couldn't measure Donna's desire. Or mine.

Now as I burned through the Arizona night with my quiet driver, I still wondered if Donna had left the door ajar for me or if she merely left the door open in her stoned fatigue. If Donna left her door ajar again in Sedona, I imagined crossing the threshold and Donna folding me into her warm breasts. The more I thought about the evening in the condo, the more I wished I had been more aggressive. Now that Donna and I were both separated, things were sure to be different.

The next morning in the condo, Ronnie told me she began crying when she and Walt started making love, which upset Walt so much he stopped. I knew why she cried. I wished it were only her loyalty to me, but I also perceived a link between Montezuma's Castle, the condo we made our temporary home, the house of our marriage, and the spirits that protect all homes from intruders.

Later that morning, after we slept a couple of hours, Ronnie and I made love, and she squeezed my chest with her wiry arms like I was her savior. "I wanted him to be you," she whispered.

When the four of us showed up in the kitchen for a late, groggy breakfast, we all seemed relieved that the tryst had not gone well. I caught Donna's eye when she speared a square of French toast and wondered if she shared my assumption that our union might have been more successful.

Harold swung off an exit. I sat up and asked where we were. He had decided to take me part of the way toward Sedona and then go on up toward Flagstaff on a county road.

After midnight, he dropped me in front of a log cabin store and gas station, both dark and deserted. Across the highway stood a matching log cabin restaurant, also closed, dimly lit by one security light mounted on a braced wooden pole, which supported a pay telephone. The one car parked in front of the restaurant, an old Chrysler, looked like it had been there for months, judging by the layer of brown pine needles on its roof and hood, but the tires still looked okay. I thought about hot wiring the beast and cruising to Sedona and a warm bed, but I figured someone would have moved the car by now if they could. I sat on my suitcase inside the ellipse of the security light, near enough to the highway to be seen by passing cars. I still hoped for one more lucky ride. I had told Donna's mother I would arrive in Sedona on Saturday, which had just become yesterday.

In the next hour, one car passed then two. I began to tire and crash; the hundreds of hot miles had taken their toll. I finally rolled out my sleeping bag on the lawn, off the edge of pavement, shaded by a pine tree from the security light. My Navy foul weather jacket was my pillow, and I kept my knife within reach underneath it. But I saw no signs of predators, only the bright blanket of stars burning cold and distant in the clear mountain air.

I lay on my back and stared upward, identifying the thick band of stars wrapped around the sky from horizon to horizon as the Milky Way. Having grown up under East Coast skies, hazy with moisture and reflected city lights, I had seldom seen the galaxy in all its glory, except for the photographs in my astronomy textbook. I imagined the core, the black hole sucking errant light and matter, creating new stars among the billions warming their own worlds, each star shining equally to me as if they dwelled on the same plane.

I wrapped my Boy Scout sleeping bag tighter around me, running through the origins of my trip and my marriage, what I was going to do, what I would say to Donna, and all the things I needed to decide, running through them in hyper speed like a quasar firing in the center of my own memory. The early days of my marriage, the brief months in California, the year on Adak, the recovery from Adak and the military, and finally the bleak Bardeen winter, all galaxies in my universe. I traced my hitchhiking trip as a voyage through that universe, inscribing connections to other times and places: Pacific Palisades, Adak, Binghamton.

But as I joined all the lines, the shape reminded me of Ronnie, her constellation burning brighter than Orion. I saw an image of her sitting cross-legged on our orange shag carpet in Binghamton, tilting her head curiously as I described the lesser constellations of my memory. When I softened my focus,

Ronnie's constellation collapsed like a condominium sliding into the sea, drawing into a single line – a trajectory away from Binghamton – away from her and curving across the sky toward the Western horizon and California. She was as distant as any star.

Chapter 7

I WAS AWAKENED by bright rays of sun filtered by pine trees. Soon, a sleepy guy in a Ford Bronco stopped. His coffee steamed on the windshield from a large triangular cup. Custom-made stoneware, it looked like an artistic interpretation of a coffee cup fashioned off planet by an alien culture.

He dropped me off before seven in Sedona. Fog clung to the ground. Tall trees pierced the gray fabric and stood out as silhouettes against the morning sky. The smell of balsam and pine was so thick it reminded me of Christmas.

Donna's street was marked on my map just west of town, about a half mile. Munching a breakfast apple from my backpack to take the edge off my hunger and breathing deeply of the sweet air, I walked slowly to kill some time before rousing Donna.

Her house was one of a development of twenty built on a stretch of flat ranch land. Few trees shaded the neighborhood, but the pine forest surrounded it in the foothills beyond. Her street was paved with oil and tar mixed with native sand, and her stucco ranch house faced the hills, away from the highway. The house looked at least ten years old, weathered by sun and mountain snow. A few evergreen shrubs grew out front along the edge of a small lawn, burned brown and worn to dirt like the yards of most of her neighbors. An old green Chevy station wagon with blistered paint sat in the gravel driveway, and next to it, a Honda 350 rested on its kickstand. I wondered who owned the Honda.

Seeing no lights inside the house, I squeezed my luggage through the wooden gate to the backyard. I thought I might catch a few more winks. A small deck jutted out from the back door and a flight of steps sloped down to the ground beside a wire pen too large for rabbits. In the quickening dawn, I barely saw the puppies at first, six of them, fat and fuzzy. Their mom, a yellow lab, watched them with lazy pride and licked my hand demurely. I thought of curling up and sleeping in their warm den, but the puppy tongues and dirty paws were sure to make me look and smell even more like a vagrant than I already did.

When I saw a light in the kitchen, I lugged my things back around to the front door and knocked. An attractive woman – not Donna – cracked open the door. A brass burglar chain cut across my line of sight. I stood on the stoop, a step down from the door, my eyes staring over the chain at her heavy bosom. She wore a dark blue robe, her blond hair mussed from sleep, and her face lined beyond her years, but I guessed she was about my age. She frowned, ready to slam the door.

When I asked for Donna, she left me standing there with the chain intact.

In a few minutes, Donna appeared in a quilted housecoat and unlatched the door. She examined me with a wry grin and ushered me into the living room. "Sit down. I'll be right back," she said with an ironic lilt to her voice. She had a way of greeting people like they were entering her lair, a place of mystery and pagan ritual. I was grateful for a soft couch and central heating.

Her roommate shuffled into the kitchen, which I could partially see from my obstructed view in the living room. She put a kettle on the stove, and I waved. She failed to notice my gesture, turning to stalk back to the rear of the house, her hair wet from the shower and swept back in a glistening mass. I stood up to stretch my legs and check the progress of the dawn over the tips of the pines through the front window with curtains edged in lace, an odd choice for Donna. She'd be more likely to tack up a Far Eastern cotton print with swirls of orange and red. Dew ran down the inside of the aluminum panes and caught on the lace. I had to take a leak.

Soon Donna swung back into the kitchen, dressed in jeans and a blue patterned flannel shirt, closely trailed by the blond woman, also in jeans and a red and white checked flannel shirt. Donna's auburn hair hung wet like the blonde's and shorter than I remembered. They chatted in hushed tones while Donna poured cereal. I smelled burning toast, reawakening my road hunger, but I had a more immediate need.

Walking up to the kitchen table, I asked, "Okay if I use the bathroom?"

Donna glanced at the other woman and laughed. "Sure, man."

"It might be occupied," the blonde added with the clear, unemotional tone of a stewardess. I wondered if Donna had other roommates.

I pivoted toward the hallway.

"Flash," Donna said to my back. "This is my friend, Amy."

"Nice to meet you, Amy."

She rewarded me with a sisterly smile and kept spreading orange marmalade on a blackened piece of whole-wheat toast.

When I returned, Donna and Amy were bent over their plates, talking in low voices. I sat down at the table and gathered the gist of their conversation. They planned a trip up to the mountains. I thought it would be fun to spend the day tromping around the woods with Donna and Amy, blowing joints and getting crazy. My spirits picked up.

"Where are you headed?" Donna asked me.

"California. I'll be seeing my friend Jack in Ventura. One of the Adak outlaws." As I mentioned Adak, I knew from her expression I had made a mistake. Her husband Walt had also spent a brief time in isolation on the muddy Aleutian island.

"Adak," Donna repeated to Amy, who smiled ironically and nodded her head as if the word unlocked a world of mutual disdain, machines and men smelling of motor oil and sweat, and beer flowing in torrents every night.

"Flash was on Adak with Walter after their orders to Vietnam got canceled," Donna said. Her voice assumed a lilting tone again, this time directed at Amy, like she was chanting a passage from memory. "Walter was only there for a few months. His father paid someone to give him a medical discharge for a bad heart. But there was nothing wrong with his heart or anything else I knew of." She turned to me. "How long were you there?"

"A year. I was supposed to go to Nam after nine months, but my orders never came. So, I escaped Vietnam twice."

"You ended up in Rhode Island."

I stared at her bowl of cornflakes. "Always lucky."

"Are you planning to crash here?"

"If it's all right," I replied hesitantly, not expecting her direct question. I had assumed it would be okay since I always offered the same hippie hospitality when any of my friends passed through Binghamton. "Last night, I was stuck in the mountains out by the interstate, and I didn't want to call you so late."

"That's right. You called my mother a couple of days ago," she said blandly. She acted like she didn't recall I was coming. I spied a wall phone next to the refrigerator.

"You gave us your mother's number in your last letter. Your mother gave me your new address."

She nodded her head, trading a dour look with Amy.

"I got a ride to Fort Worth with another Seabee who's been running dope from Mexico to Boston. But it took me longer to get here than I expected."

The mention of illegal drugs sparked her interest. "Some dudes up the road are starting a marijuana farm. They asked me to be their taster."

"I'm looking for a job myself."

"I'm going to give them a puppy. Thinking I'll give them Sneezy," Donna said, eyeing Amy who grinned in assent.

"Maybe you should give them Dopey," I suggested.

Donna and Amy showed no sign of amusement at my mild joke.

I caught the smell of Amy's toast, and my mouth began watering.

Donna recalled our party times in California for Amy's benefit, how we spent a few months in San Diego and then

Ventura after the time in the condo, while Walt and I waited for our overseas assignments. She jerked her head toward me. "How's Ronnie?"

"She's fine." I could tell from Donna's expression she expected to hear more than that. "We haven't been getting along. So, I decided to hitchhike out to California. Besides, hitchhiking across the country has always been a dream of mine." I struggled with my explanation. I didn't want to talk about Ronnie.

Donna turned again to Amy with a dark look, not unlike the aversion inspired by my references to Adak and Dopey.

"I just want to know how Ronnie is." She assumed her counselor tone. "You're having a great time on the road, but how is she feeling?"

I glimpsed Donna and sighed. "She's seeing this old guy," I began haltingly, just as a young man walked into the kitchen. His surprise appearance made me pause. Amy and Donna hardly noticed him. "That's the real the reason I left. Her scene with this guy, who's also her boss, and his sick love letters were making me crazy. She says she's breaking it off, but then it starts all over again. He's over forty." I accented Bardeen's age, not unlike the way Al described his wife's lawyer.

Donna snickered. Amy ignored me, but the young guy seemed amused.

"But how is Ronnie feeling?" Donna repeated with accents on "how" and "feeling," mimicking my speaking cadence. "You need to interrogate her feelings as well as your own."

The young guy strode over to a cabinet above the sink and fetched a box of cornflakes and an earthenware bowl with a brown and white salt glaze pattern, the same pattern as the cups the women held. He was shorter than me and stockier with light hair and a sparse moustache. He reminded me of my friend Jack, though smaller, less muscular, and his face narrower. He wore jeans patched in the ass and knees and a thermal undershirt. He was about eighteen at most. Donna was robbing the cradle. Or Amy. In either case, we might have a foursome for our mountain trip, though I was feeling less enthusiastic about the prospect.

Donna said my inability to tune into Ronnie's feelings might be the root of our problems. I had forgotten how much she liked to lecture. Amy agreed with everything she said, and the young guy paid no attention, standing at the counter and lapping up his cornflakes.

"Ronnie's having trouble deciding what she wants," I said, breaking into one of Donna's infrequent pauses. "She wants to go back to college, but she won't quit her job because of her boss."

"See, you're not tapping into her true energy." Donna looked to Amy for concurrence. "And Ronnie has more energy than any chick I've ever met."

I nodded my head, since Ronnie's personality had a quality that might be described as energy, though I was unsure what Donna meant by "true" energy. It sounded too much like a shampoo commercial.

The young guy sauntered over to the table with his bowl and spoon.

"Rob, Flash," Donna announced as I moved my elbows aside to give him room to sit. He gave me a friendly grin and extended his free hand. No one said anything while Rob munched on his cereal. Despite my cool reception thus far, I still hoped the day might turn out okay: a glowing campfire in the mountains, a few joints, and the Milky Way burning bright. Gazing up, I did not see warmth in anyone's blank expressions, and my expectations grew dimmer.

I ventured, "How's Walt doing?"

Amy frowned, furrowing her forehead and pursing her lips like I was Dopey the puppy, and I had just peed in the corner.

Donna grimaced. "He's fine. He stayed up in Seattle, and he's working for his father. I think that's what he always wanted to do. He made his choice." She studied Amy as if to say there was more to the story. "At least his parents are happy."

I shook my head. "I haven't heard from him since Adak. I wrote him a card last year, but I'm not sure he got it." I watched Donna rip off a corner of her toast and pop it in her mouth. Walt never hit it off with my cube mates on Adak, especially Jack, the Los Angeles low rider and high school dropout. Even Ronnie eventually saw his manner as condescending. He never acted that way to me, probably because our friendship began in boot camp. We knew each other as fellow serfs.

"His mother reads his mail," Donna said, still facing Amy. "She might not have given him your card."

"Do you have his address?" I asked.

"It's someplace," Donna replied dryly.

Amy got up and carried her plate to the sink, dumping her leftover toast in the garbage. My stomach churned as I watched the toast slip out of sight.

"How is he feeling?" I said, accenting "feeling."

"He's having the time of his life, just like you." Donna's smirk revealed more than she said, linking Walt and I in our treatment of our wives and our failure to tap their true energy.

She checked the clock. "Send Ronnie my love." She tilted her head toward me. "You shouldn't blame her for anything that's happened. She's never hurt anyone on purpose, least of all you. If you really understood her, you'd go back to her right now."

"A lot has happened since we were all in California."

"You think you know so much about her," Donna said sharply. "But you don't know as much as you think."

"What do you mean?" I felt the color rising in my cheeks.

"You act like an expert about something you know nothing about. I'd like to hear Ronnie's side of it."

"You haven't seen her in three years." I stood up and stared at Donna.

She was shocked by my response and so was Amy. Rob cracked a smile. Donna furrowed her eyebrows, and her face flushed. She glanced at Rob, grinning self-consciously.

He tipped his chair back. "You said I should tell you when you're acting like a bitch."

"Okay, now you told me." She recovered her lilting tone. "Now shut up about it."

Rob winked and dug into his cereal.

She sighed. "Excuse me, Flash. Let's forget what I said."

I accepted her apology with a quick nod.

Rob tried to catch Amy's eye, but she avoided him. He gave up and chewed his cornflakes. I walked over to the counter two steps and back and stood behind my chair. I would have paced farther if there were more room in the cramped kitchen. I thought about hitting the road, which would have been easy enough to do, but I didn't want to leave in anger. I took a deep breath. "I'd be happy if our marriage was the same as it was when we were all in California."

"Those days are over, man," Donna said conclusively. "I'm never going back to California. And I'm never going back to Seattle either."

"Right on!" Amy raised her fist in a power gesture. Rob chuckled over his bowl. Donna doubled her fist, raising it to eye height and peering over her knuckles at me. I always liked Donna best when she was feisty. We all paused while their power rush faded away, taking our tension with it.

Donna announced in a suggestive voice, "Rob's staying with us for a few days." She waited a minute, watching to see how I took the news.

I nodded. It was obvious he was staying there. He and Donna had a good rapport. I wondered how Amy fit in.

Donna swiveled toward Amy and back to me. "Amy and I are going camping up by Flagstaff, but you're welcome to stay here while we're gone."

"That sounds like fun." I tried to sound relaxed. "Going camping in the mountains, I mean."

"Amy and I like getting away."

"Perfect weather last night." I spied my packed bags in the living room, a self-contained camping unit, even if I no longer expected an invitation. It was just as well. I had no desire to spend the weekend talking about true energy. I studied Rob to catch his reaction since he was also left out of the camping trip. He stood and poured himself another bowl of cereal.

After Donna and Amy loaded up Amy's rusted Chevy wagon, Donna kissed both Rob and me like brothers, catching me off guard, and Amy gave Rob a hug for good measure. They clattered away, trailing a cloud of brown road dust.

Chapter 8

STUNNED BY the abruptness of Donna's departure and our tense conversation, I stood next to Rob and watched the car disappear. I had only spent twenty minutes with her after hitching over a hundred miles out of my way. I felt like a fool.

I gazed at the jagged edge of trees along the rim of the foothills under the bright morning sun and fading blue sky. The wisps of fog had dispersed unless I counted the dew steaming up from Donna's neglected lawn. I shaded my eyes, wondering what I expected from Donna after three years and why I even wanted to see her. We never really had that much in common, not like Walt and I who had met in boot camp or Walt and Ronnie who shared a physical attraction. Other than that night sipping chamomile tea, Donna and I had never crossed any threshold of desire or even true friendship. My image of Donna had only started to sharpen in the past several days after I decided to leave Ronnie and strike out on the road. I cast my eyes toward the highway and followed the white dashed line until it rose and wrapped around a steep hill, heading back toward I-10. I decided to gather my bags and leave right away.

I trailed Rob through the kitchen door. He paused at the table, lifted his bowl, and drank the dregs of milk. We shared a shake of the head at the weirdness of it all, strangers in a house neither of us owned. Rob offered to spin a joint. It might ease my lingering tension and set me up for the road. He retrieved an oriental lacquered canister from the shelf above the stove and told me to help myself to some cereal. I hesitated at first, unsure if I should eat Donna's food, but a cornflake was a cornflake, and she'd never miss a bowlful, not with Rob around.

After we got high and I finished eating, I realized how tired I was. My early morning anticipation had evaporated with the dawn.

"You knew Donna in California?" Rob asked.

"We were married then."

"That must have been cool."

"To other people." I stifled a yawn.

"I mean California must have been cool. I always wanted to go to California."

"You should go. Is that your Honda out there? You could make it in about eight hours."

"Probably break down in the desert somewhere. I don't know anyone in California." He took his bowl to the sink. "I've never been farther away than Phoenix. Never even been to the Grand Canyon."

"The Grand Canyon is worth it." I rubbed my eyes.

"I'm going to see everything, but I promised my mom I'd graduate first." He blushed. "I'm taking summer school."

I nodded. "How'd you meet Donna and Amy?"

"They shop in my mom's store." He started crumbling buds to roll another number. "They let me stay here when my father's home. My mom thinks I'm staying at Jason's."

His self-satisfied look raised my suspicions about the living arrangements. One of the women, probably Donna, liked her men young and uncomplicated. No survivor guilt from the war, no former marriages, and no fuzzy insights about astronomy and personal history. Rob reminded me of myself a few years ago when my life was one of promise and opportunity, when anything was possible.

"You look beat, man. You should crash," he said.

"Thanks, but I think I'll hit the road."

"You came here to see Donna, didn't you?"

I stared into my empty bowl.

"She can really be a bitch sometimes. Amy's worse. But they let me sleep here and all."

"She seemed surprised I was coming."

Rob waved the freshly finished joint in the air. "She knew you were coming. She talked about it. She was just acting like a bitch."

"You're right," I admitted. "She acted like a bitch."

We both laughed deeply, only stopping when I started to cough.

"It's okay to call her a bitch, but she said she'd rip my peter off if I ever called her a dyke." He grimaced, clearly believing the threat.

"What about Amy?"

"She'd rip it off just for the hell of it."

"Donna still seems to like men."

He blushed. "Don't I wish."

So, Donna's leers were more talk than action, at least as far as Rob was concerned. Maybe she had left Walt for Amy. That prospect amused me since Walt always saw himself as a lady-killer, even claiming his tryst with Ronnie was his only unsuccessful encounter. I suppressed another yawn.

Rob lit the joint. "Why don't you just crash for a while?"

I was determined not to stay, but as we passed the second doobie, my eyes rolled shut. I popped them back open with effort. Rob directed me toward the bedroom he used and told me I should take a shower if I wanted one. I thanked him and flopped on the bed, only stirring when his bike roared out of the driveway.

I woke up cold, lying on top of the blankets with a dry breeze whistling through a cracked window. The sun had dipped low over the mountains, and soon it would be dark. I thought about gathering myself together and resuming the highway, but though I had slept about eight hours, I did not feel rested. I decided to wait until morning to leave.

I took a shower, using my own soap and towel. I wandered back out to the living room, careful not to disturb anything. Seeing Donna's tan phone hanging on the kitchen wall, I decided to call my parents and let them know I was okay.

When my mother picked up, the operator said, "Will you accept a call from Patrick McCarthy?"

"Why? Is he calling collect?"

"Mom, I'm at someone's house."

The operator said, "Ma'am, will you accept the charges?"

"Oh, I don't know." She dropped the phone and yelled, "Tom?"

I heard a click as my dad picked up the phone in their bedroom. The operator repeated her request, and he agreed.

"Where are you?" he asked.

"I'm in Arizona. I'm sorry I called collect."

"I thought it might be an emergency. But it's good to hear your voice."

"Are you okay?" my mom asked.

"Yeah, I just took a nap and a shower."

"We were surprised you left," my dad said.

"I told you."

"We didn't think you were serious."

My mom's line crackled like she was shifting the receiver to her other hand. She asked, "What are you going to do when you get to California?"

"Visit some friends from the Navy and look for a job."

"Look for a job?" my dad echoed. "Why can't you look for a job here?"

"Maybe I will if I don't find anything in California."

"What about Ronnie?" my dad asked. "You have responsibilities. You can't go running around the country by yourself."

"I left her money, and I'll send her more if she needs it."

"She sounded worried when we talked to her," my mom said.

I took a deep breath. I never told them about Ronnie's affair with Bardeen and my need to escape. Ronnie wouldn't tell them either. My sister knew we were having problems, but even she was unaware of all the details. I asked, "How's Kathy doing?"

"She went to college already," my mom said.

"She started that master's program at Ohio State," my dad added with a note of pride.

My mom laughed nervously. "It's too quiet around here again."

"Now she wants us to pay for it."

"You said you'd help her," I reminded him.

"Well, you kids are old enough to pay your own way," he declared. He refused to help me pay for college, but I hoped it would be different for my sister. She had a scholarship for her BA, but there were fewer scholarships for graduate school. I reminded myself to call her.

Hearing a ding on the line, my mom said, "We should go."

"How are you both doing?" I asked.

"I'm fine," my dad responded brusquely.

"Be careful, Patrick," my mother said. "We're worried about you."

"Thanks, I'll call you from California."

"We love you," they chanted in unison.

"Love you too." I hung up and stared at the phone. The conversation seemed more awkward than usual. I wondered if something was bothering them, my dad in particular. Kathy would know.

I retrieved my sleeping bag and rolled it out in the backyard of compacted dirt, outside the dog pen. The puppies wagged and jumped on me when I fed them, slobbering my hands with crumbs of puppy chow after they gulped it down.

For dinner, I ate two peanut butter sandwiches and an apple from my knapsack, and I borrowed a glass of orange juice from Donna's refrigerator to wash it down. By sleeping outside,

I'd let the Milky Way restore my energy and the sun wake me early for my trip to California, just several hundred miles away.

The night was so hazy that I had trouble picking out stars. I lay awake, thinking about the things Donna said, my parent's concerns, and how Ronnie seemed so distant. I tried to recall how she looked the afternoon I left. She was dressed for work, wearing her blue flower print dress with a leather belt, or it could have been the long-pleated skirt that fluffed out like a square dance outfit. She liked to wear the square dance skirt with a lace blouse because the furniture customers never expected a cowgirl to recommend living room designs and color patterns. I was surprised Bardeen allowed her to dress the way she did, but I suspected he had his reasons, making him feel virile like Matt Dillon, imagining Ronnie as his own Miss Kitty.

It worried me that I couldn't remember for certain what she wore when I left. Maybe Donna's insinuations were correct, and I had not paid enough attention to Ronnie's feelings, especially how she would cope by herself. I assumed she was eager to get me out of the way, but she might have been too hot for Bardeen to handle with her husband out of the picture, and he abandoned her.

I had put off talking to her, having no desire to rerun our predictable fights, and I was unsure if I was ready to face her again. But I decided I had nothing to lose. It was about midnight her time, but she usually stayed up late.

She eagerly accepted the charges. "Where are you?"

"Sedona, Arizona. At Donna's house, but she's not here."

"Everyone asks where you are, and I keep saying I don't know." She laughed nervously. "I miss you."

"I miss you too," I replied automatically.

"I tried to call you at Rick's last night, but you'd already left. He said you slept in a waterbed." She paused. "You always wanted a waterbed."

"I changed my mind. I dreamed I was lost at sea. Shark bait."

"You should have called me. I'd save you." She laughed, recalling a standard theme. Ronnie the high school lifeguard, and me the YMCA swimming class dropout.

When I didn't respond, she turned to household news. She described Bobo's latest adventure of chewing up one of Alex Roller's saddle shoes, which we would have to replace even though Alex likely found them in the five-buck bin at Philadelphia Sales.

"Oh, that guy with the drafting job called. He wants you to call him, but I said you were on vacation."

"I'll call him from Jack's place in a few days," I replied, though I would rather find a job in California.

"He said most of the other colleges haven't ended yet, so you have time." Her voice muffled to a whisper, and I suspected the worst. I sensed Bardeen's presence in our kitchen 2,000 miles away. I avoided asking if my suspicions were true and sparking an argument. She quickly added, "Please come home, Flash. I love you."

"I love you too," I said reflexively even though I meant it. I still wondered what was happening at the other end of the line.

"How's Donna? She never answered my letter. Or maybe I didn't answer her letter."

I recounted how I spent about twenty minutes with her, Amy, and Rob before she fled to the mountains with Amy. When I tried to describe my impressions of Donna, Ronnie read my disappointment.

"Did you want to sleep with her?"

The blood rose in my cheeks. "Well, I thought she'd be happier to see me."

"She's letting you stay at her house." Ronnie laughed. "Even if she's a lesbian. Remember how she used to flirt with me? She made it sound like a joke, but I always wondered."

"Now you know," I said dryly. My mind cycled back to the condo. Donna might have encouraged Ronnie's tryst with Walt, using him as a surrogate. But I didn't want to dwell on Walt or Donna. "I had a shower and cornflakes, so I shouldn't complain."

"I'm glad you're safe."

"What about you? How are you feeling?" I paused. "Donna thinks I'm not tapping into your true energy."

She snickered. "Makes me feel like a battery."

"Or nylon stockings." I paused. "Donna says she's never going back to California."

"She was the Los Angeles hippie, Sunset Boulevard and all."

"She says those days are gone."

"I wish we could have it both ways. I guess I want it all."

I was unsure what she meant. Was Bardeen included in her vision?

She sighed. "I signed up for an art class at Robeson with Janey."

I knew our neighbor Janey, David's wife, had been taking classes at the public art center. I stared out the window at the orange sky fading over the pine forest.

"Bruce Solomon, an artist from New York City, teaches the class. He's planning to have a one-man show in October."

"I'm glad you're taking the class," I replied. "Is it expensive? I guess you could sell the rest of the weed."

"Bruce is letting me take the class for free."

"We can pay him back."

"I'm modeling for him. He says my portrait will be the centerpiece of his show."

Our silence grew awkward as I searched for the right words to say. "Are you wearing your square dance outfit?"

"He's a real artist." Her voice faded to a whisper. "I'm posing nude."

I envisioned Ronnie's nude figure in a gilded frame hanging in the entry way of the art center, an old mansion with dark stained woodwork and flowered wallpaper. But her image mutated into a Playboy foldout with David and our other friends looking up and leering.

"I'm sitting on a stool, and I have a shawl over my shoulders running down my right arm and between my legs." She paused. "He's painting me over a deep brown background. I hope I don't look too morbid."

"A lot has happened in a few days."

"Janey said I should wait and surprise you. I thought you might get mad."

"I'm not mad."

"You just don't get it, do you?"

The nightfall thickened outside the widow, and I felt a chill. "Why do you say that?"

"If it's not about Bardeen, it's something else." Her voice faded. The phone swished like she was covering the speaker with her hand. "Now you're worried I'll sleep with Bruce."

"Is someone there?"

"See, you always bring up Bardeen," she whispered. "You think he's the source of all our problems."

The blood rose in my forehead, my ears ringing. I gritted my teeth. "Maybe we need more time away to help us solve our problems."

"That was your idea. How can we save our marriage if you're in California?"

"How can we save our marriage if you're still seeing Bardeen?"

"I don't know why you called me!" she yelled, her voice welling with tears. "Why don't you just leave me alone if all you want to do is hassle me?" She slammed down the phone.

I scowled at the receiver, disbelieving for a moment that she had hung up. I yelled into the dead mouthpiece and the still mountain night. My pulse rocked hard, breaking a sweat on my face and hands. I felt like I had just leaned too close to the stove and burned my hand.

I dug through Donna's overflowing ashtray for a large roach, rolled it into a matchbook cover, and lit it with one of the exposed matches. I wondered what I should have said, and Bardeen's role in all of this.

Ronnie's comment that she wanted it all stuck in my mind. She wanted me to come home, she wanted the security of Bardeen, and she wanted Ventura beach. She wanted children. She might want Bruce the artist. In wanting it all, she also wanted none. She couldn't have both Bardeen and me indefinitely. She couldn't escape to Ventura without leaving her job in Binghamton. She might be afraid to make a choice, afraid of the risks either way. As much as I wanted her to choose, she was forcing me to choose for her.

Chapter 9

I AWOKE WITH the sun behind a thin film of fog, bright and round like a highway patrol spotlight. After one last stroke for mom and her puppies and many excited licks in return, I wrote a brief note to Donna, thanking her for the cornflakes, orange juice, and a place to stay. I wedged it in her screen door. I might return to Sedona someday but only for the scenery. Walking around to the front of the house, I saw Rob's Honda back in its space, but I had not heard him return, my head deep in my Boy Scout bag, sleeping the sound sleep of the road weary, breathing the narcotic of cold mountain air.

On the highway's sloping gravel shoulder, I swung down my knapsack, sleeping bag, and suitcase. Checking my map, I chose to head south on the one road through Sedona rather than going up through Flagstaff. I plotted a route back to I-10 and on into Los Angeles with its web of highways, some of which passed near Hollywood where I might call Diane. With any luck, I'd make Ventura that night.

An air horn blasted through my reverie and nearly blew me into the ditch. I grabbed my things and ran up to a customized red Ford pickup. We introduced ourselves. Bud was headed for Yuma, but we'd share the same route south and west for a while.

The Ford speed shifted as we peeled onto the highway like we were entering a drag strip, and my kidneys bumped and settled. The lowered suspension marked every rock and rut. A large sponge cross hanging from the mirror waved its faded pink arms like a surfer trying to keep his balance. But the ride was steady as if we were running on rails. The desert wind whipped around the pickup, hardly affecting its trajectory, and it only swayed slightly when Bud leaned out the window to spit a brown stream of tobacco juice, careful to miss the metal flake finish.

He was looking for company. By the time we hit the desert, I knew the names of everyone in his family, how his wife divorced him and moved back to Phoenix with his two little girls and his teenaged son, and how he stayed with the construction company down in Yuma, stringing power lines through Arizona and on into Death Valley and California to hook everyone up to Boulder Dam, used to be Hoover Dam until the Democrats changed its name. Now he spent his time on the road troubleshooting and connecting new developments. I wondered how he could stand the rough suspension over so many miles of highway, but with his slicked back hair and dude ranch shirt, I imagined him cruising the small town main streets with his candy apple paint job gleaming.

He pulled out his wallet and showed me pictures of his kids with squinting eyes, deeply tanned faces, and sun-bleached hair. His son had a ponytail, a tie-dyed T-shirt, patched jeans, and trouble with drugs. Bud said he was a loser, but he looked enough like Rob to give me a double take, someone I might like.

I nodded my head to the country cadence of his speech and watched the highway unwind like reels of a cowboy movie. As we sped between the crests of jagged hills and cacti, the asphalt flattened and hardened, coming into focus out of the distortion of heat waves rising from the weathered sand and rock, though it was still early morning. The mesas formed out of nothing, distant images hovering above the horizon like fairy castles, their carved and balanced stone looming above us. The day I had spent in Sedona already seemed like an intermission, a pause in the ever-running film.

Pueblo ruins appeared in the distance on a tall mesa, a magic city abandoned and left to sink back into clay dust, simple but geometric, and more exposed than Montezuma's Castle. I imagined the builders adding rooms in symmetric patterns around a central structure higher than the rest, so the whole adobe city retained its beauty and balance through the generations, another stark contrast to the sliding condo in Pacific Palisades.

A sign identified the ruins as Tuzigoot National Monument. While I stared at the abandoned city, Bud digressed into a tour guide tone, telling me the city was built by the Sinagua, before returning to his monologue about his son Buddy and the ruin he had made of his life. I began relating the pueblos and Bud's story to my own ruins, wondering if Ronnie and I ever had a golden age when life seemed easy with few debts, no military shadow, no Bardeen.

"I felt bad about throwing him out of the house. But I found his marijuana and pipe. Damn it. His mom lets him get away with anything," Bud said. "His mouth is so bad I can't believe he eats with it."

"Maybe just let him be," I suggested, sticking up for Buddy and risking a long walk in the desert.

"What do you mean?" Bud sounded defensive, surprised I had responded at all beyond a periodic nodding of my head, which gave me a further insight into his conversations with his son.

"Buddy sounds all right. You said he does well in school, and he wants to go to college. He doesn't mean any harm."

"You think it's okay to smoke dope all the time? You smoke dope?"

"Many of my friends smoke marijuana, and it doesn't seem to hurt them." I evaded his question. "Most of them have good jobs. They just have their own way of looking at things."

"Smoking dope's against the law," he persisted, "and I don't want my son doing it."

"You raised him right, and he wouldn't do anything he thought was wrong. If he was a good kid before you found the pipe, he's still a good kid."

"I think he's a good kid, but I'll never go along with his hair and his dope smoking."

"You don't have to like it," I agreed, surmising that Bud wouldn't bend much further.

"Damn straight," Bud went on. "He might be a good kid, or at least he was, but if I find more dope in the house, I'll throw him out again. I don't care what he does outside the house. And I don't give one shit what he does when he's with his mother; that's her problem."

"Throwing him out won't help him, not if you're worried about him staying with his friends or his mother."

Bud eyed my hair. "You're probably a hippie like the rest of them."

I pushed a wisp back over my ear. The ride was getting a bit tense, so I decided to play my veteran card, hoping it would work better than it did with the Texas Ranger. "I'm a veteran." I cracked a smile. "I guess I earned the right to look however I want."

"You're a vet? No shit." He looked me over like he was seeing me for the first time. He had hardly given me the chance to introduce myself, talking at me ever since he picked me up.

"I was a Seabee, Construction Battalion. An engineering aid, drafting and surveying."

"You ever do estimates for construction projects?"

"Sure, and I drew up site plans."

"I have a kid does estimating for me part time. He's going to tech school. He keeps his hair trimmed though," Bud added with a laugh, studying me again. "I really want to get Buddy a job. You know what would really straighten him out? He should go in the Army like you did. They have a way of turning kids like him around and making men out of them."

"I was in the Navy," I corrected him. "It didn't do me much good."

"But I don't want him going to Vietnam," Bud continued as if I wasn't there. "That ain't no war for anyone who wants to go on living."

I agreed as Bud plotted Buddy's life like a game piece on a Monopoly board. It was hard to tell how much effect my comments had, if any, but Bud sounded more optimistic about Buddy's future. There might be hope for Buddy and our relationships with our fathers.

I remembered the frequent fights with my dad, more about the war than weed, and how I had squashed my parents' vision for me by dropping out of college even if I did it for lack of money. My eventual decision to enlist resulted in a truce with my dad, but the arguments still erupted once he realized my hatred of the war had not subsided. At least he treated me with more respect than he once did. My sister Kathy thought he was changing his mind about the war, but I wasn't convinced. It was hard to separate his staunch politics from our tense relationship.

Bud's soliloquy continued as we burned through the desert and wound up a series of switchbacks toward Jerome. I hardly listened to what he said, finding myself mesmerized by the queer, unique beauty of the mountain town. Carved out of a cliff, Jerome was the boomtown miner's answer to the ancient pueblos, one long main street snaking up the cliff with Victorian houses and storefronts peering out over the vast dessert and barren buttes, another magic city, perched like a temple above land you knew was sacred because of the way it appeared, the warm red and brown shades of sand and rock, and the dry wind lifting your hair and spirit.

Bud said they still mined up here, but I recognized signs of a new economy, a head shop and a vegetarian restaurant, and along the retaining walls and fences, several long-haired types reclined, soaking up the view and the rarefied air. My driver preferred to ignore them, but I waved.

Bud sensed I had ceased listening to him. He tapped my shoulder and made a fist, which loomed like a threat at first, but his thumb was folded next to his fingers with "Jesus" tattooed one letter to a digit below each knuckle, giving me another insight into the challenges Buddy had to bear. Unsure what to say, I shot him a blank glance and turned back to the window.

Bud shrugged his shoulders and reached for the radio. After cycling through several static-filled stations, he gave up and continued talking about his plans for Buddy, filling the white noise of the V-8 engine, the wide tires, and buffeting wind, but I no longer tried to listen.

After Jerome, we descended from the mountains, and the scenery became less spectacular, even monotonous. The traffic thickened in anticipation of Los Angeles, still a hundred miles west. As we neared the turn off for Yuma, I checked my map to get my bearing. Bud asked me to come down to Yuma sometime, my second invitation to Yuma in three days. But we both knew a trip to Yuma for anyone who didn't live there was unlikely. I dug Larry's number out of my wallet and gave it to Bud, in case he was looking for outlaw laborers.

The sheen of sweat from my ride in Bud's pickup soon turned to ice crystals in a Cadillac DeVille driven by a quiet businessman with an endless supply of Barbra Streisand eight-track tapes and frigid air-conditioning. He floored the pedal, and we flew across the California border, invisible to the highway patrol's radar. He let me off at the first San Bernardino exit, near a Union 76 truck stop. Other than my thanks for the ride, neither of us spoke a word.

Lugging my gear to a restaurant booth, I drank my dinner milkshake and considered whether I should call my friend Diane. I had made quick time in Bud's lowered pickup and Mr. Streisand's DeVille, but I had a mind to head straight for Jack's place in Ventura. He expected me sometime tonight or early tomorrow, and he was keeping a number rolled for whenever I turned up. That prospect appealed to me, feeling drained from my depressing episode with Donna and my phone call with

Ronnie the night before. I wasn't ready to face another rejection.

After a couple of long pulls on my collapsing paper straw, I was still unsure about calling Diane, so I decided to call my sister first. I found a pay phone where I could keep an eye on my luggage and my milkshake, raising my voice over the din of idling diesel engines.

"Not so great here," Kathy said in a hushed voice. "Jeremy just showed up. He's sitting in the living room." She sighed. "I didn't realize he was so attached."

I remembered him staring at her wild red hair, freckles, and sparkling blue eyes when she brought him home to Christmas dinner with our parents. He followed her every gesture like Gatsby stalking Daisy. She had invited him as a way of keeping the table conversation away from the war and the usual minefield of arguments between my father and me, and it worked. My parents struggled to say something worthy of a college professor several years older than their two children until I suggested Billy Martin should run for president. Everyone had an opinion about the Yankees, even Ronnie and my mother. "Did you expect Dr. Jeremy to let you slip out of Oswego unnoticed?"

"It's not funny. He's supposed to be doing research in London for the summer."

"He wanted you to go."

"Yeah, great. Summer semester abroad, complete with lectures." She clicked her cigarette lighter. "I should be asking how you are. And where."

"San Bernardino."

"How lovely, but I still think you're doing the right thing." She paused. "As much as I love Ronnie, leaving her was the smartest thing you ever did."

"I remember you telling me enlisting in the Seabees was smart."

"It was," she insisted. "I hate the war as much as you do, but I didn't want you drafted into the infantry."

I was unsure what to say. I never thought I was smart for enlisting, the lesser of two evils, but at least my Seabee days were over. Now my days with Ronnie might be over too, twice a veteran. I wished I felt better about it.

"Did you hear about Dad's heart attack?" Kathy asked.

"Heart attack?" I blurted.

"He thought it was a heart attack. Later, they said it was heart strain. He's okay now." She inhaled and yelled to Jeremy, "It's Flash. You can turn on the TV. We'll be awhile." She cleared her throat and lowered her tone. "Dad wants you to come home, but I think that's for Ronnie."

"Yeah, but he didn't tell me about the heart thing." I thought back to the last time I saw him. "It's his weight."

"And the drinking. I came home tripping on windowpane acid the night before I left for Columbus, and they were too drunk to notice."

I heard a muffled voice, and Kathy called out, "In the drawer by the lamp."

"What are you going to do about Jeremy?"

"Send him away." She inhaled deeply. "I'll tell him they found an unpublished Fitzgerald manuscript in the British Library."

"When do your classes start?"

"Next week. I already met my Romantic Lit professor," she said brightly. "He has horses."

I laughed as the operator's metallic voice begged for more coins.

Kathy quickly added, "How's Ronnie?"

"She wants me to find a job."

"In California?" My sister coughed. "Poor Flash. Everyone wants you to come home."

"Except me."

The operator pinged again, and we hurried our goodbyes.

I slid back into the sticky plastic booth, stirring up the chocolate from the bottom of my shake and licking syrup off the straw. My sister sounded like her usual self, but I worried about my father. He'd never tell me how bad his health was. Kathy said it was a McCarthy family trait. She imagined us sitting around the dining room table, each with a terminal illness, dropping dead one by one, talking about the weather.

I sucked down my milkshake with Kathy's news adding more weight to the ocean in my stomach. My mind turned to Diane, just an hour away in Hollywood. Diving into my memory of her was a good antidote as it always was. I recalled the night Chief Bush introduced us at the Enlisted Men's Club on Adak. Most of the base had gathered for a USO band, "Shocked Lightning," a pleasant break in the drab military routine even if every rock song they played sounded like a Las Vegas showpiece. Imagine "Sunshine of Your Love" sung at half speed with synthesized strings and backup singers.

"Here's the lucky guy who won the Superbowl pool," the chief said, pointing at me. "This is my wife Sharon and her friend Diane. Her husband's a first class stuck on night duty at CommSta."

Diane was about my age with wavy, dark hair and dimpled cheeks, her face retaining its California tan even in the gloom of Adak. Her large brown eyes squeezed shut when she smiled, making her appear vaguely oriental, a joyful goddess. When the Bushes staggered to the dance floor, I offered Diane a taste of my herbal medicine from California. She decrypted my code for Joe's red and invited me to her house the next evening after her lifer husband left for work, obviously sharing my desire for respite from the numbing life on Adak.

Bright and playful, Diane contrasted my mood and the dull brown tundra and overcast sky. Her living room even smelled like California, thick with jasmine incense. Night after night, we talked through her husband's shift until we were hoarse. Then I would creep back to the barracks and sleep two or three hours before rising for morning quarters and speeding through the dull workday on Dexedrine, impatient to call her again. I never thought of her as a rival to Ronnie, only a friend who shared my desire to escape, until another night at the club when we snuck outside to get high.

While I rolled a number out of the pink, cherry flavored papers I had conserved along with my dwindling supply of Columbian, rolling quickly before my fingers froze, we giggled at our deceit. Above us, a security light shined yellow like the high crime lights marking the worst neighborhoods in LA, and it heightened our sense of conspiracy. We held each other while we smoked, passing the pink joint carefully, not to singe the fur on our parkas. We let the weed take us back to California, to the bright sun on Sunset Boulevard fading to white in late afternoon and glowing red as it set behind the Channel Islands, igniting the inbound fog like pink smoke.

A white spotlight flashed across my dilated eyes, and two headlights swung around and zeroed in on our huddled figures like gunnery flares centering a target. I squinted at the Marine pickup. Marines served as military police on the island. Holding the pink joint like a cigarette, I waved, hoping the driver was one of the Marines I knew, whose usual way of asking for a toke was to scare the shit out of you. But when my eyes adjusted, I recognized the Marine Commander, Colonel Swindon, always starched and polished, the last Marine I wanted to see.

I had met him a few nights before when Jack and I answered an emergency heating complaint. I was off duty and went along with Jack to keep him company and hand him wrenches. We walked toward the main door after finishing our repair, tools and footsteps clanking and echoing in the empty hallways. Compared to our quarters, ever clean and tidy, the Marine barracks gleamed with wax and new paint, and the walls were bare, except for an occasional Marine recruitment sign, more like a bunker than a living space.

A loud bark arrested us in our tracks. "You, people! Come here!"

We pivoted back to the office we had just passed. A placard identified it as belonging to Colonel Swindon. He yelled about our wrinkled uniforms, shaggy haircuts, and tipped hats when we entered his office, rattling off the list of our offenses like a machine gun. A young Marine grunt stood at attention next to his desk, so I figured the Colonel wanted to make an example for the private's benefit and put us on report. When he finally looked up at us standing in front of him, he sighed, "Shit, you guys are just Seabees. No wonder. Did you fix the heat?"

"Stuck valve in the steam line," Jack responded with measured sincerity.

I held up the broken valve like a trophy.

Swindon shook his head. "Now, get the Hell out of here," he said, banishing us from his kingdom.

I hardly expected him to be as lenient now, catching me behind the club after curfew, holding a married woman who was not my wife and smoking a joint rolled in pink papers. He leaned out and surprised me with a glint of recognition.

I greeted him nonchalantly, "Good evening, Colonel." I hoped the persistent wind would dilute the scent of our weed.

"Ain't you one of the Seabees who fixed our heat? I was so cold I thought they'd have to amputate my toes." He laughed, and I forced a smile in affirmation. "Came outside for a smoke, huh? The air's fresh out here I guess, but it's too damn cold." He cupped a cigarette in his hand.

"Yeah, we're about ready to go back in." I shrugged my shoulders at the typical weather.

He nodded, and then he eyed Diane and tipped his hat before rolling up his window and driving away.

She huddled closer as I managed to relight the number, my hands shaking from wind chill and the confrontation. We passed the joint again, but our earlier mood was extinguished, replaced by the common malaise of Adak, a sense of being imprisoned for life.

Diane looked up at me and asked, "What am I going to do with you?"

"You're doing it now." I squeezed her shoulders more tightly. But I knew her question had greater implications. The appearance of Colonel Swindon was a sign that our liaison could not be kept secret for long, not on an island of 5,000 stranded servicemen and their bored dependents, all starving for gossip to break the monotony of their regimented lives.

Diane's eyes glistened under the security light. I leaned down and kissed away a tear growing in the corner of her eye. I knew what she wanted me to say. She wanted me to take her to Los Angeles, and my first impulse was to go even if it meant going AWOL. Leaving was the only viable option.

She repeated, "What am I going to do with you?"

Gazing into Diane's brown eyes, I thought about my hatred of the military, my feelings for her, and my fears about Ronnie's job at the leather shop back home and the leatherman who might be balling her at that very moment. But leaving the island with Diane would be more than a lark. It meant divorce for each of us and a drastic change in my life and my future. I would not go back to New York, likely getting arrested for desertion, and I might regret the abrupt end to my marriage. Maybe Ronnie was simply lonely, and her relationship with the leatherman was mere friendship like my friendship with Diane had been so far.

I held Diane tighter, our thick parkas like a living membrane between us, but I could not voice a commitment. When we finally broke and traded a glance drenched in promise, I knew our moment had passed, and Diane must have sensed the same thing. Back inside, I slipped around to the bar and bought Jack a beer. I watched Diane return to her table with the Bushes, smiling like nothing had happened and dragging her coat behind her like a broken toy.

After our episode outside the club, I saw little of her. Daniel went on the day shift, ending our string of second shift encounters and phone calls, although she did invite Jack, Phil, and me to dinner one night. Phil and I saw her and Daniel at the club one other time. Daniel drank tonic water and sneered every time we burped our Olympia beers, a tee-totaling lifer, the worst kind. Diane rebuffed my attempts to talk to her, but she showed interest in Phil's plans since he was getting out of the Navy soon.

A few days later, I learned from Phil that she had made plans to leave, coinciding with his discharge. She wanted to join him on his tour of the West Coast, and Phil asked if I minded. He was surprised by her request. They had not developed the relationship Diane and I had, but my feeling of loss had subsided, and I had no hard feelings toward her or Phil. Now, sipping the dregs of my milkshake, I recalled the letters I received from both after their great escape. They parted ways after just two weeks.

I decided to call her. Diane sounded excited to hear from me, even if it was hard to hear her soft voice over the rasping phone. Her divorce had been finalized, and she hoped I would stop by. She was hosting a birthday party and I was invited.

Chapter 10

MY NEXT DRIVER had a weird tick in his neck, and his shoulders shook when he talked, reminding me of a retired boxer and instilling little confidence. But he was right. The only way to get to Sunset Court was to hike five blocks down Rockbridge, though my map did not show the intersection.

Outside Diane's door, I caught the familiar scent of jasmine incense, and a string of small brass bells jingled when she let me in. She reached up for my sweaty neck and pulled my face down for a sisterly kiss. Flickering candles lit her living room, and I heard the subdued voice of Buffy St. Marie on the stereo. No one else had arrived for the party.

I counted dozens of candles: chunky square, cylindrical, hand molded from translucent wax, glowing red, yellow, orange, green, blue, and every color in-between with free form drip patterns down their sides and a few sculpted in wild shapes like fairy houses. I dropped my baggage and joined her on the overstuffed couch behind a glass coffee table. She poured me a cup of ginseng tea, already brewing on a square mosaic platter next to a sand candle burning in the middle of a large, clay ashtray. Rings of color rippled out from the wick. Diane described how she dug the shape in sand, slowly pouring the layers and allowing them to cool. This one was flawed because the layers had bled together, but it looked perfect to me.

We began talking, and time warped around us until it seemed like we were back in her living room on Adak, sharing the excitement of the early weeks of our friendship. She sat perched on the edge of her couch, her eyes shining and a tinge of pink on her cheeks. Her hair was slightly shorter with tighter curls, but she was as vibrant as I remembered. I felt myself blush under her gaze as she filled me in on her great escape with Phil, touring the West from Washington to New Mexico in a Hertz Chevrolet before ending on a friendly note somewhere in the Painted Desert. I didn't know her husband had transferred to Long Beach about that time, and they had gotten back together for a while. She asked me to roll a joint while she retrieved a snack from the kitchen. I wished I'd showered at the truck stop.

She came back carrying two cupcakes with a small candle burning on each one. I asked, "Are you still having a party?"

"It's a birthday party," she explained softly, "for my son."

I didn't know she had a son. I had noticed a wallet-sized photo of an infant in a silver frame on the coffee table, but I assumed it was a nephew or a friend's child. She picked up the picture and held it out for me. "He's cute," I said, taking the picture. "How old?"

Her eyes glowed with a mother's pride. "He's one year old."

She retrieved a photo album from behind a row of books on a small shelf while I lit the joint. Rays of candlelight and muted colors cast wispy shadows and reflected off her dark hair and her white, beaded T-shirt, making her appear elf-like. The room itself with the candles and soft guitar music smelled and sounded magical, almost eerie.

Turning the album page by page, she described the events surrounding each picture. She gushed with stories about Billy. The photos were in no chronological order, so I had trouble matching the images to the flow of her stories. In some pictures, he looked older, especially one shot of Billy holding a red and gold rocking horse by its reins. His tow head hair seemed darker in some photos, and his face more drawn. Maybe it was the dim, patchy candlelight or Diane's Hollywood weed, but some of the images hardly looked like photographs at all, more like clippings.

She flipped the last page and turned, fighting tears, though two or three had already rolled down her cheek. She clutched my arms, burying her face in my chest and crying harder, tears welling up from deep inside. Her pain was so severe that my own throat constricted and eyes moistened.

Finally, her breathing settled into a normal rhythm, and she gazed up at me, her long lashes wet, teardrops like glitter reflecting the candle flames. She raised her face like she wanted me to kiss her, so I did, and despite the agony of the moment, I enjoyed it, my first real kiss since I set out from Binghamton, a kiss of need, of rescue.

She nestled against my chest while I fumbled on the table for a roach clip and relit the joint, unsure what else to do. I was hitching a ride in her world. We smoked and listened to the stereo. The next album dropped, and Neil Young sang "Helpless." Diane leaned over and pinched out the birthday candles, which had burned down to the pink frosting.

Breathing deeply to control her voice, she admitted the photos were cut from magazines. She had never seen her son, but she knew what he looked like. Every time she saw a picture that resembled him, she cut it out.

"Do you think that's strange?" she asked.

"No," I answered, trying to hide my discomfort. I wanted to believe her, thinking her loss must have focused itself into a vision, an image of the boy she had never seen. "How do you know what he looks like?"

"He was inside me. I felt him grow, and I talked to him. Sometimes I still feel him inside me, and I think he calls me at night. I'm his mother. I will always be his mother."

I chugged my cup of tea and asked her where Billy was now. She jumped up like I had just dropped a lit roach on her lap and grabbed the teapot in one motion. Sighing, she patted my shoulder and returned to the kitchen for more hot water.

With fresh tea in our cups, Diane described how empty and guilty she felt after the great escape with Phil evaporated, and she realized she'd deserted her husband. Her return to Los Angeles and all the places she and Daniel used to go – the Santa Monica pier, the observatory, Disneyland – all reminded her of the man he was before his military brainwashing. His hair had trailed halfway down his back. He got high and read books. He was her first real love. She began to associate his change in character with his transfer to Adak. The isle of the damned that turned her freak husband into a lifer.

Daniel was a part of her life, and she wanted her life back. I found it hard to understand how she could want a lifer Jesus freak for a husband, but I flashed back to my own early marriage and how I wished Ronnie and I could recover our days in college and our months living on the beach in Ventura. I understood her impulse if not her love for Daniel. After they got back together, Diane thought she might be pregnant, but Daniel didn't share her excitement. He knew he wasn't the father since they had only been sleeping together for two weeks.

She paused, and the corners of her mouth trembled. "I think Daniel was right. Billy doesn't look like him. Billy has a much fairer complexion and a smaller nose." She peered at me over her teacup. "Don't you think he looks like you?"

"Like me?" I jerked back. My knees nearly upset the coffee table. I took a deep breath and tried to absorb her comment. Beside the fact that I was two thousand miles away, still stuck on Adak at the moment of conception, she and I had never slept together. I always thought our relationship was too hot for a casual fling, but I had never projected it this far.

"I knew you would love Billy. You always understood how I felt. Maybe that's why he looks like you." Her voice faded into tears. "Looked like you."

I pulled her close and completed her story in my mind. Daniel forced her to give up the child rather than face him day after day. My mind spun between her loss, the smiling faces, and my surprising role in it all.

"Billy's in Heaven," she whispered. She clutched my shirt in her fists and wept.

Stroking the back of her head, I surveyed the room, still alight with candles and ethereal shadows, more of a séance than a party, a ceremony to pacify the dead or ease the loss of the living.

"I can't believe he made you have an abortion," I said possessively. "How could he do such a thing?"

"Oh, no," she whispered. "Daniel would never want that. He doesn't believe in abortion." She paused for a breath. "Billy is my spirit child. But I think he would have stayed if Daniel loved him like I do."

"A spirit child?"

"Billy was a part of me. I could feel him. I think Daniel could feel him too, though he'd never admit it."

My head was spinning. She hadn't been pregnant in a physical sense. A spiritual pregnancy? I held her closer and kissed the top of her head, wishing I could stare down into her mind and better understand what was going on there.

She wiped her tears on a birthday napkin and poured us another cup of tea. She handed me a cupcake and urged me to eat it. Angel food with chunks of cherries. At first, I had little appetite, but my road hunger, enhanced by her Hollywood weed, overcame my somber mood.

"It's okay, Flash. He's with Jesus." She told me her plans for Billy, going into detail about the bicycle he would receive at his fifth birthday and how they would ride together.

Her moist eyes glowed in the subdued light of the flickering sand candle, wax pooling and nearly snuffing the wick, throwing soft shadows across her face like tiny hands of her spirit child as if she were cradling him against her breasts, making me more wary of her party mood and how she drew me into her spirit family as the estranged father. I wasn't prepared to be a spirit father, and I began to question my decision to seek her out.

Sensing my distance, she asked again, "Do you think I'm strange?"

"No, you're not strange." I assured her reflexively, crumbling up my cupcake wrapper and looking into her bright eyes, still wet with promise. But the thought of spending more time with her made me feel queasy, and I knew it wasn't the cupcake. "I'm just surprised. I didn't know you had gone back with Daniel, and I didn't know about Billy." I pinched a crumb and added, "Maybe you need to let go of him."

She moved away and handed me the canister of weed. "Here, roll another joint." Our eyes met in a brief impasse, and we stopped talking for several minutes, listening to David Crosby singing, "Deja Vu."

When the record changed, I wondered what I might say to comfort her and reignite our earlier mood. Then the doorbell rang, and Diane jumped up like it was a drug raid. "It's Daniel," she whispered, her eyes wide with fear. "Daniel, my husband."

"Is he coming for the party?"

"No, he doesn't know about the party. He wants to borrow my car." She rolled up the cupcake papers and birthday candles into my napkin and wiped the coffee table, sliding the ashtray into a drawer. She pushed me toward the bedroom and grabbed my backpack with one hand, dragging it across the gray carpet. I caught on to her intent and picked up my suitcase and sleeping bag, carrying them to the bedroom.

"Get under the bed," she ordered. The bell rang again. "Coming!" she screamed.

"You're kidding. You really want me to crawl under the bed? You're not married anymore. We weren't doing anything wrong."

"Please get under the bed," she insisted in a tone a mother might use with a toddler. I squeezed under the bed frame, plowing small balls of dust, and she shoved my sleeping bag, knapsack, and suitcase after me along with Billy's photo album. With all my luggage and my gangly six-foot frame, it was a tight fit, but once she straightened the blue flowered bed spread, which hung towards the floor with little white tassels, the bedroom could have passed a moral inspection from Grandma Roller, provided I didn't cough or scratch. She ran across the hardwood floor and let her husband in.

Hearing Daniel's exasperated voice, I wondered about his state of mind. I had only met him a few times on Adak. He was about my height with a swarthy complexion and a closely trimmed moustache, reminding me of gangster movies from the fifties: the face of a repressed murderer, despite his Bible-thumping demeanor. I couldn't imagine how he could be a lifer and a Jesus freak, and remain legally sane. By now, he might be psychotic, and his military training had taught him how to handle guns.

I concentrated on remaining quiet, imagining the ocean and the stars, the beach and midnight surf in Ventura. As the pulse in my temples slowed, I began to hear their voices in the living room with greater clarity. They were praying. I recognized the tones and cadence from my months of living above the Rollers back in New York. They prayed in loud proclamations, punctuated by several "Alleluias" and "Praise the Lords."

They signed off, and I heard their footsteps coming in my direction. I tried not to breathe.

Diane retrieved something from the bureau across the room, and they began talking about Jesus like He was sitting in the living room eating a cupcake.

"Jesus says a man and a woman should live together. They are part of the same flesh," Daniel said as he sat down on the bed with the mattress bulge of his ass pressing against my chest.

"Praise the Lord," Diane replied in a luscious whisper. "But we aren't married anymore. Jesus wouldn't approve of our living together out of wedlock."

"We lived together before we were reborn in Christ."

"Yes, but we were living in sin."

"We were happy."

"Yes, we were happy. And I still love you." She walked over to the bed, and Daniel's weight shifted, allowing me a deep but silent breath.

"Why do we keep teasing ourselves like this? When we both want to be together?"

"I didn't say I wanted to live with you, Daniel. Jesus says we must make these choices carefully. I've prayed and prayed about our relationship, but I still haven't been called with an answer." She crawled onto the bed beside him, just above my thighs.

Neither of them spoke for a suspenseful moment, and I suspected the worst, thinking they would make love. I wondered if my injuries would be slow and gradual, beaten into a liquid gelatin like bread dough in a kneading machine or fast and messy like soft metal fed into a punch press.

Finally, Daniel whispered, "Our divorce was only a secular divorce, granted by the lawyers and bureaucrats. Jesus never approved of our divorce."

"Our divorce was in our hearts," Diane replied, remaining firm. I heard some wet sucking sounds, and then another moment of relative silence. "Daniel, I really can't tonight." She rolled off the bed.

I was saved.

He followed her across the room and pleaded with her again before finally giving up. As they left the room, Diane asked him if he was going to the lecture tomorrow night by Sam-Raji Wilson.

"I don't trust that guy," Daniel said. "Used to be a pagan. Now he's Christian."

"He's a Buddhist and a Christian. They say he's been reborn nine times." Diane paused. "He teaches people to listen to their thoughts because thoughts can deceive you and distract you from the real message of Jesus."

"You know I believe in Jesus, but Sam-Raji Wilson makes a lot of money selling his books and tapes."

"Melanie's going to his retreat in Colorado. It's free."

"Melanie loves that new age stuff," Daniel grunted.

"She's not that bad," Diane countered.

The front door creaked open, and Daniel thanked Diane for loaning him some money. He reminded her to meet him at five tomorrow, when his car repair should be done.

I dragged my stuff back out to the living room. Diane sat on the couch stunned like she had just survived a car accident, a close call. I felt just as worn with dust bunnies clinging to my damp jeans and shirt. I needed a thorough cleaning, inside and out.

"I didn't know he was coming," she said in apology. "And thank you for crawling under the bed." She picked a clump of lint from my shirt sleeve.

"That's all right." I forced a grin. "But I still don't understand why you wanted me to hide."

"It wasn't you. It was Billy."

"Billy?" I decided not to question her logic. "I left his album under the bed."

"It means a lot to me that you love Billy." She clutched me around the waist and tucked her head into my chest.

I dropped my bags even though I was ready to leave. I wanted to be polite because I was still hitching a ride in her world, but now I was looking for an exit. She broke her grasp, motioned me toward the couch, and retrieved her canister of weed.

I looked into her eyes, recalling again all the secrets we had shared, and I decided to stay for one number. We recovered by talking about how long ago Adak seemed, a few years extending to several light years of displacement. Her living room felt that much smaller, collapsed by the weight of the past and the lingering presence of her unborn son and her husband, memories in spirit and flesh, even though we avoided talking about them. They seemed less important now that they had made their appearances and left Diane and me to ourselves.

She brought out another plate of cupcakes, but my appetite had vanished. The cupcakes now sat like relics, along with her smile and the stack of records she restarted after Daniel left. Like my presence on her worn couch.

I relit the joint as she studied me closely, and I tried to understand how her needs had given birth to Billy and kept her tethered to Daniel. She wanted to help them like she wanted to help me, though she was unsure what any of us needed.

Catching my eye, she asked, "Have you thought about accepting Jesus into your life?"

I coughed on my hit. "Well, this morning a guy in a lowered pickup showed me a Jesus tattoo on his knuckles."

"I understand how he put you off, but you should think about it. Jesus could help you."

"I think Mick Jagger could help me more."

"What?" She looked astonished and offended.

"I'm sorry," I said. "I used to believe in God, but I guess I grew out of it."

She eyed me sympathetically, convinced I really needed saving. "I can help you find Jesus," she whispered.

I studied her expectant stare, wishing she had not brought Jesus into our discussion. But if I were going to pray with someone, I'd rather pray with her than Bud. "Diane, I'm not ready. You have to be ready for Jesus, and I'm not ready." She ran her fingers through my hair and stroked my neck, sending tingles down my back. "Especially now, with my separation and everything, I'm feeling too vulnerable. Now isn't the time to be born again. In any religion."

"It's the best time."

"Not for me." We held our stare for a long moment, her offer and my refusal hanging in the air between us like a thick cloud.

I finally excused myself, saying I had to be in Ventura by morning. Jack was expecting me. I gave her his phone number and promised to call her again the next time I was in LA. I didn't say I'd be more likely to call if I knew Jesus had moved out and taken a couple of ghosts with Him.

Chapter 11

AFTER A FEW short hops into the maze of LA freeways, my ride dropped me off at a Sunoco station with a phone booth. Two older guys in tattered khakis studied my untidy pile of belongings. One with yellow eyes and an unhealthy red flush said, "What you got there, pal? You lookin' for a place to stay?" He glanced at his buddy. "Let's have some fun, men. Let's party."

"I'm on my way out of town," I said, digging into my pockets to call Ventura, twenty cents for the first three minutes.

"Any spare change?" he asked.

"You probably have more money than me. Do you have any spare change?"

His comrade, pupils dilated like black holes, was hardly interested in my meager prospects. They gave up and headed toward a Mercury idling beside the full-service island. I found three dimes lodged deep in my pocket.

Jack sounded sleepy, but he asked me to call again when I reached the Ventura exit off 101, so he could drive out and fetch me. I told him about the special message I was carrying from Rick, which Jack decoded, making me feel like a Hollywood outlaw despite my fatigue. Then he said he was holding a letter for me, and my mood faded.

"A pink envelope," he informed me, impressed with Ronnie's taste in stationary and her apparent devotion. She must have sent it soon after I left, and before we argued over the phone in Sedona.

"That's great. My wife's tracking me down, and I'm not even there yet."

Jack laughed easily like he always did, but I knew he expected a different response. Back on Adak, we treasured our letters from home like Holy Scriptures. But there was no way to tell him the entire story in less than three minutes. I had to save my last dime to call him later. "Thanks for coming out to get me. I'll see you in a couple hours."

"There's a joint rolled just for you."

A gardener's truck rescued me from another conversation with my buddies. I sat on a bag of starter soil in the breezy flatbed, breathing the moist scent of young roots tied up in burlap. My pack leaned against a row of seedlings intended for a rich man's yard. Dirt clods bounced around me, each moist ball ready to sprout with new life. I tried to imagine the gardens they might become, but the thought of Ronnie's letter kept intruding. Maybe I should toss her letter without reading it, wondering if she would bug me again about yet another unborn child.

I twisted my legs sideways to ease the strain of sitting on the packed soil. Even if some of my friends, like David and Janey, were building their own families, I wasn't ready for fatherhood, spirit or flesh. The flatbed jammed my tailbone, shuddering and pounding over every rut, but I shrugged off the discomfort. I wanted movement and change, and soon I'd smell the cool, salty ocean breeze.

Changing rides after I left the bright neon of the city for the softer glare of residential neighborhoods, I found myself listening to a thundering Grateful Dead tape, with "Casey Jones" cut in several times between other tunes, cruising in a genuine woody station wagon driven by a freak with long, healthy hair and dirty teeth. He asked me where I was headed and then turned up the volume. We wound up a hilly, two-lane highway, where he left me off on the rim of a canyon. According to my map, I was still on a road to Ventura, but my driver had chosen the scenic route.

I stood on the narrow shoulder, soaking up the view. The San Fernando Valley flashed like glitter in the lingering sunset as I stared over the cliff from my perch, but my vision evaporated in a flash of high beams behind me. I turned warily, expecting a cop, but I spied an old delivery van with two young women checking me out. One who looked about fifteen with a Red Army star painted on her cheek leaned out the passenger door and asked if I was going their way. Since the van was pointed in the right direction, I hopped in, complimenting her star and squeezing awkwardly behind her copilot seat as she slid forward to give me room. I pushed through a curtain of stringed beads hanging behind the two front seats and crawled into the back with my sleeping bag, knapsack, and suitcase in tow.

The interior resembled a hippie living room with no windows, painted the bright green of frogs in comic strips. Five people reclined in comfort. An old institutional mattress, several home-stuffed pillows, and a patchwork of blankets, sheets, and fabric remnants circled a wire spool where three candles in differing stages of meltdown were wax-soldered to the wooden surface. In the center of the spool was a large art deco ashtray, orange with brown spots, like it had been rescued from a lawyer's waiting room, though it was filled with ashes, roaches, and incense sticks. More incense sticks, most of them burning, were stuck in the cracks of the spool, along with a hemostat roach clip. The walls of the van were hung with Indian bedspreads, one red with blue and white patterns and another orange with red markings like stylized leaves. I crawled past the wire spool, dragging my stuff to the back where a pile of traveling gear was stacked against the tire wells. I kept my sleeping bag for a backrest and removed my shoes, observing that everyone else was shoeless, most of them sockless. Not wanting to appear too forward, I kept my socks on.

I settled into the thick smell of marijuana and incense, along with the sudden closeness of my fellow travelers. They stared at me, waiting for me to say something. I mumbled, "Hi," and flashed a smile, but I realized they wanted more. I counted three women, all younger than me, one guy younger than them, and an older guy in his late twenties, who was the most stoned of the group. His dilated pupils reminded me of the hippie I met earlier at the gas station. He had a dark complexion with a drooping moustache, heavy eyelids, and a small droplet of spit on the corner of his mouth, which no one else seemed to notice. The younger folk waited for his reaction.

"I'm Flash." I extended my hand to him. "On my way from New York to visit my buddy in Ventura. Thanks for picking me up."

"Thank Faith," he replied. "She's driving." He lurched forward to grab my hand, missing on his first try and shaking my hand heartily while steadying himself on the wire spool. "Call me Joshua. Everything we have is yours." He said it like he meant it. "We're on our way up the coast for a little camping."

"San Luis Obispo," announced one of the girls, who identified herself as Valarie. The rest of the crew introduced themselves as Julie, Laurel, and Bark. I think he said "Bark," but it might have been "Bart" or "Mark." His voice suffered from herbal bronchitis. The girl in the Red Army uniform called back, "Alicia." Valarie produced a large Ziplock bag of weed and commenced rolling with Joshua's assent. Valarie winked as she rolled, and I complimented her technique.

We smoked and coughed in the enclosed van, the open front windows doing little for air circulation, soon becoming seriously stoned, everyone talking feverishly. Smoking in the van was like sticking your head in a bag of smoke or inhaling several bongs without taking a breath. Valerie probed me about my route west, and the other riders seemed interested, so I told them my adventures, editing for effect. I had brought my new friends as far as the Texas Ranger episode when Laurel interrupted.

"Joshua would have told that pig he didn't recognize his authority. They can't arrest anyone who isn't part of their government. You should have stood up for your independence."

"He wouldn't have cared what I thought about the government and his authority," I replied. "I was breaking the law, and he had a shotgun."

"It's an unjust law. You should have told him so, rather than trying to talk him into letting you go. You shouldn't have acted so friendly."

"I wasn't trying to make friends with him. But he did let me go, and that's all I wanted. What would I gain by going to jail?" Her advice annoyed me, but I tried to stay calm. I didn't want to offend her or the group since I had little desire to thumb another ride. But somehow her twisted reasoning reminded me of Ronnie's complaints about my enlistment, how I should have refused the draft, refused jail, and refused to move to Canada, striking a noble stance that was hopelessly impractical.

"Joshua would have gone to jail on principle," she went on. "He's been in jail a lot of times. And each time it was because some pig was unenlightened, and Joshua tried to teach him. Joshua believes it's important to carry his message to everyone even if it means going to jail for what he believes in."

"That's admirable." I glanced at him. He might endure jail better than me. At the moment, he was oblivious to anything, eyes shut, slumping lower in his pile of pillows, his chin jammed against his chest, fixed in a benevolent smile. He hardly looked like a prophet, though he appeared stoic and even mystical in repose. Maybe he owned the van.

"I don't think it's wrong to try and stay out of jail," Bark spoke up. "The joint sucks."

"You were only in county jail for three weeks, so you don't know that much about it," Laurel reminded him. "Joshua was in federal prison."

"You've never been in jail," Bark retorted.

"All jails are bad," I said diplomatically. "Especially now when they send up so many people for drugs or politics, and they mix them in with the real criminals. Some county jails are worse than prisons."

Valarie caught my eyes and said, "He's right about that, you know."

Laurel nodded reluctantly. "Joshua says they arrest us because they're afraid of us. They know we're the future, and their ways won't fit. They hold onto power by repressing us like peasants in the middle ages. Joshua says we have to show them the error of their ways and teach them that love is the answer."

"Pigs don't believe that," Bark replied. "You can't teach them about love and stuff."

"Joshua says we have to try and teach them, and if they don't listen now, they'll listen later, after the revolution. Then they won't have a choice," she said firmly, looking around for agreement.

Bark raised his fist like a club and waved it in the air, and everyone copied his gesture, even the two in the front seats who extended their fists through the bead curtain, warming at the thought of revolution. They chanted, "Power to the people. Right on," repeating the John Lennon phrase over and over, and their chanting finally aroused Joshua.

Struggling to push himself upright, Joshua grinned with pride, though his expression carried a hint of irony. He said, "Children, children, children. Let's join our hands together, and then we'll share a joint with our new friend."

We linked hands, swaying and singing the refrain until it sounded like a Hindu mantra, "pow-er-to-the-peo-ple-right-on," a Zen rock meditation, a sense of oneness, extending to me as one of their chain of chanters. The bus grew warmer with our energy. I enjoyed the moment, and I liked it even more when the van swung around a turn, and I found myself pressed closer to Valarie. When we broke our chain of hands, Valarie rolled a ceremonial number.

She rolled joints all the way to Ventura, and we kept smoking, while Julie and Laurel lectured me about Joshua's life and teachings with Laurel providing most of the instruction. Faith eventually tuned the radio to an underground FM station, drowning the conversation. I sat back and concentrated on the music. Joshua slumped in his cushions, meditating, or sleeping.

As we approached my exit, Valarie leaned over and whispered, "Laurel's not usually this bad. It's because you're new, and you don't know about Joshua. I think it's better to let people get to know Joshua naturally, over a period of time. That's how the rest of us got to know him. Laurel's only been traveling with us the last week."

"A recent convert," I said.

"So am I, I guess, but I'm not as new or as serious." She sat up and looked into my eyes like she was trying to probe my mind. "You're welcome to stay with us."

Her offer took me by surprise. I glanced around, but no one else could hear us.

"My friend Jack is expecting me," I replied automatically. She was slightly older than Laurel and Bark, eighteen or more. In the dark interior of the van with her long, brown hair falling across her face and wire-rimmed glasses, it was difficult to tell what she really looked like, but the softness of her voice, and her empathy promised more than I could see. She rested her hand on my forearm and swept her hair back as if sensing my appraisal. She took off her glasses and tilted her head, revealing her wide eyes and soft cheeks. We studied one another, leaning closer together. My mind grew lighter, my neurons cooling like smoke in a water pipe. She was a woman I might like if I got to know her.

When we parted, she said, "Come with us, Flash."

My immediate thought was to go with her, and she knew it. I was ready to follow her anywhere. But I shook my head. Hers was a hard invitation to decline, even if my attraction was enhanced by the bong van.

Drawing her near, I explained, "Don't get me wrong; I might go with you if you were by yourself, but I'd never fit into your group. After the Navy, I'm not good at following anyone."

The van lurched to a stop. Valarie touched my cheek and whispered, "I understand how you feel. I'm not sure how long I'll stay with them either."

In the background, I could hear Laurel lecturing the others on prison etiquette, but she paused and called out to me, "We love you, but don't take any more shit from the pigs."

Valarie and I locked eyes, but we knew we had to break off. I wished I could offer her a place in my own van, which I would have to go out and steal somewhere. She looked toward Joshua, whose eyes were closed, and grabbed a loosely knit shoulder bag, digging out a felt tip pen and scribbling a phone number in the palm of my hand, pressing hard to make the ink stick. She said it was her sister's number in Santa Barbara, and she planned to stop there for a few days. She kissed me on the cheek for good luck.

I dragged my baggage from the rear of the van and backed through their living space. Everyone shook hands with me and patted me on the back like I was an old friend. I squeezed behind the passenger seat and stepped into the cool night air, not too far from a phone booth. While Alicia waved and closed the door behind me, the van crept forward. I heard Joshua awaken and call out for a fresh number. I had arrived in Ventura at last.

Chapter 12

I WOKE UP late the next morning in Jack's living room. My sleeping bag was stretched out alongside a round oak tabletop without legs. A large glass ashtray and two thick candles, one purple and the other blue with pink chunks, rested on a red and white checkered tablecloth with a shiny plastic sheen. Huge pillows sewn from remnants circled the table, each one a different patchwork of patterns, and in the corner squatted an old legless upholstered chair alongside a dark wooden pole lamp. I heard pans clanging and water running in the kitchen.

I pulled on my jeans and pressed back my oily hair before shuffling into the brightly lit kitchen. To my sleep heavy eyes, the morning light flashed off the white appliances and walls like an alien sun going supernova. I squinted and blinked several times before the shadows converged into recognizable shapes.

A young woman watched me and flashed a cute smile when I turned in her direction.

"I can tell a man who needs to get his head straight." She poured me a cup of coffee and sneezed, shielding the cup. "This damn cold," she sniffed, waving her hands when she talked. "I'm Sara. The boys are all at work."

"Hey, Sara," I stammered. "I'm Flash." I took the hot mug and set it down on a round Budweiser coaster on the old wooden kitchen table. A large glass ashtray held a smoldering cigarette and an unlit roach. It was hard to keep up with Jack's romances, but when he picked me up from the truck stop on 101 last night, he said that Sara had moved in a few weeks ago.

She was married to a Navy medic shipped overseas. I caught myself staring at her sleek tan back.

"Of course, you're Flash." She set down the coffee pot, turning toward me and motioning me to sit. "We were worried. Jack didn't sleep much before you called."

"Sorry about calling so late. Hard to predict when you're hitching."

"For sure." She leaned over and pecked me on the cheek, much to my surprise. She wore her chestnut hair short, framing her round, pleasant face. Soft circles lined her brown eyes, now red from her cold. Tall and thin, she wore a white Ventura Community College tank top, no bra, and jeans ripped at the knees. She was barefoot with toenails painted light blue. She wanted to cook me breakfast.

"Let's just start with that roach." I leaned back. "Glad Jack rescued me. His beetle was one of the few cars I saw at the truck stop."

"That's my bug. Jack rides his hog when it's running." She took the roach from my fingertips and secured it in a small brass clip. She relit it with a quick puff, careful not to touch the roach with her lips. "Hey, looks like you got someone's number," she teased.

I glanced at Valarie's scrawl on my palm and blushed.

"You must be having some trip so far. Chicks writing their numbers on your hand, so you won't forget them."

"We just talked for a while." I reached for the roach.

She read my embarrassment and responded in an ironic tone, "It's cool, man. Don't worry. I won't tell anyone."

I inhaled and balanced the roach on the edge of the ashtray.

She tapped my hand lightly. "It's okay. Jack looks up to you like a big brother, and you can't do anything wrong in his eyes or mine for that matter." She studied my ring finger, still bearing the telltale lines. "Must have been hard for you to leave your wife. I'm married too, you know."

She held up her bare ring finger and blew her nose. "Married two years ago when I was seventeen. Then he went off to Nam and accused me of sleeping with everyone." She shook her head. "Not true. I was loyal then."

"Sounds worse than my marriage." I sipped my coffee and cracked my shoulders.

"Can't believe I put up with it, but I was younger then." She broke into a cough. "This time I met Jack."

She described the night at the enlisted men's club in Port Hueneme, the Seabee home station, a few miles south of Ventura. She was drinking beers at the bar with her girlfriends after bowling. Jack teased her when he came up to order a pitcher, saying her arms were hardly strong enough for bowling, but her score was higher than his. After a few more rounds, she was drunk enough to tell him about her marriage. "Jack is so easy to talk to. He said I deserved better and my husband was thousands of miles away. I was a free woman."

She stopped to blow her nose and light a cigarette, tilting her head back. "Jack makes me feel free, never any demands or conditions. He gave me a ride home on his hog. That was some ride, and me so drunk I thought I'd fall off." Watching the soft curves of her arms and her graceful gestures, I imagined her squeezing my back as I punched a motorcycle through the cool Ventura night.

After a second cup of coffee and two pieces of toast with strawberry jelly, I accepted Sara's suggestion of a direly needed shower in preparation for a trip to the laundromat. I copied Valarie's phone number to a corner of newspaper and stashed it in my knapsack before stepping into the tub. Her looping script recalled her soft touch in the bong van and her eyes glistening with promise when we said our goodbyes. She must be about Sara's age, just what I needed, a sensual escape from the Bardeen winter. I had plenty of time to find a job and worry about how I'd reconcile the dregs of my marriage.

I found a fresh yellow towel waiting for me after I rinsed off my road grime, but hanging on the hook instead of my clothes were a pair of gym shorts and a T-shirt, probably belonging to Jack because the chest was roomy. Sara found me a pair of flip-flops. I could pass for a California native.

While we waited for our clothes to wash and dry, we sat on the curb outside the laundromat, soaking in the sun. Sara smoked cigarette after cigarette, switching to Newports because the menthol helped her cold. "I still visit Richard's family. His mother doesn't know about Jack, of course. I keep my apartment near the base because of his family and because, well, you know, Jack."

"You know him better than I do."

"I've only known him two months. I know he loves me, but I'm never sure if I should give up my apartment. It costs a lot of money."

"Best to keep your options open."

"For sure. Do you think Jack wants a long-term relationship?"

"Not sure where his head's at now." On Adak, he claimed a continuing love for Sue Knapp, though it never stood in the way of other liaisons. "Last time I saw him was at Logan Airport in Boston." Sara's eyes flashed with interest, so I continued. "His battalion stopped in Boston to refuel on their way to Spain. Ronnie and I drove up to there on a lark, hoping to see him. The guy at the gate said Jack's commander wasn't letting anyone off. I told him Jack Ferro was my brother, nearly killed in Vietnam four times. I might never see him again. Finally got him to call the plane and ask if they'd make an exception. Soon enough, Jack came jogging across the tarmac, and we skipped out to a parking deck to smoke a couple joints."

Sara jumped up and ran into the laundromat to feed the dryer more quarters.

When she returned, I picked up my story. "Jack had just learned his battalion was exempted from going through customs, but he left his stash behind. I gave him our film canister of buds, and Ronnie didn't complain. We both wanted to get on the plane with him."

Sara lit another Newport.

"About three weeks later, we received a shoe box from Germany with some chocolates and about an ounce of hashish wrapped in foil."

"He tried to bring hash home after his tour because it was so good and cheap," Sara added.

"But he threw it in a trash can at the airport when he found out they had to go through customs on the way back." I completed the story we both knew. "What a bummer."

"He said it was like throwing his hog away. He planned to make enough money off the hash to buy a bike. Bought one anyway, one that needs a lot of work."

After feeding the dryer again, we went back to Sara's bug to blow another number. She shook her head. "I can't believe you and Ronnie got stoned with Jack in the airport."

Oddly enough, I sensed a chill even in the dry heat, recalling another time at an airport. I had slept on plastic chairs in Seattle on my way home from Adak, wondering if I would find Ronnie shacked up with the leatherman. Glancing into Sara's tired eyes, I imagined Ronnie in New York at that very moment, leading her double life with Bardeen, just as Sara led a double life with Jack, with her husband thousands of miles away.

"Is something wrong?" Sara asked.

She was poised to listen, so I went on. "I'm wondering how Ronnie must feel now that I'm gone again and how you must feel."

"Can't say how she feels, but I still love Richard. I remember the best times like painting his car and driving down to Mexico. Dancing at the club. Then I remember him saying I lived like a pig because the floor wasn't shiny enough, worrying about shit like that. Jack's different. I love him, but he might decide it's not his trip anymore and tell me to move out."

"How can you love them both?"

"I just do. I don't think about Richard all the time when I'm with Jack. And when Richard was home, I was with him."

"I can only love one person at a time. True love, anyway."

"It's not like that for me. Most days I love Jack, but I still think about Richard." She stubbed out her cigarette on the curb. "Richard's coming home in July, about the same time Jack's getting out. Another reason we haven't made anything permanent."

"How about Richard?"

"He doesn't know about Jack. If he did, he'd kill me. I doubt he could kill Jack, even if he wanted to."

I watched Sara reach for another cigarette. In some ways, it was easy to empathize with Richard's homicidal anger. I bent back and twisted my neck to relieve my hunched position. "Maybe we should get Richard to kill Bardeen," I suggested. "Bardeen's the old fart my wife's seeing. You tell Richard that you're seeing him, not Jack. Then, Richard kills Bardeen and gets arrested. Problem solved for both of us. "

"That's the weed talking," Sara laughed, but then grew serious. "I just want Richard to be the way he was. Jack says I should face him and tell him I'm leaving for good. Jack says I owe him that."

"Might be the right thing to do, but escape is easier."

"You're going back, aren't you?"

"Never said I was going back."

"What does Ronnie think?"

"She thinks I'm coming back."

Sara shook her head. "Wow, man. You have some unfinished business."

I stared into Sara's bloodshot eyes as she sniffed, blocking a sneeze before it finally erupted. Sara might be right. At some point, I had to face my unfinished business.

She stroked my shoulder. "I'm glad you decided to come out here, and so is Jack. You have plenty of time to decide what you want to do."

When Jack roared up the driveway on his Electra-Glide in the late afternoon and burst into the living room with a knapsack slung over his shoulder, Sara and I were lumpy, hung over from weed. We stood up from the sawed-off table and welcomed him home. He hugged us one at a time and stood back, scanning us with a curious expression on his face like we were an old couple he had just come to visit. But he laughed easily and plopped his knapsack on the table, his thick arms and chest straining his khaki T-shirt. With his blond hair swooping across his tan face and day-old beard, he could have stepped out of a surfer poster. Sara's eyes followed him like radar.

She retrieved an old Coca-Cola serving tray with a small pile of weed and a few flavors of papers. She did the honors of rolling while Jack dragged a pound of dope out of the sack, proud of his afternoon score like a primitive hunter bringing home fresh game for the table.

Despite Jack's herbal wealth, I retrieved Rick's gift ounce and asked Sara to roll from Rick's bag because it now belonged to Jack and, by extension, the house.

"Wow! Thanks, Rick," Jack crooned. "And thanks, Flash."

We spread out a couple sections of the Los Angeles Times on the sawed-off table and dumped Jack's pound. We soon separated the buds and leaves from a pile of stems and a smaller pile of seeds.

"Look at all these sticks," Jack said. "Hate to throw them away."

"We could make tea," I suggested.

Sara set a large saucepan of water to boil on the stove just as another Seabee in khaki fatigues shoved through the front door, cradling two giant pizzas. His timing was perfect. My munchies were peaking, and the sticks were starting to look like food. Tall and lanky, he had chiseled features like Peter Fonda, and he moved with the smooth grace of an athlete as he set the pizzas on the round table. I leaned back as he pulled one of the stubby chairs closer, perching his long arms and cracking his knuckles loudly like he was snapping twigs for a campfire, sending a shiver down my neck. "Seth White," he said, extending a large hand across the table to me.

"Flash here." Taking his hand, I expected him to crush my fingers as easily as his knuckles, but his grip was restrained and friendly.

He shot me a curious glance, bending his arms around the ashtray like he was ready to deal a deck of cards. Sara emerged from the kitchen with a roll of paper towels. From the corner of my eye, I saw Seth watching her too.

Even after spending the day with her, I couldn't help admiring her fresh beauty and the way she beamed with late afternoon sunshine and the promise of an evening party. She kissed Jack on his forehead as she tore off towels for each of us. I flushed with envy, even a hint of possessiveness, with the way she swung her lithe frame around Jack, treating me formally like a guest even though she knew me better than that.

"Seth and me are headed to Maine when we get out of the suck in August," Jack abruptly announced.

"That's a long way from California," I replied, surprised at the revelation. I had rather hoped Jack might be staying in Ventura to ease my transition from New York.

"For sure," Jack said. "Seth will make sure I don't get lost."

"Mainards don't get lost in the woods," Seth nodded as he got up to queue Black Sabbath on the stereo. Jack asked him to follow it up with CSNY.

"His uncle's a builder, and he's loaning us a house," Jack gleamed, gazing at Seth like his mentor. I wished Jack had shared his plans, but it had been two years since we endured Adak together, when we were closer than brothers and Jack had looked up to me, a few years older and married.

"We'll have everything we need," Seth told me with soft confidence, "and we can make anything else we want." His wide arms flexed under his short-sleeved khakis as he reached for another slice, and I believed him.

"Outhouse and hand pump in the kitchen," Jack said. "Everything but heat."

Seth shrugged. "There's a stove and acres of wood."

I tried to read Sara's thoughts about the primitive utilities, but she just winked at me with a mouthful of pizza. I wasn't sure if she was joining the trek east. Once the water boiled, I got up to stuff the heap of stems into the pan and turn it down to a simmer.

"What happened in Hollywood?" Jack asked me.

"Diane got her divorce, and now she loves Jesus."

"What a loss. You should give her another chance."

Sara poked my shoulder. "Is she the chick who wrote her number on your hand?"

"Whoa! What's this?" Jack gibed.

"That's another story." I deflected their teasing and went back to stir the pan with a wooden spoon.

Black as espresso, the tea tasted terrible, requiring several squirts of honey from a clear plastic bear. The living room grew quiet as I took my turn rolling a couple of joints. Seth's eyes started to close, and before long, he passed out.

Sara slumped against Jack's shoulder, her peaceful breaths hypnotic, and my chest synchronized with her rhythm. Jack gently poked her awake. "Did you give Flash his letter?"

"No, I forgot. I'll get it for you," she said, starting to rise.

"Nah, it can wait," I replied. I'd forgotten about the letter too, foggy with tea and focused on my thought of calling Valarie in the morning, even though my image of her blended with Sara's sleepy allure.

Jack scanned the room. "It's not even nine yet, and my party buddies are falling out."

We listened to the record changer drop "Four Way Street," and as the Crosby, Stills, Nash, and Young concert got underway, Sara and Jack drifted into sleep. I wasn't far behind. I awoke briefly when Seth, then Jack and Sara shuffled off to their bedrooms.

Sara returned with the letter and softly brushed the hair on my head. Her touch was electric, and I reached for her hand. For a moment, I hoped she might join me on the pile of pillows, but she soon pulled away.

"God, I love California," I mumbled as I fell into the anaesthetized sleep of a surgery patient.

Chapter 13

THE BRIGHT CALIFORNIA sun sliced between the living room curtains. I squinted and peeled my lids open. The house was quiet; everyone else was sleeping off the tea, but I arose alert with a desire to start fresh in California.

On the edge of my sleeping bag, I saw the pink envelope with long loops of Ronnie's handwriting resting on the sawed-off dining room table. I thought of burying it unopened beneath the drying apples, peanut butter, and squished bread in my knapsack. I stared for several minutes at the familiar stationary, finally unable to resist the temptation.

On Adak, Ronnie's letters always smelled like her fresh skin and light perfume, the Oil of Olay she used at night, and her Cover Girl makeup. I could conjure up her image even before I read her letters, and she seemed to talk to me, sitting on my bedside with her ironic smile, one corner of her mouth dipping slightly as she described her latest crumby job, the idiot bosses, and her fellow sufferers. Her letters traced her days like a diary, drawing me in like I was part of her life back home.

But when I ripped open the pink envelope and tried to breathe in Ronnie and the trapped molecules of damp New York air, all I smelled was paper as if the dry desert had evaporated her body scents.

"Dear Lover," she wrote, applying the same opening phrase she always used. "It seems funny to call you that now, but that's the way I still feel about you. I still miss you and wish you'd come home. You should see Bobo. I think he misses you even more than I do. Every time he hears someone coming up the stairs, he runs to the door and then to the window and tries to look out. When he realizes you're not coming, he goes back and lies down behind the director's chair. He's pathetic. He even runs over to the car door to see if you're there when I let him out. Tonight, I got a ride home from Bardeen because our car wouldn't start in the morning, but he only stayed long enough to try and start it. Bobo ran up and peed on his leg. I couldn't help but laugh. Bobo also dumped the garbage again, and Grandma Roller says she's going to call the police next time. David gave me a jump and charged the battery. He said the radiator is leaking. I tried to give him a couple joints, but he wouldn't take them.

"I hardly ever see Bardeen, except at work. He gets mad whenever I talk about you, so he's mad most of the time. I just stay home with Bobo. I can't believe how good I'm being. Janey and David had me over to dinner, and I said I'd baby sit Martin on Saturday night. I hope they don't find me tied up in a chair! Your parents called after you left. I think your dad has a health problem, but he wouldn't talk about it. You should call them and Kathy. I'm worried about her too. My mother called and offered to drive out here to get me, but I said no. That's all I need.

"I've been following your trip in my mind, so you might feel me in spirit. Sometimes I feel like I can touch you. I know you're having some great adventures, but I hope you think of me sometimes. I can't wait for you to get home, so we can plan the rest of our life together. Say hi to everyone in California, and hurry home. Have you seen our blue surf yet? Last night, I dreamed we were watching it together.

"Love, Ronnie."

I read the letter two more times, and my hands were sweating when I folded it up. I never read her letters without emotion, and this one affected me even more because of its relaxed tone, so unlike our frustrating conversation two days ago. She wrote the letter before we talked. Her letter didn't mention my failure to provide a stable income, father her children, or her other well-worn complaints. She was avoiding Bardeen. My first impulse was to roll up my sleeping bag and hike back out to Highway 101. One lucky ride might take me all the way to New York.

I watched the morning grow bright, replaying her words in my mind and searching for clues behind her careful script. I tried to decipher my emotions. She wanted me to believe things were different, that Bardeen was pushed into the background, and our marriage was ready to resume its unsteady course. But he still offered her rides, and Bobo still ate garbage, though he deserved a steak for peeing on Bardeen's leg.

Ronnie's state of mind might be like Sara's, missing me most on nights when Bardeen failed to break away from his wife and daughter and left her alone to brood, not unlike her moods before I left. I missed her too, but not enough to close the distance between us.

I buried her letter deep in my knapsack and happened across the slip of paper with Valarie's phone number. I shoved it into the pocket of my jeans as I dressed, thinking I'd call her later. As I pulled a comb through my tangled hair, I heard the Seabees rising upstairs for another meaningless day at the base.

Sara appeared first, wearing a clean halter top and blue jeans for her visit to Richard's mother, who lived nearby in

Oxnard, and her lunch shift at Pedro's. Her tanned, firm stomach reminded me of Ronnie and how her skin felt warm to the touch after a day at the beach, but I shook off the sensation. Now that I was well rested, I wanted to hit the beach myself and wash out my memories in the ocean breeze. I rolled a breakfast number.

Jack was the last one up, and the first thing he did was dial the duty officer to report a serious flu bug. I passed him the joint, and we began planning our day together as Seth complained Jack had already taken too much sick time.

"So what? They can't fire him," I commented, repeating the standard Navy joke.

Jack was unmoved. "In two months, they'll have to get by without me."

Seth shrugged and bit into his peanut butter toast.

"If you can forgive me, how about Yosemite this weekend?" Jack cracked a grin. "Flash has never been there."

"That would be perfect," I said, drawing on the joint and recalling how Ronnie and I had never made it there during our stay in Ventura. When I had called Jack to say I was headed west, my desire to see Yosemite was second only to the beach.

"Of course. I love that place." Seth checked his watch and strode out of the kitchen with a warm but muffled goodbye. We heard the low rumble of his Buick, and Black Sabbath blared as he pulled out the driveway.

"Mr. Responsibility," Sara said as she got up from the table to leave.

Jack called to her in a mock serious voice, "Hey, aren't you going to start the hog for me before you go? A biker mama's supposed to kick start her old man's Harley before he goes out in the morning."

"Start your own hog," she said over her shoulder. "A biker should get his electric starter fixed. You fix the starter, and I'll turn the key for you."

"Is that right?"

"For sure." At that, Jack leapt up and grabbed her from behind, tickling her under her ribs until her high-pitched laughter and screams persuaded him to stop. In their struggle, one of the bangles flew off her wrist and rung against the wall like a ricocheting bullet.

Jack retrieved the bracelet and renewed his plea. "I guess that means I'll have to start the hog myself."

Sara swung out the door, throwing an impish grin and reminding us to be good boys in her absence.

We watched the screen door flap shut.

"She's pretty feisty," I said, imagining how different she must act around her gung-ho husband.

"She thinks she's pretty tough, and she's getting worse all the time."

"It's your fault."

"Yep, I guess it is." Sipping his coffee, Jack offered to cruise the town and check out some of my old haunts down by the beach.

"I'd like to call a woman I met on the way here."

"For sure. But we can't fit three on the hog. Ask her if she has a car. And a sister."

"She might be staying at her sister's." I was surprised at Jack's eagerness. "You better be careful. Sara might come after you."

"She can't catch my hog with that bug," Jack said. "Besides, we ain't done nothing yet."

"Doing nothing isn't what I had in mind."

"Hey, I'm still a free man. Sara's the one who's married."

Valarie answered the phone and remembered me right off. I had expected her sister to answer and tell me that Valarie and the Joshua bong van were smoking up the highway somewhere in northern California. She agreed to meet us near the wharf in about two hours. Her sister had the day off and a car. Jack and I rolled a baggie of numbers, and after an agonizing half-hour trying to kick-start the hog, it finally popped when Jack threatened the vintage Harley with his welding torch.

Before I left New York, I had assumed Jack lived on Ventura beach, ideally the same block where Ronnie and I had lived. But the small rental he shared with Seth actually stood closer to Santa Paula, seven hilly miles from the ocean. We roared out a back road where Jack eased the heavy bike up to ninety, our eyes watering and our faces pressed flat with the wind. The rush was our reward for having to kick-start the monster. Jack tipped the hog toward the sea, and we sped downhill. The air smelled wet and salty as we approached the beach. We passed through pockets of invisible fog with sudden drops in temperature and moisture clinging to our cheeks.

South of the wharf, we wheeled into The Cove, a restaurant and bar near where Ronnie and I had lived. The place was named 'Sandcrab's' now, and a soft pink poster advertised disco dancing. Jack said The Cove was almost bulldozed for new condos like the ones sprouting up behind it. Gone were the huddled groups of hippies smoking their joints in peace, the youthful panhandlers, and guitar players. All that remained from my three-year-old memories were the palm trees and the ocean, along with a few older houses.

We cut across a couple of streets to our former apartment building, but I had difficulty picking it out at first because of the new construction. I looked up the street toward the beach and muttered, "Holy shit. They put up a wall."

"That's the state park," Jack informed me. A sign announced to all former users of the "free" beach that the park was closed after dark. A state park dune buggy zipped by as we peered over the wall. I flashed back to our evenings on the beach with the continuous party where we wandered from fire to fire, joining any ring of quiet revelers who passed their joints as if they had known us forever. One night, we came across a sunset wedding with torches and candles that Ronnie and I joined in passing, and we helped the couple celebrate their new union well into the night and finally toasted them with our own consummation under the bright stars, an image now reserved for owners of beach property with ocean views.

We swung the hog around and headed for the wharf, pulling into the parking lot near the entrance gate, but there were no park rangers charging admission that day. We locked the bike and boosted ourselves over the sea wall, crossing the deep sand and climbing out on a breakwater built of huge boulders to smoke a joint and bide our time until Valarie arrived with her sister. A sailboat tacked up the coast toward Santa Barbara, and three surfers caught waves off the point of the breakwater, steering their boards clear of the rocks. Inhaling the rich sea mist and feeling the sun evaporate the salty sheen on my white skin, I stretched my arms and leaned back, as far away from New York as the continent would allow, on the shoreline of a new life. My mood enhanced by Jack's weed, I sensed the edge of the continental plate dipping into the ocean beneath me, and the waves rich with brine, rising up from deep tide pools and licking the stones with life, mussels, barnacles, urchins, and water thick with sand. My jeans dripped with splashes of incoming tide like the rocks around me. I felt free, elated with promise like a species yet to be discovered, breathing deep gusts of salt air.

Climbing back over the breakwater to the shore, we walked along the foaming waves. Sandpipers dodged our footsteps, scooting down the wet sand when each wave retracted, waiting until the last moment before running away, fishing the edge of the surf.

We leaned against a concrete abutment on the lip of the parking lot where we could see the arriving cars. We continued to study the waves and soak up the ocean air. Posing like Greek heroes in sunglasses and colored T-shirts, we brazenly smoked another joint as we waited. Finally, a blue Chevy with two young women pulled up nearby, and we watched them stare at the sea while stealing sideways glances at us.

After a few moments of exchanging meaningful looks, Jack said, "Hey, let's go." He stood up to approach the car.

"That's not Valarie and her sister."

"So what?"

Leaning into the passenger window, Jack asked the icebreaker question, "Would you ladies like to get high?" From their easy assent, it was apparent they were spending their day like we were.

"Mind if we smoke in the car?" I asked, looking inside. Both smoked cigarettes and the small pullout ashtray overflowed. The woman on the passenger side reached back to unlock the rear door.

Jack held her gaze. "Why don't you climb in the back with me? Flash can sit up front."

Continuing to eye Jack, the passenger combed her dark hair with her fingers, reaching for the door handle as Jack and I shuffled back to give her room to get out.

Just then, the car surged forward, and the two women squealed and waved at us from the windows as they twisted out of the parking lot.

Jack laughed. "The high school tease and I fell for it."

We lit another joint as a light blue Datsun crept past the empty ticket booth. I recognized Valarie tightly holding the steering wheel and scanning the lot. She pulled over when she saw me and whipped off her glasses, shaking her hair free like she had when we met in the haze of the bong van. Her long, brown strands with lighter highlights fell across her bare shoulders and her yellow frilled halter top. Under the bright sun, she looked less like Sara than I remembered, a long face with dark eyebrows, thick red lipstick, and teeth slightly bent behind an amused smile.

Her sister eagerly crawled into the backseat with Jack and announced herself as "Marty," but she preferred "Mame." Her long hair fell down her back and arms. Long hair usually turned me on, but hers was not her best asset, its dull black color accented by pale skin. She wore a blue, silk blouse with several buttons open at the top and tight fitting black knit pants. Her quick laughter brought an echo from Jack.

Valarie helped me with the seat belt, which Mame had twisted in her eagerness to change seats. A self-conscious blush spread across Valarie's round, pink cheeks. I smiled, and her eyes began to relax, her face settling into an ironic grin. She pulled up the straps of her halter top and the waist of her loose jeans, hardly disguising her voluptuous figure.

As the Datsun began to fill with the acrid smoke of our joint, Mame asked how Jack and I knew each other. I was reluctant to talk about my military experiences with strangers, but Jack didn't share my reserve. He told them we had met in the Seabees, and he went on to recount how we became friends.

"Flash and our cubemates Rick and Phil were suspicious because I looked like a low rider when I got to Adak. Short, greased back hair. But I don't look like a low rider now." He pulled on a loose strand of his thick, blond hair while sucking a hit off the number. "One day, we went tundra sliding, and Flash lost the keys to the Dreadnaught."

"Phil's old black Buick," I added.

"So, I hot-wired it."

"You did a righteous job," I recalled. "We had to solder in a lamp switch because the car was permanently hot-wired."

"What's tundra sliding?" Mame interjected.

Jack nodded his head and waved her off to continue his thread. "Two switches. Ignition. Takeoff," he called, slapping my headrest. "Flash bought it from Phil when he left the island, then Flash sold it to me when he left, and I sold it to some airman. Great party car." He flopped back in his seat and pulled Mame over for a sloppy kiss.

"Still is, I bet. You could smoke a strip of upholstery and get high," I said. Valarie smirked as she glanced at her sister and Jack entwined in the backseat. After a moment, I prompted him, "Tell them about tundra sliding."

"Oh yeah. First you drop some acid. Then you climb up a tall hill covered with tundra like a steep haystack. Stand with your back to the slope, pull your parka hood over your head, and fall backwards."

"Like a human bobsled," I added. "Twisting over stones and whipping around curves." I showed them the technique of holding your arms at your side and tucking your chin, relaxing to keep from having your limbs ripped off by sharp protruding rocks.

"Safer than bobsledding," Jack assured Mame, who seemed ready to try anything with him.

Valerie shot me a questioning stare, her lips curled to the side, very alluring. I figured she might go tundra sliding, but I'd hate to hide her soft cleavage in a parka. She fumbled in the ashtray for a roach, but I produced a fresh joint from my baggie.

Mame called from the back seat. "You dudes should come up to Santa Barbara with us this afternoon." She buried her head in Jack's face, hands roaming under cloth, bodies sliding toward a prone position. In a muffled voice she added, "We can blow numbers and get crazy."

"Mame! I don't believe you!" Valarie blurted.

Jack looked up, blinking his bleary eyes. "Yeah, let's cruise north."

Valarie threw the car into gear and twisted the wheel with force as it stuttered uncertainly out of the parking lot. Mame's head fell into Jack's lap.

"Looks like we're headed to Santa Barbara," I said.

Valarie replied in a confidential tone, "I just want to get out of here before they get us arrested."

But there were no other cars around, and no cops. I leaned toward her, careful not to interrupt her driving, her brow furrowed in concentration through her head of weed.

At the intersection, she turned right, not left, swinging the car south onto Harbor Boulevard. She reached over and patted my thigh. I rested my hand on top of hers.

Mame called up to the front seat, "Hey. I thought we were going to Santa Barbara."

"So you say," Valarie said curtly.

Another of Mame's buttons had popped open.

Jack erupted with enthusiasm, "We've got plenty of weed, and we can pick up some beers."

Valarie turned to face her sister in the backseat.

I reflexively reached for the wheel.

"Why not?" Mame asked. "Everyone's welcome. They're cool."

"Welcome where?" I asked, now curious.

"At our coven," Mame said.

Valarie shook her head. "I can't believe you. You're not supposed to tell anyone. The coven's supposed to be a secret."

"I won't tell them about the ceremonies," Mame argued. "The coven itself isn't secret."

"A coven's where they have witches, isn't it?" I tentatively asked Valarie. "Joshua's crew didn't look like witches."

"Joshua was just giving me a ride. He's too spiritual. I believe in the power of the body and nature."

"Works for me," I replied, but I began to feel apprehensive about the promise of the afternoon. I couldn't help thinking about Alice Cooper biting the head off a chicken.

"Besides, I told Joshua if he tried anything with me, I'd cut him." Valarie swooshed her hand like she was holding a blade and shot me a threatening look, stunning in its intensity, before wiping it away. She sprouted a self-conscious smile to convince me her gesture was a joke.

"Yeah, we're witches," Mame said brightly. She stuck out her tongue to reveal a pentagram tattoo covering its narrow tip. The tattoo was a sickly blue, standing out from the background of pink flesh. Jack tried to keep smiling, but he looked a little ill, having already tasted the branded tongue.

I found it revolting and wondered if Valarie had one just like it.

She did. She licked her lips unconsciously as if reading my mind. She turned to face Mame again. "I can't believe you," she chided. "You're not even a witch yet. You only started training two weeks ago."

"I'm a warlock," Jack announced. "And so's Flash."

"No," I corrected him. "I'm an anti-warlock." I forced a laugh, wishing the coven were part of Valarie's joke. Neither of the women laughed.

"We *really* are witches. At least I am," Valarie said seriously. She reached between her breasts and pulled out a silver medallion stamped with a pentagram, its lines resembling woven straw. The rim of the medallion was lacquered black, and the medal had the tarnished look of an ancient coin. She held the medallion by its chain like she was hesitant to touch it, igniting a shiver in the back of my neck. I recalled Egyptian amulets and larger Incan medallions I had seen in museum cases and how those artifacts emitted a residue of magic. I drew back as I would from a radioactive nugget before trying to convince myself her medallion held no more magic than a buffalo nickel.

"You guys aren't afraid of witches, are you?" Mame asked.

"No way," I said. "You two seem safe enough."

"I guess we are. It's the others I'm worried about," Valarie replied with a cold emphasis on the word, 'others.'

"Do you sacrifice animals?" Jack asked a bit too casually.

"We love animals and all living things. Witches celebrate life," Valarie explained.

"Tell them the truth," demanded Mame.

Valarie shot Mame a deathly look that would have stunned a chicken. Her face startled me, and I leaned toward the open window. Jack also caught Valarie's threatening expression. "That is the truth, and you know it, Mame."

"You are such a dictator!"

"I should tell dad you skipped school today!"

"Skipped school?" Jack asked Mame, forcing a smile.

"You're sixteen," Valarie reminded her.

"It's my life!" Mame yelled back at her sister. "Whether I go to school or become a witch. At least I tell the truth."

"You better not say anything more," Valarie commanded in a deep voice.

That ended the conversation. For a long, tense moment, the car was quiet, except for the breeze whistling around the sharp edges of the old Datsun as it rattled along the coast. Valarie continued to scowl, and Mame settled into a deep pout, shifting her attention between Jack and the road with a few furtive glances toward her sister and senior witch. She still leaned against Jack, but he was no longer embracing her, his grin fixed like wax. Jack had obviously changed his attitude toward underage women in the years since Adak. Valarie's hand lightly stroked my thigh, but her touch felt about as sensual as a nurse. So much for a carefree day at the beach with a couple of wild women. I wanted to escape before I became altar meat even if their identity as witches bothered me less than the thick tension between them. Hardly a party atmosphere.

Finally, I said, "Wow, I just remembered Jack has to work this afternoon. The chief will kill him if he doesn't show."

Jack shot me a surprised glance, but he nodded his head.

"Thought you had the day off," Valarie said.

"I was stretching it," Jack explained. "Thanks for keeping me straight, Flash."

We hadn't driven far from the wharf, so Valarie swung around. Her tension eased as the car rolled to a jerky stop, and Jack and I jumped out. Mame climbed into the front seat with a lingering gaze at Jack. Valarie said I should call her again, and I judged by her glare toward her sister that she regretted bringing her along. We waved as they puttered away.

"Talk about coitus interruptus," Jack said as he fired up a roach. The parking lot was still deserted. "Those women were too weird, even for me."

He squinted and caught my eye. We erupted with laughter, coughing out our hits and spitting gray exhaust like Valarie's old Datsun.

Retreating toward the wharf, we passed a fresh joint and walked down to a dry stretch of beach where we dug easy chairs in the sand, sculpting deep impressions for our bodies, arms, and legs, still laughing about the witches and our lack of pickup skills.

"I was pretty inept with women on Adak," I reminded him.

"You were only half-hearted about it because of your wife back home. You could have had Diane, and she was the pick of the litter. I still think you should give her another chance."

I shrugged. "My success on this trip has been about the same, except I'm trying harder."

"Did Sara tell you about her dream?"

"What dream?"

"Two nights ago, she dreamed she met a tall, dark, good-looking dude, and she ended up sleeping with him. I laughed about it because her husband's a red head, and I'm about as blond as they come. Then I thought about you. She'd never met you, but you fit the description in her dream, and you were due to arrive in a couple days. She started asking a lot of questions about you. You two had quite a day together." He gave me a knowing look.

I sat up, shocked by the dream. "Geez. You're not accusing us of anything are you?" Despite my denial, I was flattered.

"No, of course not," he said, staring into my eyes. "Wish I could say the same about Sara."

"That's between you and Sara."

He grinned and pushed me down in the sand, and I pushed him back., our brief tension blowing away with the sea mist. Jack and I seldom disagreed, but I recalled the first day we met when he casually lit a cigarette in my face, a gesture left over from his low rider days. I told him to back up. He laughed, and I found it impossible to resist laughing myself. Jack had that impact on people, one of the ways he stayed alive on the LA streets.

Jack's revelation had a weird effect on me as I lay back in my sand chair. I had plotted my trip with Donna and Diane in mind as if connecting with them might restore something I'd lost during the bleak Bardeen era. Knowing Sara might be attracted to me gave me a fresh perspective.

"Sara asked me about you," I said. "She wondered if you'll stay with her after your discharge."

"Ha." Jack rolled over and reached into the baggie for another number. Only two left. "She's the one who doesn't know what to do. She can't decide if she wants to go back with Richard. I think he fried his brains in country, and now he talks like some John Wayne Marine even though he's a corpsman. Acts like a Nazi, everything in its place."

"She worries about you going to Maine."

"Who knows what I'll decide to do once I get the military madness out of my head. I like the idea of getting lost in the woods." He relit the joint and passed it to me. "Hard to know what will happen."

I recalled the life of the military, a distorted reflection of real life, a controlled environment with a sense of stasis, nothing changing. For those stuck inside long enough, the military world became normal and the outside world surreal. Jack was leaving one world for another, just like Rick and I had before him, feeling like pioneers in our own country.

We passed the burning roach, its coal invisible in the hot sun. I relaxed into the warm sand, growing sleepy from the sun and the progression of loosely rolled numbers, projecting a new drafting job, a new apartment near the beach, and a new woman at my side. I gradually dozed off, dreaming it was Valarie lying next to me, casting a spell and me trying to stop her, unsure what her spell might conjure. Then Valarie's image softly faded into Sara. She said she was waiting for me, but not as Jack had feared, only waiting to give me Ronnie's letter. As she handed me the pink envelope, her hands and face dispersed like a wisp of fog, and Ronnie emerged. I breathed the scent of her makeup and sensed her warm skin lying next to me in the sand. A cool gust of wind shook me awake, the air freshening as the sun dipped into dusk.

Jack woke up about the same time and said he was ready to scare up some dinner. It was just dark enough that we might see the blue flashes in the breaking surf, but Jack reminded me the eerie glow was caused by plankton, and their abundance depended on the season. We were a few weeks off.

Chapter 14

When Jack and I roared up his street, we found Sara's bug with all four doors open, blocking the driveway. Jack slowed to an idle and swung the hog onto the brown lawn. Sara emerged from the front door with a handful of clothes on hangers, and Seth followed with a cardboard box.

"What's this?" Jack forced a grin as he parked the bike and pulled off his helmet.

"Nothing's wrong," Sara replied, leaning into the VW and hooking the hangers. She stood and adjusted the elastic band of her halter top, facing Jack and dropping her hands to her hips. She wore a troubled expression. "It's Richard," she said. "They're sending him back for a two-week training class."

"That's weird." Jack eyed her and glanced between Seth and me.

"Some new field procedure." She shrugged her shoulders. "All the corpsmen have to go."

"They're flying Richard all the way back from Okinawa?" Jack furrowed his brow.

Sara returned his disbelieving stare with a stoic look of acceptance, reminding me of Ronnie when the Navy changed my orders and scrambled our lives. "He's flying in on Sunday."

"What are you going to do?" Jack asked in a softer tone.

"I'm moving some of my stuff back to the apartment to get ready. But I'll be back here tonight."

"We should talk." Jack's voice lowered to a whisper.

Sara's eyes began to cloud as she rested against the door frame. Still holding the box, Seth looked like he wanted to say something. Jack pushed past him and wrapped Sara in his arms. "You know I don't want you to go."

She buried her face in his chest. "I have to."

Jack stroked her hair and kissed the top of her head. "Maybe this is your opportunity."

Her shoulders began to rock as she fought back her tears, and Jack's helmet dropped from his hand and thudded on the gravel.

Keeping his head down, Seth set the box on the beetle's roof and mumbled, "She's not ready, Jack."

Jack swiveled toward Seth, who retreated to the front door, passing behind me.

"I'm sorry, Jack," Sara said in a husky voice. "You weren't here when I got home, so I dumped it all on Seth."

"It's okay. I'd do the same thing," Jack said.

"Mr. Responsibility." She tried to smile. "I should talk to Seth."

"That's between you and him."

I headed to the bathroom to wash the sand out of my eyes and gulp a glass of water. When I returned to the living room, the front door was open as they left it most evenings, hoping to catch a cool ocean breeze. Sara stood in front of her black bug staring up at Seth, talking softly and reminding me of Fay Wray taming King Kong. A few inches taller than Jack and me, Seth had an angular strength with wide shoulders and large hands splayed at his side and rhythmically flexing as if he was following a song in his head. A construction foreman would fit him with the largest hammer. Despite my slight jealousy about his close friendship with Jack and now Sara, I perceived his quiet charisma, a natural leader, someone a crew would follow on a job site without question. Or follow to Maine as Jack intended.

Seth gave Sara a quick nod and turned toward the kitchen door. I heard the screen slap shut as Jack strode out and kissed Sara goodbye. Her sandals slipped on the gravel getting into the car, and Jack caught her fall in his outstretched arm like a dancer.

After she left, Jack stood there, watching the empty street. Finally, he turned and called toward the house, "Time for dinner."

The three of us piled into Seth's old green Buick, reminiscent of my Dreadnaught on Adak even though Seth's car was several years newer and rode much higher on its suspension. A shrunken head molded from black rubber with black nylon hair, closed eyes, and a panting tongue hung from the mirror. Seth slipped in a Black Sabbath cassette. We filled up the beige interior with billows of burning weed as we sat back on the soft upholstery and retooled our mood. When Seth rolled down his window at the drive-in *taqueria*, the attendant threw back his head and inhaled deeply, grateful for the free hit.

That ride turned out to be the best part of the weekend.

Jack's Harley clanged ominously when he arrived home on Friday night. He didn't come inside right away, so I stepped out to the driveway where his bike billowed gray smoke.

"Not a great day," Jack said, rubbing his eyes. "The Navy stuck our battalion with military training for the next two weeks."

"Thought your battalion wasn't going back to country."

"Go figure." Jack dropped his jacket on the parched lawn.

I shrugged and studied the bike, but I couldn't identify the source of the smoke. The entire engine smoldered.

"Could be worse," Jack said, throwing a positive spin. "The Marine barracks are full, so they can't make us stay there like last time."

"What a bummer," I muttered, recalling my two weeks at Pendleton a few years before. "Place reminded me of Cool Hand Luke."

"Wonder if I'll see Richard out there," Jack mused. "Never met him. Wonder if that's where the corpsmen are training."

"Better not get wounded." I replied sarcastically, recalling how the medics manned the medical tents during military training and practiced their skills by treating strap on plastic wounds.

"Speaking of wounded." Jack glanced at his bike as it continued to smoke. He turned to me. "Sorry about Yosemite, Flash. Have to put it off."

"Family comes first." I patted the handlebars and tried to hold my breath, avoiding the oil rich fumes. Jack spent the weekend nursing his hog with no success.

Jack's dreadful day, and mine by extension, repeated over and over like an eight-track tape as his mindless military training dragged on. I soon ran out of things to do, other than look for a job.

Two weeks later, I pushed through the screen door to the kitchen and handed Sara the keys to her bug. She rose on her toes and planted a quick peck on my cheek. The sweet buttery smell of cookies filled the kitchen. Lately, I had seen her more often than Jack since she often stopped by the house in the afternoon, and each time, she baked him something. On Monday, it was cupcakes with cherry frosting. Today, she had come early to loan me her car.

"Doesn't look good," she said, eyeing my expression and turning to pull open the oven door before I had a chance to respond. She scooped the brown cookies off a pizza pan and onto an unfolded newspaper laid out on the kitchen table. Chocolate chip. Jack would be pleased.

I waited for her to drop the spatula and hot pad on the table and start spooning out another batch. She wore a yellow headband to complement her gray T-shirt and orange gym shorts. "Interviews went well enough," I said. "But no bites."

She paused and shot me a sympathetic glance.

"Met several engineers from Northrup," I continued. "They had a big layoff."

"That sucks."

"Now they're applying for drafting jobs." I helped myself to a warm cookie, hoping it would calm my frustration. "Why hire a draftsman when you can get an engineer for the same price?"

Sara went back to her batter. "They're hiring at Pedro's Cantina where I work."

"Thanks, but I've been drawing for years." I pulled out a chair. "Even before the Seabees."

"Pays better, I guess." She picked up the pan and slid it into the oven, checking the wall clock. She reached for her cigarettes and sat down.

I shrugged. "Means I can work fewer hours while I'm going to college."

She leaned forward, the deep neck of her tee shirt framing her firm cleavage as smoke curled around her smooth face. "Not for me," she said conclusively. "College I mean. I like feeding people. Probably sounds lame, but I'm good at it."

"You are," I stammered. "These cookies are great."

Sara nodded as she lit a roach with her cigarette and handed it to me. She was right about her domestic prowess. Her movements around the kitchen reminded me of a dancer, perfect but casual, as if every muscle knew its role and performed with the least effort. Watching her reminded me of the evenings when I cooked dinner with Ronnie. Though she hated to cook, leaving most of it to me or the phonebook, Ronnie had a similar athletic grace, mesmerizing in its simplicity and sexuality.

Sara lined the newspaper with another row of cookies. "How's Jack?" she asked. "I miss him."

"They get in late and leave early."

"Same with Richard."

"Only two more days."

"Hope Jack wants me back." She flashed her cute smile. "At least he has my cookies."

"I'll try to save him some."

Sara protectively raised her spatula like a hatchet.

After she left, I found myself pacing around the sawed off table in the living room, Jack's guitar strapped to my neck, playing the opening riff from "Iron Man" over and over again as if I was trying to coax something new from the progression Seth had taught me. I sat down on the floor pillows and strummed "Mr. Tamborineman," my favorite tune, rerunning my failed interviews and wishing I could forget them. I set down the guitar and stared at the dirty picture window and the old blue and yellow sheets hung like curtains from a bending rod. I never noticed the sun-bleached sheets in the evening when the house was filled with pot smoke and loud music, only when I was alone. I felt edgy again, the way I had before I started my trip, dampening the Ventura dream I'd carried all the way from New York. I was unaccustomed to so much idle time.

Before I landed the two fruitless interviews, I'd called every draftsman ad in the newspaper, though there were fewer jobs than I expected. The two interviews were oddly similar with stuffed vinyl furniture and instant coffee in Styrofoam cups. The recruiter abruptly ended the first one after I confided my desire to return to college in the fall, but there was little chance he'd hire me anyway with the crowd of engineers in the waiting room. The second interview ended about as quickly though I never mentioned college. As I rattled back to Jack's place in Sara's bug, I blamed Nixon's creeping withdrawal and its effect on the defense industry, affecting all engineering jobs, including temporary summer drafting jobs.

Returning Jack's guitar to its case, I took a few more laps around the sawed-off table before deciding to hitchhike the seven miles to the beach. I changed out of the presentable interview clothes I had borrowed from Jack: wingtip shoes, perma-press black slacks a bit high at the ankles, and an extra-large pin stripe dress shirt.

Stepping outside, I soon rallied, slipping the confines of the living room like a felon on parole. I tried to ignore the chafing on my thighs from the swimsuit under my jeans as I walked, and I gave up extending my thumb. There were few cars on Foothill Road, but it wended its way to the beach by the shortest route. I could have asked Sara for a ride or called up Valarie, but I was in no mood to talk to anyone. The wide parched yards on the outskirts of Ventura gave way to large irrigated mansions as I descended with a punishing heat on my back and a cool breeze wafting my face. By the time I reached the state park, I walked lighter. My sweat almost purged my interview failures.

I evaded the ticket booth in case they charged pedestrians and hopped the wall. Near the secluded spot where Jack and I had shared a number, I lit up again, but I felt weird smoking alone. My vintage memories of Ventura beach featured Ronnie as another natural element along with the sand and the salt breeze. The beach was a moment that should be shared like the joint in my hand.

I set off in search of our old apartment, wanting a closer look than my flyby with Jack on his hog. I found it pinned between a new condominium and a stucco house under construction that sprawled over two lots, including the one where I'd bought the bag of Columbian for my trip to Adak. I hardly remembered the duplex now gone, but I remembered Joe's red.

A placard on the door of our building advertised an apartment for more than double the rent Ronnie and I had paid. No wonder Jack lived up in the hills. I stared at the bleached and sand-scratched door, feeling my dream of Ventura adjusting to the rent and intensifying the discomfort I experienced smoking alone like a spirit returning to a life that no longer existed.

There must be other places with cheaper rent, assuming I eventually found a job, and with that thought, I headed back to the beach, stripping to my swimsuit, and wading into the surf. I remembered all the times Ronnie and I had played in the waves and how her smooth skin dried to a salty haze, so our love making when we returned to the apartment felt primordial like creatures spawned by the sea. Alone, my swimming became more exercise than play, diving into the tubes and catching their power.

When I paused to catch my breath, a large shape crossed the edge of my vision, just beneath the surface, several feet away. I froze, standing in water up to my chest and scanning the layers of translucent water. Refracted images on the bottom broke and rejoined, fading in and out of focus in the cups of waves. I cautiously extended my toes to test their solidity, hoping they were rocks and weeds and knowing anything moving might be a threat. Better not to disturb them. If I knew how to swim, I might just paddle away, but I had to know the danger before I moved. My attempt to swim might summon the shadow, my splashes resembling a wounded fish or seal, igniting its predatory instinct. Running could be worse. Like ringing a dinner bell.

I saw it again, looping around me. My pulse quickened as it faded back into the layers of light and shadow. I hardly breathed. My senses tuned to survival, trying to identify the shape and its angle of attack. The dark form rose with one fin breaking the skin of ocean. Shark. I swiveled toward shore, trying to run with the water clinging to my legs like mud, my arms flailing. I struggled to emerge, one heavy step after another. As the depth receded, I strode faster, splashing out of the water and reaching the safety of dry sand with my lungs and pulse pounding. I checked my skin for signs of blood, making sure my hands and feet were still attached.

Just offshore, a dolphin flipped out of the water as if it was amused by my feverish thrashing but not as amused as a group of teenagers a few yards up the beach, cracking up and pointing between me and my pursuer. I breathed hard and leaned over, resting my hands on my knees, and watching the dolphin. Finally, it joined another dolphin a few feet farther out, and I lost track of their sinuous dives. I heard one of the kids laugh again, closer this time, and I had to join him, caught in the irony of the moment and recalling my jokes with Ronnie about how her dolphin-like swimming skills would save me from sharks, an image with a new twist. I had escaped Ronnie and fled all the way to the Pacific Ocean, and now she was chasing me back to shore.

"You okay, man?" the kid asked. "You can tell dolphins from sharks because they like to play."

"Right, sharks don't play," I muttered between breaths, wondering how I could tell the difference before a shark bit off my leg.

"I'm Lobo." He grinned through a pockmarked face and offered me a swig of Ripple from a half gallon jug. A spider web tattoo draped across his shoulder.

I declined the wine as his friends gathered around, shouting introductions over the crashing surf. They congratulated me on my escape, and Lobo questioned if I was really from New York, eyeing me like an alien species. I told them I had to be back in New York before dinner.

The long walk uphill fanned my sense of displacement. Maybe it was the heat, but I also thought back on my trip from New York, how my friends questioned why I was leaving, what I was planning to do in California, and what I hoped to find. During my trip west, the answer came easy – all about escape – and I assumed Ventura would be the way I left it when the Navy shipped me to Adak. I remembered Ronnie asking me what I had expected from Donna, and I wondered what I had expected of Diane, Jack, and even Valarie, all faces in my dream of Ventura. Outside of my dream, I knew they each had built their own lives extending beyond what I remembered or projected. I had to find my own life.

Chapter 15

After a shower, I sat alone on the floor pillows in Jack's living room, stretching my tired legs, and squinting at the evening sun slanting through the bedsheet curtains. Ronnie's letter lay across my lap, the pink stationary stained by sweat from my Coke can. I waited for the clock to tick past seven, so I could call her collect with evening rates. We hadn't talked since Arizona, and I'd avoided rekindling our fights.

Ronnie's voice was warm and chatty, but I knew how fast that could turn. She wanted to hear about my time in Ventura. I told her about my day at the beach with Jack, leaving out Valarie and the coven.

"That's one day," Ronnie said. "What else?"

"Well, Jack lives up in the hills, and everyone's working."

"I thought he lived on the beach."

"The beach is pretty far. Believe me. I walked it."

"You can always come home," she said, making it sound like a joke. Her voice changed to a serious tone. "We got the last GI check, and we won't have enough for next month's rent."

"I interviewed for a couple jobs. I'll keep looking."

"What for? I think you have a job. That guy Johnson where you applied before you left called here three times." Ronnie sounded upbeat. "Come home. Problem solved."

I paused to process the news. If I had a job in New York, our finances would improve, assuming I decided to hitch back home, but that wasn't our only problem. I wanted to avoid bringing up Bardeen and turning the phone call into another depressing impasse. "Okay, I'll call Johnson."

Ronnie sensed my reluctance. "Flash, I love you. I know you're worried about Bardeen, but I'm only seeing him at work. I'm concentrating on my painting class with Janey, and I even picked up an application to start college in September like you wanted. Solomon said he'd write me a reference."

I shook off the mention of Solomon, her painting instructor, wondering if he was still drooling over his nude portrait of Ronnie, and if he was a substitute for Bardeen. I chose my words carefully to avoid our usual fights. "I love you too, but I just got here."

"Two weeks ago."

Our conversation paused, and I filled the silence. "I talked to Kathy. My dad thought he had a heart attack, but they decided it was heart strain."

"Hope he's better," she said in a measured tone, avoiding her usual rant about his drinking.

"He says he's too ornery to die." I glanced at the clock, calculating the minutes and the charges. "And Dr. Jeremy showed up in Columbus."

"Ha! I could have predicted that."

"But Kathy's new Romantics professor has horses."

"Poor Jeremy has no chance. Are you going to stop in Columbus? Help Kathy throw Jeremy out?"

"Maybe I should," I replied, sidestepping Ronnie's implicit question about my plans and thinking my sister hardly needed my help. I still hoped a job might materialize in

California. I gazed outside to see Sara's bug and Seth's Buick arrive about the same time. Jack hopped out of the Buick and ran to her car door.

"Call me again soon," Ronnie said, subtly reminding me that I should have called sooner. As I hung up the phone, my spirits rose. Despite the mention of Bardeen and Solomon, it was the first conversation I could remember that had not erupted in anger. I hoped we were entering a truce, helped along by my careful steps across the no man's land between our trenches.

Sara and Jack shared a few words and a long, lingering kiss through the bug's open window. Sara puttered away as Jack stepped through the front door with a sour expression.

"Richard's staying through the weekend," he said. "It keeps getting better and better."

"Only a few more days."

Jack faced me with a gleam in his blue eyes. "Well, my training's done tomorrow, so we can finally hit Yosemite."

"I can use a trip to Yosemite."

"Yosemite, got it," Seth echoed as he passed through the living room, munching a cold slice of pizza. He headed directly to bed after their long day in the desert.

Jack slid open the bedsheet curtains, hoping to see some sunset color through the thickening haze. We retrieved the rest of the cold pizza and fresh Cokes, pushing the candles and ashtray to one side of the sawed-off table to make space for dinner. Jack restacked the pile of CSNY albums and turned on the stereo while I rolled a joint.

He waited until after dinner to ask me where my head was. I knew he was asking about Ronnie, not my job search, but I suspected he was also asking when his living room might be cleared out, even if he'd never say as much.

"She says things are different. I wish I could believe her," I said.

"If you want to believe her, it means you believe her already."

"I might believe her a little, a mile or two, but not three thousand miles, not enough to hitch all the way back to New York." I sipped some Coke to cool my throat. "What about you?"

"You know I ain't happy about Richard coming home, but I only care if Sara wants to be with me when she's with me. She'll be back here Sunday night." Jack paused for a moment. "I'm getting out about the same time he's finishing his tour. We'll see what happens then."

"I wish I could feel so open about Ronnie."

"I never said I didn't want to snuff Richard's ass. That's only natural." He cleared his throat, poking me playfully. "But I'm new to this steady girlfriend thing, not like you."

His gibe recalled the kidding I endured from my cubemates on Adak when I was the old, married guy, though we were all about the same age. "Not anymore."

"Ronnie's begging you to come back. What more do you want?"

I slid the ashtray closer and picked up the roach clip, ignoring his question.

Jack leaned forward. "What's happened to you, man?" he asked with a smile. "Up on Adak, you always knew what you wanted. You had your life together."

"I'm not that different."

He looked out the window as if he were scanning the night sky through the fog. "You're letting Ronnie and that guy Jardeen control your life."

"Bardeen." I struck a match and fired up the roach.

"Whatever. You're waiting to see what she's going to do and then you decide what to do."

"I decided to come out here."

"But she's still in your head, man. You didn't really get away from her."

"That'll take time."

"But you're still talking to her on the phone. She even wrote you a nice long letter." Jack shifted his weight in the sawed-off chair. His eyes were heavy.

I took a quick hit from the diminishing coal and set the clip on the ashtray. "Seems funny to talk about my marriage the way we talked about the Navy all those years."

"You lost me, man."

"You want to be free of the Navy, but you get used to how they control everything. You're stuck in a rut, and it's hard to realize when you're finally free. My separation from Ronnie feels that way."

"I can't wait to have that problem," Jack replied sleepily. "Getting out of the Navy, I mean. Two more months and I'm free."

As Jack trudged off to bed, I decided to call Johnson in the morning, and try again to flush a job out of the Ventura want ads, hoping I could conger a way to stay in California. Returning home to Ronnie would feel like defeat after escaping her affair and enduring the long days of hitchhiking to Ventura, but I'd have to make a decision soon. I fell into a restless sleep without any conclusion, shifting for comfort between the pillows and the hard, wooden floor.

Well before dawn on Sunday morning, the three of us loaded up Seth's Buick and set off for Yosemite, winding high into the Sierras. We caught the morning light filtered by ponderosa pines as we descended into the valley. Crammed in the backseat, I saw little of the mountain scenery until we reached the parking lot at the base of the falls.

Crawling out and stretching my legs, I craned my neck to see a torrent of water shooting out over the peak of a mountain. After a quick joint in the safety of the car, we ate a brunch of Twinkies and crackers, washed down with Coke. We carried a handful of candy bars for lunch along with the ever-present baggie of rolled joints.

We hiked along the rushing stream until Seth led our small caravan over a short pipe fence, past a sign warning of imminent danger, and up a series of passages between huge boulders. From the bottom, the falls looked like one continuous drop all the way down, but as we ascended, we could see three or more major falls cut deep into the cliffs, all linked together by steep cascades and rapids.

I set off on a side route, and after a few steps, I looked back to see my friends following me. I crept along a ledge that angled up toward the main path along the opposite side of a jutting cliff. I pressed my body to the ancient stone as the shelf began to narrow. My hands and feet gripped the chinks and edges tightly and safely, a sure-handed chameleon out for my daily scramble on the rocks. Moving slowly to test each hold before I trusted it with my weight, I felt the sun warm my back and the face of the cliff, while the cool wisps of spray floated down around me. To each side, a faint rainbow extended into the distance, and each ray of refracted light formed its own spectral target of color.

A high-pitched scream pierced my reverie. "He's going to fall! Daddy, look! He's going to jump!" I gazed down for the first time and realized I had crept out a narrowing ledge above a shear drop of about a hundred feet. Below me, two boys and their father stood on a pile of rocks, staring up and pointing. I froze, pressing myself to the stone face, but I gradually recovered. I had taken a wrong turn, and my path was blocked. I waved down to them before retracing my steps and returning to the wider section of the ledge with my friends shuffling ahead of me.

We wound up and up, past chipped boulders, broken like giant's teeth. Some of them were larger than houses, and many had fallen hundreds of feet down the sheer face. I imagined the stones forming a steeper cliff before the river started its slow process of decay. Back in the lead, I paused now and again to wait for Jack who was next behind me, disappearing around one cliff and then another. I caught brief glimpses of Seth, farther away, resembling a spirit, wavering and translucent in the rising heat waves, with the mist and the auras around the jutting rocks lit now with brighter rainbows and trails of light color, verdant greens, and hotter pinks. Winded from my climb, I breathed the colors through my skin like a rock lizard.

When they caught up to me, my friends were out of breath too. We stopped by a shallow pool cut in the rock, The Devil's Bathtub, according to Seth. The torrent was gentler here and fell at the rate of a typical shower, except the water was a constant glacial temperature. It was oddly quiet, though we still heard the roar of the falls around us. Seth and Jack took off their clothes, and I joined them. The icy water soothed my superheated feet, and I lay back, watching the curtain of rainbows mutate in the mist around us.

Jack began humming a Graham Nash tune, "Military madness, it's killing our country," a song he'd often sung in our cabin, the abandoned building up on Adak. The melody brought me back to our time on the island. We had always talked about home, our friends, our families, and how we wanted to live and love, building our future lives. Those were the times when Jack proclaimed his love of the week, and I decried my separation from Ronnie, cut apart by the military. I had sensed her near, a missing body part my nerves still remembered, her head resting on my lap as I sat cross-legged on the rotting cabin floor.

The freezing water brought me back to the present, and like a vague idea I could hardly articulate, Ronnie materialized in the periphery of my vision, reclining behind me in the pool, another spirit among us. Her skin gleamed like a dolphin. I stared into her star-like eyes, flashing with the brilliance of a new sun. She reached through the rainbow mist of the glacial falls, crossing the distance between us.

Just as she had during all those lonely moments on Adak, Ronnie's spirit pulled me back to our life together in New York. She'd been the focus of my love then, and everything else I missed revolved around her, an extension of her ethereal presence. My family, friends, and my desire to go back to college all drew meaning from her. Now she called me again, and I began to realize my thought of building a life in Ventura was a pipe dream rising from my need to escape, and it should remain a dream. My life was still in New York, as it always had been, even if I remained unsure what would happen between Ronnie and me. Jack and Sara were right. All signs were pulling me home. Like a comet reaching the farthest edge of its trajectory, my life in New York drew my orbit eastward, back toward Ronnie's star. I raised my voice to join Jack's tune.

We finally crawled out of the water, our limbs numb with cold, and we baked ourselves dry on the rocks. Our descent was slower, and it was dusk by the time we rejoined the tourists at the base of the falls. The rainbows had faded by then, but the fog began to rise around us.

Seth drove us out of the park, and Jack fell asleep on the back seat, oblivious to the Black Sabbath tape pounding through the stereo. Sitting in the passenger seat, I found myself mesmerized by Seth's shrunken head, rocking to the music until I lost consciousness on the third replay of "Iron Man."

Chapter 16

Sara's beetle was back in its spot when we pulled into the driveway after midnight, but I didn't see her until breakfast. A griddle of pancakes sizzled on the stove next to a small saucepan of maple syrup, and the percolator hissed with the promise of fresh coffee. Jack and Seth followed the sweet oily smells into the kitchen right behind me. My goodbye breakfast.

We agreed to rendezvous in New York or Maine later in the summer after Jack and Seth received their freedom papers. I was happy Jack's migration plan included Sara.

"Flash, if you come to live in Maine, I'll build you a cabin," Jack offered.

I glanced at Seth, but he was busy smearing butter on a stack of pancakes. I recalled how his uncle's old farmhouse came with twenty acres, mostly forest.

"I'm already building a cabin for Sara and me." Jack continued with enthusiasm. "You can help me pound nails."

Seth nodded with his mouthful as if to say Jack's endorsement was enough for him.

"I'll think about it," I replied. "But I'm signed up for next semester." Sara eyed me over her cup, and I could tell the invitation also came from her. Moving to Maine might sound better once I confronted the remains of my marriage in Binghamton, if things didn't work out.

After a fat joint to seal our farewell, the Seabees clomped off to work in their heavy boots, and Sara drove me out to 101.

We topped off our caffeine at a Dunkin Donuts while I waited for the commuter traffic to clear. The juke box played Johnny Cash, and the sugary scent of the restaurant carried a faint tinge of diesel fumes from a row of semis idling outside, drawing me toward the highway.

"Your home life with the boys made me miss my place back east," I said. "When you were gone last week, it felt like a barracks."

"I'm not their house mother, you know. Even if the boys sometimes act like I am." She grinned. "Don't go telling Ronnie I'm a house mother. I just take care of Jack, and he takes care of me."

"She'll get the right impression when I tell her you kick start his hog in the morning."

"Fat chance." She sipped her coffee. "I can't believe you only borrowed twenty bucks for your trip home."

"One monster milkshake a day."

"At least you have a job waiting. Jack said the guy offered you a lot of money."

"Yeah, but he hasn't seen me yet." I self-consciously reached behind my head and checked the rubber band around my snarled hair.

"For sure, but you'll do fine." She gave me a serious look. "I'm glad you're going home. Jack says you and Ronnie belong together."

"I'll find out."

"So many changes in the next couple months. You going back to New York, Richard coming off his tour, Jack and Seth trucking up to Maine." She paused. "Jack acts like he wants me to come, but you know Jack." She lit a cigarette and swiped the match to blow it out. "I won't know how to live without the Navy sending my men away."

I flagged the waitress for another cup of coffee. "In some ways, it's worse for you and Ronnie."

"I think Jack understands that." She dabbed the coffee ring in her saucer with one of the thin napkins. "But he wanted me to break up with Richard last week. I couldn't do it, not on his way back to Okinawa. He's on standby and might end up back in Nam. I owe him that much."

"You did the right thing," I said, recalling how I worried about Ronnie and the leatherman when I was stuck on Adak. I wondered if knowing the truth would have made me feel better or worse.

"Jack's a good man but hard to read." She flicked her cigarette. "Even about Maine."

"You can always come to Binghamton," I said impulsively, quickly adding, "I mean you can stay with Ronnie and me." I blushed at my blunder, but Sara didn't seem to notice.

"I hope you work things out with her." Sara reached for a fresh napkin as I sipped my coffee, only lukewarm. I chugged the rest, and she leaned over and kissed me platonically, ending my California escape.

I settled for a series of short, hot rides from one interchange to another, with long waits in-between, as impatient drivers flew by to their next traffic jam. By the time a beautiful, young divorcee and her red-haired toddler son picked me up, I was parched and oily, my throat dried from breathing exhaust, and my usual good humor strained.

Joanne was so calm in the crazy traffic that I soon relaxed and enjoyed the drive out past San Bernardino, where she was taking Mike to visit his grandmother. The boy looked like trouble, as all freckled boys do, but he bided his time in the car talking to Joanne or me or his stuffed monkey with equal sincerity, or combing and trying to braid my hair, which hung over the seat in a nested tangle. Joanne had taught him well; he was gentle with his comb, but I can't say he made much progress. I figured my hair would never recover from several thousand miles of hot sun and wind.

Joanne was light haired and tan, and she wore blue jeans and a bikini top. She was soft spoken, and I strove to hear her over the rush of air through the open windows. Mike ignored us as we shared a joint, and she queried me about my trip so far. Impulsively, to my surprise, Joanne said I might crash at her mom's house, since my journey through LA and its suburbs had taken most of the day, and I wouldn't make Las Vegas before nightfall. Although her voice carried no hint of romance, I wished I had met her on my way to California, when I was bent on escape. I amazed myself by declining her invitation, unsure how serious it was and hoping one lucky ride would make up for the time I'd lost. As always when I began a new trip, I was anxious to log miles.

After we finished the joint, she inserted an Allman Brother's tape, *Live at the Fillmore East*, and turned it up. I sat back to watch the housing developments pass as Joanne's expression continued in a soft smile, unaffected by the heat or traffic. She was locked in her own world, bobbing her head to the music, and stealing occasional glances to the car seat in the back where Mike had nodded off. Maybe it was the Allmans or my vector to Las Vegas where I planned to visit Phil Briones, but my mind drifted back to my first night on Adak when I met Phil and offered to share my stash of Joe's pillowcase red.

That night we bounced down a series of gravel roads extending far from the base lights and any signs of humanity. Phil had organized a car party with Billy Sullivan and Jerry Fenn in the old, black Buick that I was destined to buy from him a few months later. On the dash balanced two small bookshelf speakers wired to a portable cassette deck blaring "Elizabeth Reed." As the honored guest, I rode shotgun next to Phil. My job was to keep the speakers from falling, which was not that easy. Blasted by rain and wind, the car rocked on its collapsed springs and scraped bottom as we drove through deep holes and pools on the abandoned road. Lightning burst through the thick clouds and revealed a mountainous landscape, devoid of trees, with rivulets of water flowing down and across the road, as if we were cruising up a stream bed.

My new comrades laughed and said not to worry. Phil produced a bong, not wanting to waste my precious weed by rolling joints, and Billy handed around a bottle of sweet Taylor Pink Catawba wine. Wasted and not at all comforted by their claims about the safety of the road and the sturdiness of the Buick, I thought we might die.

"We don't call her the Dreadnaught for nothing," Phil said, patting the cracked dashboard.

We swung down an even narrower path, and Jerry yelled up to Phil, "You can't cross here! It might be washed out!"

"It's cool," Phil yelled back. "We were up here in a Jeep last week and the road was fine. No problem!"

"But the tide's high, and it's storming!" Jerry persisted. "And this ain't no Jeep; it's the fucking Buick!"

"Hey, Phil," crooned Billy, "Jerry says it's raining!"

But Phil would not be diverted from his planned route. "We have to show Flash what Adak is really like."

The road narrowed to one car width with an ocean of water on either side. A wave crashed up and over the car, inspiring Jerry and Billy to hoot with pleasure. I clasped the wine bottle like a crucifix when a second wave crashed up from the other side and doused the car again. Waves washed us from both sides in a sickening rhythm as the old Buick continued to inch along.

Finally, I burst, "Where are we?" I felt like the Pharaoh crossing the dry bed of the Red Sea with walls of water crashing down.

Phil turned to me. His voice echoed the calm, rhythmic drone of a tour director. "To our right is Lake Andrew, really a large lagoon, and to the left is the Bering Sea. Lake Andrew is fresh water."

"Not for long," Jerry chortled. "Looks like the sea wants to take it back."

After one high wave teetered above us and collapsed like an office building, Billy yelled, "Punch the damn pedal. I ain't drowning tonight!"

Phil pushed the speed up to about ten miles per hour, which was all he dared, given the Dreadnaught's suspension and the condition of the road if it was a road. We finally turned off the estuary and climbed to drier ground, over gravel with rocks the size of watermelons, where we stopped to finish the wine and quiet our nerves before returning to the base, my initiation complete. Less than a day after I got off the flight from LA, and I knew what Adak was like, a washed-out road with waves crashing from either side. Every time I thought about Phil, I remembered how we parted the sea in the Dreadnaught that first night we met, our friendship sealed by the Bering Sea, surviving even our tenuous triangle with Diane.

Back on the smooth concrete interstate extending east from LA, Joanne pulled over to the side of the exit ramp for San Bernardino and let me out with a peck on the cheek. I blushed, even though my face was already pink from the blistering sun, and shook her hand. Watching her disappear into the heat waves and dust, I stared at the tail of her car. I might be crazy for choosing a night of hitching across the desert instead of a night at her mother's, even if I was trying to get home. Her mother must have air-conditioning. But my mind was set on New York and whatever awaited me there.

After a half-hour of unrelenting sun, a quiet guy in a pickup took me out past Barstow where I waited for another ride, beginning to fade like a desert mirage. I yawned, hoping I would not have to roll out my sleeping bag on the hot rocks and mesquite spikes. Worse, I needed to take a crap.

There were no bathrooms, of course, and no scrub bushes tall enough to hide a squatting man. I should have remembered to replenish my emergency supply of toilet paper. I searched through the fast food debris along the shoulder for any napkins or tissues that might qualify. After I gathered a suitable stash, I walked far enough from the highway that the speeding cars, if there were any, would be unlikely to notice.

From my immodest squat, I spied an old man watching me from the shoulder. He was walking toward Las Vegas, and all he carried was a translucent plastic jug. He glanced back at me several times.

By the time I scrambled back to the highway, he was gone. No cars had passed. I peered ahead into the distorted heat waves for a sign of him, but I saw nothing except the endless tongue of highway, the looping power lines, and the parched desert brush. While I wondered whether the old man was flesh or vision, a car honked on the roadside behind me, a late model red Dodge pickup.

The driver was a few years older than me, clean-shaven and light haired, and he wore a Dodger baseball cap and a Hawaiian shirt imprinted with blue palms. As I climbed in, he gestured toward a notepad on the dashboard. He pointed at his ears and mouth and shook his head. Through a series of notes back and forth, I learned his name was Brian Hooper, he worked at Lockheed, where he had lost his hearing, and he was on his way to Las Vegas for vacation. He wrote "Girls!" on the pad. His anticipation was contagious, but I was only glad to have a ride to Phil's place.

He pulled a makeup compact out of the glove compartment and tapped it while pointing toward my nose. Inside the compact, I found white powder, a razor blade, and a stubby straw, but the road was too bumpy to chop and carve lines. I gestured to Brian with a series of wavy hand motions. After he pulled onto the shoulder, I snorted a couple of thin lines and recognized the cocaine burn. Brian shaped a wide, thick line and vacuumed it up with gusto. "I'm on vacation!" he scrawled on the note pad while I fired up one of my numbers with his dashboard lighter.

We got on famously as my fatigue dispersed, and the miles sped by. I invited Brian to join Phil and me for a night on the town, but he wrote "other plans." Phil had said something about trouble with his fiancée Tara when I called him yesterday, so he was free. He had started his own business painting houses, and he might give himself tomorrow off.

It was dark when we caught our first glimpse of Las Vegas. The town rose like an alien spaceport with brightly lit towers and flashing colored lights, out of place among the stark browns and muted greens of the surrounding desert. Driving down the strip in slow traffic, our eyes adjusted to the brightness of noon, and when we turned down Phil's residential street, we plunged into suburban darkness. Stopping at Phil's address, Brian scribbled "directions to brothel?" on his pad. I shook my head and waved as he drove away.

I crossed the thick lawn of a white three-bedroom ranch, like those in any American city, but it seemed oddly normal just a few blocks off the strip. Phil's father answered the door, reluctant to let me in. As soon as he realized I was Phil's friend from the Navy, he introduced himself as Bob. Phil was away at his fiancée's, not far, and due back any minute. Bob was shorter than Phil but cast the same wide smile. His tan arms hung from a white T-shirt. Phil's mom trailed into the living room, adjusting an earring. She wore make up, heels, and a dark blue dress with a sunset pattern. She stared at me as I crossed the threshold, shedding dust after my long day on the road. She turned and paced out of the living room. Bob gave me a quick shrug and pointed to a rug near the door where I dropped my baggage.

"Here's Phil now," he said as an old brown Ford pickup pulled into the driveway.

Phil swept me into a tight hug. His smile showed the tips of his teeth beneath his thick gunslinger moustache, his ruddy complexion peppered with flecks of paint. He wore Seabee-issue greens, bleached by the sun and splashed with random color.

"Gotta show you Las Vegas," he chanted. The gleam in his eye reminded me of that first night on Adak.

"Should be drier than the Dreadnaught."

"In some ways." He flicked a wave at his dad and led me to his pickup. He'd left the engine running, and we made a fast escape. Before we hit the end of his block, I lit our first joint. His tour route wove back and forth across the strip, crossing parking lots and side streets to avoid the worst traffic, as he pointed out the sights. At one hotel, we backed into a garage, surprising the attendant who froze in mid yell when Phil completed a three-point turn and peeled away.

A few blocks up the strip, he slowed to a crawl and joined a line of cars entering the Circus Circus garage. He waved off the parking valet, and he sped into a spot in the valet section beyond the sight of the booth.

"Local plates," Phil shrugged as I tried to catch my breath from his motocross driving. "They probably think I'm here to work."

I tucked in my stained T-shirt and brushed off my jeans as we entered the casino, walking past the din of ringing and flashing slot machines.

"They don't care how we look," Phil said as we watched a woman with a blond beehive sweep her winnings into the hem of a black skirt riding up her plump thighs. "Only one thing they care about."

We entered an alcove that resembled a restaurant except for the trapeze artist swinging overhead and the loud music punctuated by squeals of occasional winners. Phil picked a table near a large stage jutting into the middle of the room. White lights flashed along the edges of the runway, contrasting with the ambient red glow.

I leaned close to Phil and asked him how he was doing. I thought he would tell me about his fiancée, but he wanted to talk about Diane. His version of their great escape in the Painted Desert was different from hers. Diane had described their ending as a mutual parting of ways, but Phil described it as a Christian revival for her and a stunning withdrawal for him. He had hoped for a longer commitment.

I could hardly hear his deep voice over the droning bass of "The Pusher," as a dancer with tight, red shorts and a beaded white sweater swung down the stage with another dancer behind her. They wore wigs of shiny silver hair and gold lipstick, appearing more mannequin than human.

The next song was even louder, "Born to Be Wild," with an extra organ track. Even though Phil was speaking into my ear, I only caught random words. I tried to listen, but I zoned out, staring at the colored lights pulsing between the white strobes along the stage. They reminded me of the airfield light show we had arranged for Phil's last night on Adak before he left with Diane. The promise of a few joints had convinced an airman in the control tower to run a test with red, yellow, and white lights flashing up and down the runway and around the edges of the aprons and taxiways, igniting the low hanging clouds. The Adak light show surrounded us like we were sitting inside a giant pinball machine, not unlike the casino show.

Phil tapped my arm, suggesting we get out of there, which we did. He grabbed the check for our beers and burger baskets on the way out. Walking into the silence of the parking deck felt like diving underwater. Neither of us broke the spell as Phil drove down a series of side streets away from the strip.

He pulled into the gravel driveway of a house under construction. A cement mixer and two sawhorses stood in front of a double garage next to a red Toyota Corolla with no rust. A stack of plywood and a pile of crushed stone filled the dirt yard, and a yellow tarp draped over the far end of the house. A light shone from the living room window.

"Welcome to Phil's place," he said proudly, extending his arms like an MC.

"You built it?" I caught his excitement.

"You bet. Just one bedroom now but we'll have two more. Looks like Tara's here. Let's meet her."

We followed a dirt path and climbed three concrete steps to the front door where a small woman stood behind an aluminum screen door. She hopped out under the porch light and sprouted a soft laugh that caught me off guard at first, sounding a bit like Diane. Her dimpled cheeks and curly hair also recalled Diane, but Tara's hair was darker, and she wore deep red lipstick and gold hooped earrings, accenting her smooth brown complexion. She was easily as attractive as Diane but more exotic. Her smile emanated warmth as Phil introduced us. She wrapped him in a long kiss before pushing him away with a somber expression.

"I'm still mad at you," she said.

Phil laughed. "Thought we'd talk about it later."

"Now is later."

He glanced at me and back to her. "But you have to go to work."

"Flash can go rescue Diane," she said with a lilt.

"What?" I sputtered.

"Later," Phil said.

Tara reached behind her and grabbed a shoulder purse resting inside the door. With another wet kiss for Phil and a quick wave for me, she swayed to the Corolla, and we watched her car crunch down the driveway.

"She does the books for her dad at night," Phil said. "He's a contractor, how I met her." He stepped inside the house. "She takes accounting classes during the day."

The walls were hung with wall board and draped with tapestries. A line of bare studs marked the wall to the kitchen. "Easy entry," Phil said.

"What about Diane?"

"She called yesterday." Phil shrugged. "I shouldn't have told Tara, but I don't like secrets."

"Me neither," I replied, admiring the large kitchen, complete except for the exposed sub-floor.

"She was looking for you. Calling from some place near Denver."

We strode past the master bedroom, finished with carpet, a new bed, and dressers, and we stopped at the end of the hallway, which was blocked by a sheet of plywood. "The kid wing," Phil said, pointing skyward at the distant future.

"Why should Tara care if Diane was looking for me?"

"Tara's got her Latin thing going, hot and cold," Phil laughed. "Just like my mom."

I remembered his mother's cold stare.

"But there's also history," he went on. "Diane wants someone to come to Denver, but she wants you, not me. Tara thinks I want to go, but she should know better."

"What about Daniel?"

"Shipped him overseas."

"Daniel was stateside when I saw her in Hollywood." We retraced our steps to the living room. "She was stuck on Jesus."

"Same thing when she showed up here about six months ago. I had just met Tara, but we weren't dating yet. Diane stayed with me for a week. She acted almost pagan like on Adak. Until one night when she said Jesus told her to do something. The next morning, she called Daniel and left."

"Chasing saints," I said as we left the house. I lit a joint and tossed the match in the dirt. "She mentioned a religious retreat in Denver."

"Makes sense." Phil took the doobie and stared back at his unfinished house. "Part of me wanted to go. Diane always has that effect on me."

"Something's wrong." I stood next to Phil. "With Diane, I mean."

Phil nodded in agreement as I sorted through my feelings about Diane, more complex than Phil's after my recent visit. Despite her strange spiritual beliefs and her personal ghosts, her spirit child, and her lifer husband, she had always cared about my state of mind. Even if I wished for more at times, she was a loyal friend. I had an obligation to call her at least. I found myself wondering about Billy. Phil might not know about him.

We stubbed out the roach and climbed back into the truck. When we pulled up in front of his parent's house, Phil switched off the engine and pocketed the keys. I looked at him uncertainly, unsure what we were doing. My baggage was here, but I had assumed we would end up at his place.

"I'm sleeping here tonight. Could be a few nights," Phil said. "Tara wants it that way."

"She's staying there without you?"

"She'll get over it. She always does."

His parents' house was dark. I quietly retrieved my stuff and rolled out my sleeping bag on the soft green lawn in the back yard. Phil joined me for a nightcap joint, and we lay back and stared at the stars, hardly visible above the muted glow of the strip.

Without warning, the lawn sprinklers clicked on, and Phil ran to turn them off. I caught a few cool drops that dried quickly in the desert breeze. When he returned, he handed me the torn corner of a phone book page with Diane's number in Denver scribbled in the margin.

Phil got up early to drop me off at the I-15 interchange. Dressed again in his old Seabee uniform, he offered me a chance to work with him for a few days and build up my stake. But I was anxious to keep moving. With a few lucky rides, I should make Binghamton in four days.

Chapter 17

My chances of getting a ride out of Las Vegas looked bleak. I counted eleven hitchhikers at the interchange, none of them happy to have more competition. Many had waited more than a day, standing or sitting all night while I slept in Phil's backyard. The troopers stopped by every now and then to order the hitchhikers back up to the top of the entrance ramp where no cars passing on the interstate could see them, so their only chance to escape the relentless heat came from the occasional cars leaving Las Vegas. My rideless brothers had formed a line, in the American tradition. I could plan on waiting a day or two for my turn.

My road map revealed another interchange, also serving Las Vegas, a few miles north. I figured traffic going in my direction might use that route. Staring into the brightening horizon, I made out the concrete overpass marking my destination. The other hitchhikers thought I was crazy to walk that far, and they saw me off like frightened settlers sending a scout into Apache territory, thinking I'd never survive.

Streaming with sweat, I trudged between the mesquite and sage brush, avoiding tin cans and other debris of civilization but seeing no living creatures. About halfway across, I passed an abandoned trailer where someone had tried to raise a ranch out of the parched soil, which resembled concrete more than any topsoil I remembered from my rural childhood. A few fence posts, baked to thin gray sticks, marked the corral, extending out past a rusted water trough. I stumbled and jumped back in shock before realizing I'd only caught a strand of barbed wire, not the clutch of a rattlesnake.

My slow progress brought me close enough to the interchange to see the cars careening down the entrance ramp and heading away from the neon temples. I spied an old man walking along the shoulder, his limbs as thin as branches of mesquite. I recognized his blue coveralls and his long-sleeved T-shirt from my trip into town, and he was still carrying a gallon plastic jug and no other belongings. He was headed into Las Vegas like he had been when I saw him before, but he was coming from the opposite direction. He continued along the shoulder and looked toward me as I approached, but I lost sight of him behind the mound of the overpass. When I finally reached the highway, he was gone.

He might be a mirage or a spirit of the highway, hitchhiking between a series of nameless towns. If my luck failed to change at this ramp, I might end up just like him with my skin drying and tightening with the sun and age, and my baggage crumbling to dust while I waited for a ride out of the desert.

But within minutes, I was reclining comfortably in a Volkswagen bus with John Taylor and Sheila Villa, relieved that my hot trek had paid off with a quick ride. They made me feel like I had stepped into their living room, offering me Coca-Cola and snacks, and asking me if I felt all right after waiting so long in the hot sun. I relaxed and offered to share my last Jack number.

I sat behind John on the floor of the van, staring at his shoulder-length blonde hair tied back with a bronze clip. Sheila turned around from her passenger seat.

"Don't you love his hair? I'm jealous of it," she said. "Why don't you sit on one of the pillows?" She was about my age, a few years younger than John, and she had a healthy, tomboy look with auburn hair and a sprinkling of freckles.

"Those pillows have been around. Across the country, all the way up to Nome on the Alcan Highway, and down the coast. You can't hurt them," John said, ignoring Sheila's comments about his hair. He went on to tell me how they'd met in Hawaii and how they'd been traveling together for six months.

John stopped in his travel log and said, "Hey, look at that old guy walking on the median strip. Looks like he's been walking in the desert for days."

He was the same spirit I'd seen twice before, still carrying the plastic jug. As I watched his image disappear behind us, Sheila said, "Maybe I should've given this to the old man, but you can have it." She produced a souvenir sewing kit from Caesar's Palace. I thanked her and shoved it into my backpack.

"Flash, we won't get you to New York very fast, though we're headed that way," John informed me. "We're planning to see the Grand Canyon and some of the national parks before stopping to visit Sheila's friends in Denver. We're camping at the North Rim tonight."

"You can roll out your sleeping bag by the bus," added Sheila.

I decided a ride was better than no ride, and I wouldn't gain much by waiting for another car to get me to Denver, where I planned to call Diane. Although I wanted to make it home, I was both in a hurry and not in a hurry. I was beginning to miss Ronnie more now after our positive phone conversation, which seemed like an analgesic to our sick relationship, but I was still unsure what I might find in New York: a new life or an illusion, promises as ephemeral as the spirit of the highway, and the stark, Bardeen wasteland stretching past the horizon.

Sheila was waiting for a response, so I nodded and told them a bit about my marriage and my trip as John steered the bus into the national forest, and the pavement gave way to gravel. By the time we stopped for the night, we were still several miles from the Grand Canyon. John pulled off the narrow road under a bright canopy of stars and the silhouettes of ponderosa pine. Their rich, dry scent reminded me of my night near Sedona, several hundred miles south.

Under a Coleman lantern hissing white light from a hook on the van's ceiling, my hosts sat across from one another at a fold-down wooden table, stained mahogany brown. Sheila spread a blue flowered tablecloth, which matched the curtains. She squeezed into one of the bench seats and left room for me, but I preferred lounging on the pile of pillows.

They invited me to share their dinner, which began with John's killer hors devours, a Triscuit cracker topped with a slice of cheddar cheese, a dab of Dijon mustard, and a slice of stuffed pimento olive. Sheila produced a large bottle of Gallo burgundy and three sturdy, short stemmed wineglasses. While John replenished the hors devours, I helped Sheila fry burgers on the propane stove.

Once we quenched our munchies, we reclined and listened to the soft wind rustling branches outside. John leaned toward me, pointing with a cracker.

"As a veteran, I hope you don't mind me saying I was a conscientious objector."

"Good for you," I replied.

"I appealed to my draft board in Boston when I got out of law school. They'd opened up the rules by then."

"You had to be a Jehovah Witness your entire life at my draft board, and they still declined most of them."

Sheila looked at me sympathetically as John paused to fire up a roach.

"I did alternative service at legal aid," he said exhaling. "Then I stayed on and built up a stash of money for this trip."

John's revelation impressed me. He was the first lawyer I'd met in the flesh, and the first lawyer who seemed altogether different from Nixon and his henchmen. But as I took the joint from him, I felt a thread of resentment. His escape sounded easy after my efforts to avoid Vietnam, and how the war had scrambled my life and my marriage. I remembered those early days in college with Ronnie when we protested the war, caught up in a common purpose that pulled us closer together. We knew a guy, Bruce Horford, who spent the summer of love in San Francisco, while I worked two jobs to pay my tuition and eventually ran out of money and had to quit school anyway. Bruce brought back the true gospel of protest, saying we had it all wrong, though no one could figure out what he meant. But I learned how money and privilege made a difference, allowing some to stay in school or pay for a medical discharge like my Seabee friend Walt.

I passed the doobie to Sheila and studied John's sincere expression. Although the cards had fallen his way, he wasn't bragging about his good fortune like Bruce and Walt. Listening to John brought back the edges of my two-sided guilt. When I talked to my veteran friends like David, I felt guilty for not going to Vietnam, not getting wounded or dying as so many of my other friends had. With Ronnie and now John, I chided myself for not standing up more strongly for my convictions against the war.

"I'm glad you avoided the suck," I finally said. "And you helped people."

"Mostly landlord stuff but thanks."

"Flash, I hope you didn't go to Vietnam," Sheila said, leaning for the roach and patting my shoulder.

I shook my head and found myself telling them about my stint as battalion clerk on Adak after a few months in the drafting department, when I had launched a personal mission of converting my boss, the highest ranking enlisted Seabee on the island, something I seldom mentioned to anyone.

"Chief Bush was a hardcore lifer," I said. "Every morning, he gulped the cold, black coffee left over in his cup from the day before. Even on Mondays, when the dregs had an oily sheen, floating with orange fungi." I paused for a second to adjust my cramped leg on the pillow. "But he surprised me by listening when I started telling him my arguments against the war. He knew I hid in the head during rifle practice, and he never saw my name when I made out the duty rosters for inspections and military training. He said I was the best clerk he'd had, so he let me get away with that stuff."

"The military isn't far removed from feudal law." John shook his head.

Sheila began filling a pipe with hashish they had preserved all the way from Hawaii. "It's great how you stood up to him," she said.

"Well, when you work closely with someone, the feudal separation breaks down." I took the pipe from Sheila. "Like guards and inmates, I guess." I broke into a cough and passed the pipe to John.

"Anyway, I had orders to Vietnam after I left Adak, but they never came," I said when I regained my breath. "Bush called Washington once a week to rap with another Chief, a buddy of his in the Pentagon who made Seabee personnel assignments. Bush did his best to get us tours in country, knowing how much we wanted to do our duty."

"That's draconian," John blurted. "They shouldn't have the right to choose fates for other people."

"Well, they did. Bush said I was going to the tenth battalion, and they were preparing for a tour in Cam Rahn Bay. He was happy for me, like he was doing me a favor. He probably hoped the tour would change my mind, so I could fill a body bag like the other good Seabees."

John and Sheila blanched at my mention of body bags. She relit the pipe and passed it to me.

I inhaled and held my breath for several seconds. "But I never received the manila envelope with my official orders and my day to leave the island came and went. When I finally asked Bush what was going on, he said I was getting orders to Newport, Rhode Island, but I was extended on Adak for three months." I cracked a smile. "I hated Adak, but it meant I'd have less than a year left in my enlistment, ineligible for foreign duty."

"They found an administrative way to change your orders," John surmised. "They want to get rid of anyone who might cause trouble, the assholes."

"Maybe your Chief got you off," Sheila suggested.

"That's possible," I admitted, "but they probably lost me. I got lucky."

"Did you ever ask him? I think you changed his heart after all," she said.

"Nah, I didn't want to risk losing my orders to Newport."

"They silenced you, that's for sure," John said. "But that's my radical opinion as your lawyer. You avoided going to Vietnam, and you did it in a creative way. You out-smarted them."

"It's incredible," agreed Sheila.

I coughed on my hit but caught the smoke in my cheeks and pushed it back down. "This hash is incredible," I squeaked, holding my breath. I wasn't proud of my escape from Vietnam any more than I was proud of my decision to enlist in the first place. Deep down, I knew the impersonal randomness of the Pentagon bureaucracy was more likely to have saved me than anything Bush or I might have done.

John seemed to hear my thoughts about enlisting but not in the way I hoped. "I commend you for changing your mind about the war," he said.

"I didn't change my mind."

"But you enlisted."

"I had no choice." I stared at John. He furrowed his eyebrows before breaking away and reaching for a farmer match to relight the pipe.

"He's right, John," Sheila nodded. "Most guys never had a choice."

"I agree the system is unfair," John allowed. "But there's always a choice."

I bit my tongue, not wanting to let my simmering thoughts spoil the evening. I admired John's unwavering perspective about the war as I admired Ronnie's, but I had felt trapped, both then and now.

Sheila asked John, "Would you have gone to jail if they denied your CO petition?"

John turned toward me as I examined my stockinged feet. "Flash, did you petition your draft board?"

"I looked into it after I dropped out of college, but no, I didn't." I leaned back on the pillows and stared at the darkened window. "Not much point with my draft board."

"There's Boston, and there's everywhere else," Sheila said.

John shrugged, cracking a grin as he sucked down a hit. "Well, at least you avoided Vietnam," he gasped.

Sheila nodded in agreement, fetching John a swallow of burgundy to cool his smoky throat. "Maui smoke is the best," she said. "I'll be sad when the hash runs out. Not as good as Maui weed but good enough. We'll have to go back to Maui, right John?"

"You bet," John agreed. The bus grew quiet, and I blamed my talking about the war and conscription. But John's mind was already cruising a different highway.

"Our contract's up in Denver," Sheila informed me. "I'm stopping there to see some friends, and John says he might just drop me off and continue east. But we might renew our contract again. We've been renewing it ever since Maui. First, it was to tour Alaska, then the West Coast, and then to head out to Denver." She went on to describe how she met John while she was working in a hotel bar on Maui, and how they spent several weeks camping there and several more weeks on the big island while the bus was parked at his cousin's house in Seattle. "John saved my life. I was into some sick habits with the people who hung out at the bar, and John would have none of that. He parties, but it's not his life."

She leaned against his arm and stroked his shoulder.

"Wait a minute, I thought partying was my life," John responded with a smile. "Just like dope is hope. No hope without dope. Maui was like paradise, but I guess even paradise can get to be too much after a while."

"Does the ripe fruit never fall?" I said, trying to quote one of my favorite poems from English class, also one my sister Kathy liked to recite on Sunday mornings. To their questioning glances I added, "No change in paradise. Like a still life painting, lifeless."

John grinned wistfully. "You make Maui sound like your island in Alaska, but I remember some philosopher, probably a racist, saying that human progress was more likely in colder climates because people had to struggle to survive."

"Like Egypt," gibed Sheila. "I guess the pyramids were built in a blizzard."

We laughed at our jagged line of reasoning.

"Where Maui has sand Adak has rocks," I said. "Instead of bikinis, Adak has plenty of parkas and very few women. But it does have a volcano."

"So does Maui," Sheila said. She started loading up her bamboo bong for a good night hit.

Soon enough, we were all falling asleep, Sheila and John on their air mattress in the bus and me in my Boy Scout bag just outside. I closed my eyes and reran our conversation about how the Navy miraculously lost my orders to Vietnam. John and Sheila sympathized with my predicament, and Sheila at least understood my compromise to enlist. I had seldom known that level of support from Ronnie.

I remembered all the times she said I never should have enlisted, and I should not have gone to Canada either. I should have simply denied the existence of the government. Now, I wondered if she realized my new job in New York, the one she was so happy about, would be working for a defense contractor, even if it was the only job available. Another compromise to make a living. Even in the best of times, when our marriage resembled those idyllic days before the draft lottery, I always thought there was something missing, like I had failed.

In the morning, the van skidded and shook along the gravel road until we came to the smoothly paved driveway for Grand Canyon National Park. The morning was chilly and clear, so we could see all the way across the canyon to the south rim. The throngs of tourists were muted by distance, but I sensed their presence, recalling how Ronnie and I had stood on the opposite cliff a few years ago during our dash across the country after boot camp, fearful about my Vietnam orders and another pending separation, still clinging to the innocent love of our first year of marriage. I squinted across the chasm as if I might see us standing there, remembering how grateful, and even surprised, I had felt when Ronnie stuck with me through boot camp and my transfer to California and military training. She said our love was stronger than the war, even if she disapproved of my enlisting. If our younger selves could see me standing here, I wondered what she would think of me now. I'd find out soon enough.

I tried to stare down at the Colorado River to shake my mood, but I couldn't get close enough to the fence, blocked by the crowd of white-legged tourists in Bermuda shorts, soft colored polyester shirts, and straw hats, all taking pictures of one other. Threading my way down the path until I found an open spot, I spied puffs of fog along the river like clouds from an airplane. At each bend in the trail, the view was slightly different, sunlight and shadows drawing new shapes and shades of color. A large man bumped me from behind, excusing himself as I reflexively grabbed the rail. I realized John and Sheila had wandered away.

I found them outside the souvenir store. John held a Grand Canyon sun visor for his mother, and Sheila waved a propeller on a stick, saying we needed a toy. As we waded through the crowd back to the van, a well-oiled group of sightseers in Hawaiian shirts, standing next to a tour bus, laughed and pointed at us, impressed by our ponytails. I tried to ignore them, hoping to preserve the transcendent views I had just enjoyed, but I could see John's mood darken

"This country is run by fascists," he said as we rolled out of the parking lot. "Even if no one realizes it, not even the fascists themselves. In this country, if you call a man a fascist, ninety percent of the time he should thank you for complimenting him on his lifestyle and world view."

I spun Sheila's propeller as she loaded up the bamboo bong. Every time we emptied their film canister of Maui weed, it refilled like magic. John waited for my reply.

"You're right," I said as I took the bong. "Even in the Navy, most guys never complained about their lack of freedom. That's why my friends and I kept to ourselves and never let anyone else know we were getting high." I sucked a hit and passed it back.

"The same with most families," John opined. "They just watch TV every night and never question anything. *Ozzie and Harriet* is definitely Nazi propaganda."

"You're going a bit too far, John," Sheila commented. She held the bong and lit it for him, so he could keep his eyes on the road. "Ozzie and Harriet aren't Nazis. They might be straight and conservative, but they aren't Nazis."

"Well, they aren't card-carrying Nazis," John allowed. "But they reinforce the same middle-class values — the Christian, heterosexual, family unit — where dad rules the roost, and mom looks after the family's emotional needs."

A green station wagon with camping equipment tied to the roof honked and passed us. John calmly ignored the faster car as he always did, but the conversation was getting heavy.

I said, "I can see Ricky goose-stepping in a stiff wool uniform while Ozzie and Harriet look on in pride."

John returned a smile at the image of Ricky in uniform.

"I wonder if he still has his rock band." I added. "Maybe he's changed his head."

"Might be why they're off the air. Wasn't Wally his big brother?"

"You're thinking of Beaver."

"Aren't you guys hungry?" Sheila interjected brightly. "What should we have for lunch?"

John gave up his reverie at the mention of food. "Yeah, time for munchie mitigation. We better eat that sliced ham we bought in Vegas."

I scrambled around the cooler and pillows, helping Sheila assemble sandwiches while staring at the other worldly scenery of Utah unfolding around us. We were headed for Zion National Park, but to me, the green mileage signs were ticking ever closer to New York.

Two mornings later, they dropped me off at a truck stop near Denver where we said our goodbyes, and Sheila pressed a fat joint into my palm. As the bus headed toward Sheila's friends, John waved with his free hand, and Sheila snuggled up under his arm, signaling another renewal of their contract. I spied a phone booth and dug out Diane's number.

Chapter 18

Diane's vibrant voice usually raised my mood, inviting me to share her joy. But when I called her from Denver, she spoke in a suppressed tone, sounding even worse than Phil had described, like she was calling from a hospital room or a prison cell. She begged me to visit her and gave me an address in Boulder. I was eager to maintain my eastward momentum, but she conveyed an unspoken need that I couldn't ignore, not when I was only an hour away. I knew her well enough to confirm that something was wrong.

The address led to a large brick suburban mansion south of town. Through the wide driveway gate, I spied a swimming pool and a few smaller buildings that looked like plywood gardening sheds from Sears, but they had windows and curtains like children's playhouses. A dark-haired woman in a white cotton dress and sandals answered the double oak door. Direct sunlight from a high window silhouetted her figure and obscured her face. I pulled my eyes away and asked for Diane as a well-dressed couple slid behind her and out the door. Following her inside, I saw a dozen people in a large living room with an arched ceiling, accented by a gray stone fireplace and chimney. The women wore dresses, and the men sported ties and coats, all pinned with nametags like it was Sunday morning.

The greeter turned to face me. She was about my age, and I felt the impact of her high cheekbones and pouting lips. She had the smooth, chiseled face of a glamour model, cold and distant despite her beauty. "I'm Melanie," she said softly as I glimpsed her nametag.

Melanie, I should know who she was. Her deep blue eyes drew me closer, but my feet gripped the floor like tree roots, not wanting to approach any further in my dusty road wardrobe. "I'm Flash." My voice sounded disembodied in the open space like it came from a speaker in another room.

"You're Diane's friend. She told me so much about you." Melanie's warm tone calmed my apprehensions. She told me to leave my luggage by the door and waved me toward the couch. Before we crossed the slate floor, Diane appeared in front of me, bouncing on her toes like she had just appeared out of the mist. She wore a green silk blouse with puffy sleeves and a brown skirt. Her golden link necklace matched the glint in her eyes, twinkling as always.

Melanie touched Diane's shoulder and retreated through a doorway to a room lined with foldout chairs. Three other women entered the living room from the courtyard, crossing in front of me and following in her wake.

Diane waited for them to pass and glanced around. "You look great," Diane lied as she pulled down my neck for a hug.

I stood back and admired her blouse. "You came here with Melanie?" I asked, finally connecting the name I had heard two weeks ago when I was breathing dust under Diane's bed in Hollywood. "Daniel didn't seem to like her."

"Not really," Diane smirked. "He doesn't like what she says about Jesus. But there's more to it than that."

The look on her face conjured up an image of her stiff ex-husband making a pass at Melanie, raising the ghost of a smile on my lips.

"But she has a thousand ways of saying no," Diane continued.

A man in a tweed jacket and a woman in a frilly blue dress sat in the armchairs across from us, nodding toward Diane and eyeing my patched jeans and gray T-shirt. Diane glanced at the couple furtively like she was worried about something. Maybe how out of place I looked.

She sandwiched my right hand between her slender fingers and asked, "How's Phil?"

"Sends his best. He wishes he could have come."

"I knew you would stop to see him." She eyed me expectantly.

"How's the retreat?" I asked, unsure what she wanted.

"The retreat is giving me new ways to think about Jesus. It ends this weekend. Sam-Raji asked me to stay longer."

"I thought you were working at your mother's store in LA."

"She understands." Diane patted my hand. "You could stay here too. Spend the weekend."

I stared into her brown eyes, recalling our evening in Hollywood when she wanted me to share her life with Jesus and Billy. Her voice on the phone this morning had sounded so desperate and different than it did now. "You know I'm not ready for this." I waved my free hand to encompass the expansive room. The people across from us watched me sympathetically. "I should hit the road."

She stood and slipped behind me, her hands resting on my shoulders. She kissed my ear, sending tingles down my neck. "I want to show you my room," she said.

We entered one of the toy houses, just large enough for four single beds, one for each wall. Diane shut the door and told me to lean against it. She dragged out Billy's photo album, a small suitcase, and her shoulder purse from under one of the beds and quickly pulled her dress over her head and shoulders. I had never seen her naked – or nearly naked – before, and I was too stunned to look away from her petite figure. She wriggled into jeans and a T-shirt, pulling on a pink Santa Monica sweatshirt. Someone knocked. She shook her head, raising her hand to tell me to stay in place. She leaned behind her bed to grab a photo wedged partway into a seam in the paneled wall. Billy.

"Sam-Raji wants me to give up Billy," she said. "He says my love for my son is hiding the truth of Jesus. Only he doesn't say love; he says illusion. Billy's not an illusion."

"You could have left."

She folded her skirt and blouse, placing them on top of the album in her suitcase. "He says Jesus allows no other spirits but the Holy Spirit. He wants me to choose Jesus or Billy. I know that now."

"Diane, you could have left," I repeated with a bit more emphasis.

She shook her head and pressed the lid shut, snapping the latch. "I thought I could convince Sam-Raji, but I have to protect Billy." She looked up at me with her trusting eyes, and I realized something about her that I must have known before at some level. She seldom acted on her own. She needed me to help her, and her need was sincere, just as her love for Billy. In that moment, I felt like another projection of her mind as if I truly were Billy's spirit father as she had suggested in Hollywood.

"You're the only one who loves Billy," she said.

No, I believed she loved Billy, not the same thing. I studied the photo on the bedspread of Billy wearing red overalls and holding a foam basketball in front of a pale blue background. I could make out the shadow of newsprint on the other side. She slid the picture into a side pocket of her purse.

"Flash, take me with you."

I already figured we were leaving the retreat together, but her eyes projected something further. I assumed she would be heading west. "Where do you want to go?"

"Take me to New York."

"I can't take you to New York." My face grew warm.

She rested her hand on my arm. "Not like that. I mean just travel together."

I leaned against the wall by the door, trying to process her request. A few weeks ago, I would have gladly traveled anywhere with her, just like Phil had done after they left Adak, and a part of my brain was telling me to say yes. But I also knew I couldn't spend that much time with her without hoping for more, and now I wanted to focus on returning to Ronnie, whatever that might mean. My life was complicated enough. "I don't think it would work," I finally mumbled.

"I understand," she said warmly, patting my hand and moving to the mirror to comb her hair and load her purse. She mentioned helping her mother get ready for a craft show in Hollywood. I watched her scan the room to make sure she had everything, and I realized her request to me had been an experimental candle, and now she was discarding that design.

She squeezed my hand and motioned me away from the door, swinging it open and shoving past an unhappy woman who scowled and said, "It's my room too, you know."

Outside, I heard a door open from the back of the house as Diane pointed me toward a side gate. She paused to change hands as a large figure crossed the courtyard in front of us and squatted down on a cement bench meant for three people.

He turned to face us. His appearance was shocking at first, even though I had seen Sam-Raji Wilson's photo on paperback books. He reminded me of Jesus in Gethsemane, the print hanging above my mother's bed, with long wavy dark hair, a full beard nicely trimmed, and long fingered hands pressed together in prayer. He wore an exceptionally large white shirt, tailored and hanging like a robe over white slacks, but his body was shaped more like a Buddha with a large belly pressing the buttons of his shirt. He must have weighed three times more than Jesus. I wondered if a cross could hold him.

He acted surprised to see Diane with her suitcase. Worried creases in her forehead betrayed her hope to avoid him.

"Diane, please don't leave the retreat early," he called in a soft, warm voice that raised harmonics in my bones. There was no mistaking his charisma, extending out from his massive body like a magnetic field. "Jesus wants you to stay."

"You said we could leave any time," Diane replied, her eyes lowered and her voice hardly above a whisper. She held her suitcase in two hands like a barrier between her and Sam-Raji as we passed closer to him.

Several people had gathered, following Sam-Raji from the main house, but I caught no sign of Melanie. The side gate was slightly open.

"Jesus says you are one of us," he whispered breathlessly. "He has a purpose for you."

I knew from the way he stared at Diane what purpose Sam-Raji had in mind, more for him than Jesus. I wondered how many ways Diane could say no. Then I heard her say it softly, "No."

Sam-Raji pretended not to hear her, continuing to peer at Diane.

"She said no," I said, making sure my voice was loud enough.

"Diane, don't let your thoughts get in the way of your real feeling for Jesus. Your thoughts can deceive you."

She glimpsed up at me and then toward Wilson. Her face flushed. "What about Billy?" she asked.

Sam-Raji wore an empathetic expression, his head bobbing. "You know what I say about Billy. Don't leave because of Billy. Stay because of Jesus."

He shot me a sidelong glance as if assessing my attitude toward Diane's spirit child. I knew Billy was important to her. Her love for him hardly rivaled Jesus who held the largest space in her heart, sadly enough for the men in her life, including me, but I found myself rallying to her defense, not as Billy's spirit father or Diane's estranged spirit lover, but as her friend.

Diane mumbled, "I can't stay."

Again Sam-Raji gave no indication he heard her.

I glared at him. "She said she can't stay."

"You have no say in this." He pointed me toward the gate.

"Don't give me orders," I said firmly.

"Please, Flash," Diane implored me. She faced Sam-Raji with her eyes lowered. "I can't stay. My place is with Billy."

I took a step toward the gate but stopped, realizing I had left my baggage by the front door. If I went back to get my stuff, it would give Sam-Raji Wilson more time to knead Diane's wavering mind.

As I froze in place, staring toward the house, Melanie swayed through the throng, carrying my suitcase, and holding my knapsack and sleeping bag away from her white dress to avoid getting it soiled. She whispered in my ear, "You and Diane should leave now."

With a farewell flick of her hand toward Diane, Melanie slid in front of Wilson and rested her arms on his immense shoulders. Everyone stared as Melanie kissed his cheek like she might kiss a horse.

I gently pushed Diane out the gate ahead of me, juggling my baggage.

Outside, Diane sighed, "I want to leave, but I want to go back."

"Jesus will always take you back," I replied. "You told me that yourself."

We crossed the street, and Diane paused, staring over her shoulder. Melanie broke away from Wilson, leaving him sitting like a statue as she retreated across the courtyard.

Halfway down the block, I lit Sheila's joint and passed it to Diane, cupping it in my hand in case any suburbanites were watching. Once we reached the artery road, I stashed the roach in my pocket, and we quickly hitched a ride. Diane's good looks enhanced my usual luck.

In the backseat of the car, she performed a breathing exercise, inhaling several deep breaths and extending her arms forward with her eyes closed in meditation. After a few minutes, she leaned her head on my shoulder. "I'll never forget this, Flash."

I shrugged. "Gave me an excuse to see you, and I got to meet the famous Sam-Raji Wilson."

"He's changing his name to La-di-bal," Diane corrected me. "He had a new vision."

"He needs a new diet."

She ignored my comment and eyed me reflectively. "I tried to leave. But he talked me out of it. He can be very persuasive." She looked away.

"There's something about him," I agreed. We sat silently for a couple miles, winding out of the hills, and merging on to the highway. "But I don't get his thing about Billy. Unless he wanted all your attention."

"Not for himself. For Jesus."

I shook my head in disbelief. I almost said she didn't need anyone like Sam-Raji to tell her what to do, but I realized she might not agree.

"Everything he does is for Jesus," she continued.

"That explains the second helpings."

Diane studied my sarcastic expression and finally cracked a smile. "I hate to know what you think of me now."

"I worry about you." I turned to check the road signs. In Denver, I planned to catch I-70 and resume my trajectory east after dropping Diane near the airport. She said she had money for her flight home. My next stop would be my sister's apartment in Columbus, Ohio for a real bed and a well needed shower, about two days away. Facing Diane, I added, "You're on a spiritual journey."

"I guess that's true. But you're on a spiritual journey too. Even if you don't realize it."

"Nah, my road's out there." I said, pointing toward the highway.

Diane glanced out her window. "New York."

I jerked away. Her words reignited the part of me that still wanted to escape with Diane and let Ronnie have Bardeen, but I knew it wouldn't work out that way. Diane would likely retreat to Daniel and Jesus as she had done with Phil in Las Vegas, and I might regret giving up my marriage. Better to stay on my current plan, I kept repeating to myself.

As an afterthought, Diane added, "I'd like to meet Ronnie. I hope you work it out."

Resting my head on the cold glass, I pondered how awkward I'd feel if Ronnie and Diane met one another but returning to Ronnie felt awkward as well. However much I wanted to believe Ronnie's desire to resume our marriage, I sensed a certain hesitation on both sides, or maybe it was the way she dismissed Bardeen so easily during our last conversation as if he had ceased to exist. Ronnie might question my sincerity, holding Bardeen offstage in case our reconciliation failed.

Glimpsing Diane's soft eyes, I recalled the spark of our initial meeting on Adak. Our friendship had survived Daniel, Billy, Sam-Raji, and the tatters of my marriage, from the leatherman to Bardeen, and my own self-doubts. Ronnie would see her as a rival. Though I hardly expected Diane and I would ever pursue a real romance after all that had happened, I might need her help one day to spring me from a bad situation, returning the favor I had done her.

"I hope you'll come back to California," she said.

"You know I love California."

Chapter 19

In the late afternoon, I stood near an entrance ramp on I-70 just across the Kansas border when a semi pulled up. The air horn blasted twice before I realized the trucker was waving at me. Ears ringing, I jogged up to the cab and stopped. I had never climbed into a big rig before, but I spied the rungs leading up from the wide, lower step. My host leaned out the passenger door, reaching for my bags, and I scrambled up behind them.

The deep seat felt luxurious, with plenty of space behind for my luggage. The cab had air-conditioning. After two days in the hot, tight space of John's van, I relaxed like I was riding an easy chair down the highway.

The trucker introduced himself as Joe Sherman, and he firmly shook my hand. A few years older than me, he had the friendly demeanor of a fishing buddy. Judging from his deep tan and sinewy arms, he spent his days working outside when he was off the road. He had thick, black hair combed back from his clean-shaven face. A handsome man, Joe reminded me of the woodsman in a Field and Stream ad.

Soon after we rolled on to the interstate, he reached into a compartment in the center console and produced a square plastic box like fishermen use to store lures. Inside were several dozen pills of assorted colors and shapes, both capsules and tablets.

"You're going to need these because we're driving all night," he informed me. "Or you can sleep."

His voice tailed off, nudging me to take the former option. Joe wanted company on his long trip to Kansas City with his load of wheat.

Seeing I was unsure which one to take and how I studied the pills like a jar of candy, Joe advised me, "The black ones are the best."

"We call them black beauties," I replied, agreeing that the large capsules were the obvious choice, much stronger than the white crosses Rick and I had taken on our overnight trip to Fort Worth. I washed one down with saliva.

"You can take more later. They're right here, and you can get them whenever you want. Just don't leave them on the seat, okay?" He told me how the Kansas state troopers kept a keen eye on truckers, often pulling them over at night. He figured they got bored on the quiet prairie. He turned to me. "How come someone left you off in Hayes?"

"Guy said he was looking for food."

Joe smirked and shook his head as we passed a family station wagon. The cab rode high enough off the ground that it felt like we were flying over the car in a 747. He tucked behind a tall moving van and ticked off the miles to the next exit.

"We need to stop for beers," Joe announced, swinging the rig off the interstate and into an all-night grocery. "We've got a long dry ride ahead of us. You drink beer, don't you?"

"I might drink a couple." The black beauty had begun to kick up my pulse and dry my throat, and the hundred-degree heat of the afternoon had hardly declined. A brisk warm wind blew dust and chaff across the dimly lit parking lot. Joe gave me the money for a couple of six packs of Coors and a bag of Lay's potato chips. He didn't want to be seen buying the beer.

Before we left the store, he scanned the parking lot to make sure it was free of troopers, but as we approached the truck, he whispered, "Shit, it's that fucking Kershaw again. Hurry up and put that bag under your shirt."

There wasn't enough cloth in my T-shirt to pull over the bag, so I just wrapped it in my arms and slunk over to the passenger side of the cab. Anyone watching me climb into the cab had to know I was carrying something bulky, about the size of two six packs, however much I tried to conceal them. Joe popped one open below the windshield, and I copied him. He nodded toward a stunted willow in the corner of the parking lot, where a trooper car sat with his lights out.

"That's Kershaw's M. O. He's hell on truckers."

Back on the highway, Joe coaxed the rig up to eighty or more, and we streaked past a few surprised cars before abruptly pulling off in an unmarked parking area. He shut off the engine and all the running lights and told me to get down. One thin line of trees separated us from the road.

A few minutes later, we watched a patrol car whiz past, and Joe chuckled, "Couldn't arrest us at the store. Ain't illegal to have beer unless you're on the road. He had to wait until we were moving."

"Can't he wait again?"

"He could, but he's miles up the highway by now. Besides, we look like most every other wheat truck out here, and he'd need to be right on our ass to read our plates. We'll just wait a couple more minutes and head out. Hand me that box of uppers, will you?"

Joe was right about our escape. We saw a few more troopers, and Joe waved to each one, but none of them pulled us over. We sped along in mind and body, while Joe rambled on about his wife and two small boys. "My brother works my dad's farm now, and I help him when I can. Thought about buying some land myself. But I like driving better. The rig's mine, clear in three years. I might get a loan for another rig and start my own company or just stay independent. My wife wants me to farm and keep regular hours, but the only thing farming ever did for me was keep me out of the draft. I still go to the National Guard two weeks each year after the harvest, enough military for me. Don't get why so many of my friends volunteered out of high school." We agreed on that.

"Yeah, I'm heading home to my wife, anxious to start my new job." I found myself sounding like a good ol' working boy and family man, just like Joe.

A young woman appeared in the headlights on the side of the interstate, waving her red jacket above her head and signaling for help. Joe pulled over just past her, and she ran up to my side of the cab and climbed up the steps before I could roll down the window.

Joe warned me, "Be careful, Flash. Never can tell about people out here in the middle of the night."

She looked harmless enough to me.

"Please give me a ride," she pleaded breathlessly. "I've just been in an accident."

"Where's your car?" Joe asked, reaching for his CB radio, and turning up the monitor.

"Back there, behind the trees. We drove off the road." When she saw Joe holding the handset, she said, "Please don't call it in. I don't want any trouble with the police."

"You were driving?" Joe asked.

"Is there anyone else in the car?" I asked.

Joe looked at me. "Shit, if someone's stuck in the car, we better help him."

"No, he's okay. I just want a ride out of here." She was desperate to escape.

"What about the car?" Joe's eyes probed the brush along the shoulder.

"He drove my car off the road." She started to cry. All this time, she had been hanging on the side of the cab.

"Are you sure he's all right?" I asked. "We can't leave him out here."

"He can drive my car back. It wasn't hurt that bad."

Joe leaned across me and spoke calmly, "I have a winch. We can crank it up and pull your car out, and then he can drive your car back. Why don't you come on up here rather than hanging on the door? What's your name?" He motioned for me to let her in, and she scrambled over me and sat on the center console.

"Sherry," she said with a deep breath. "I'm from Manhattan."

"Joe from Hayes."

"Flash from New York but not Manhattan," I said, hoping to calm her down, but my joke fell flat. She gave me a quick, apprehensive glance at the mention of New York like I was a

Doberman Pincher, and she wanted to make sure I was friendly before getting too close.

She wore tight pink shorts and a loosely flowing silky white blouse, and she had streaked blonde hair cut about shoulder length, blown wild by the wind. Her tears had not smeared her makeup; she hardly needed any. After I closed the door, her sandalwood scent filled the cab like nerve gas.

Digging behind his seat for a blanket to soften Sherry's perch on the console, Joe asked, "Where's your car?"

"Let's just go," she implored. "Can you drive me home to Manhattan?"

"We're truckin' all the way to Kansas City, Kansas. Glad to drop you off," Joe nodded. "But only take a few minutes to pull out your car."

"I don't want to go back."

"It's okay. We'll go back with you," I said, sensing her fear. "Otherwise you'll have to pay for a tow truck and wait until morning to get your car."

"You don't understand," she pleaded, gripping my arm. "I don't want to go back. Just take me home. Please."

Joe and I shared a shocked and chilling glance. We both wanted to catch the bastard who hurt this vulnerable woman. But we'd never find him in the dark unless she told us where she left him and the car.

I recalled helping Diane that morning, which now seemed so civilized compared to my speedy trip across Kansas, pulsing with black beauties, avoiding the law, and rescuing another woman in distress.

"Are you sure you don't want us to go back and get your car?" Joe asked one last time as he engaged the gears and steered the rig back on to the highway.

"No, please. Let's go," Sherry said, trying to regain her composure.

"I can call the troopers on the CB, or we can stop and make a report at the next exit."

She ignored Joe's persistent offers and stared straight ahead into the approaching headlights. She took a few deep breaths and relaxed her rigid posture.

"Are you thirsty?" I asked. "All we have is beer."

"Sure, I'll take a beer." She popped open a Coors, and Joe held up his can in a casual toast. He offered her an upper for the road, which she declined at first before choosing a blue speckled tablet. A mild one, according to Joe.

Joe and I sped miles ahead, talking like crazy and waiting for Sherry to catch up. She hardly said a thing about Joe's trucking business and his fleet dreams, but she relaxed when I started rattling about school. She was an English major at Kansas State, a couple of semesters ahead of me, planning on becoming a teacher. She finished off her second beer while I was still nursing my first. Joe called for a rest stop, and she seconded.

Inside the men's room, Joe said, "I'm depending on you."

"Depending on me for what?" Catching Joe's expectant glance, I had the uneasy feeling I was being recruited for something. I already had an inkling of what he wanted.

"You don't believe her story, do you? There's no way it adds up. She wouldn't give us any details. I think she picked up some guy or he picked her up, they were screwing on the side of the road, and then he pissed her off. So, she left him there and flagged us down."

"Seems worse than that," I argued, though I still wondered why she refused our help. I tried to see her point of view through my black beauty haze, wondering what Ronnie or Kathy would do in a comparable situation. If Ronnie wanted to get away from someone, she'd flag down a car just like Sherry. Kathy would apply her razor wit to wriggle out of the problem, and if that failed, she'd also run for help. "She's probably embarrassed."

"That was an act. She just wanted a ride home."

"You saw how scared she looked."

"Sure, but she wouldn't let us pull her car out, and she didn't want me to call it in. She was working us for a ride."

"Even if she was, there's no harm in it."

"She's easy, or she wouldn't have been in that situation."

"I don't see anything wrong with what she was doing, if she was doing anything," I said, surprised at his moral judgment.

Joe went on, "She warmed up when you started talking to her."

"We were talking about college." I tried to pull down a fresh section of the towel roll, but it was broken, so I shook the water off my hands.

"That's what you think." He winked at me. "I'm depending on you to loosen her up, and we can both get a piece."

"What do you mean?" I asked, though I knew what he meant. Under his intent stare, I raced through my options, none of them good. I could adopt a strict moral stance and drag my luggage out of the cab, but that would leave Sherry alone with Joe. I doubted she would join me for a restless night trying to sleep on the pet exercise lawn while we waited for the morning traffic. Better to go along with Joe on the surface and protect Sherry. But in the dark pit of my mind, I wondered if Joe might be right. With all three of us loaded with speed and beer, anything might happen.

"Trust me," Joe confided as we left the men's room. "I have an eye for women like her."

Sherry sat on the lower step of the cab waiting for us. She appeared calm; her earlier episode was all but forgotten.

Back on the highway, we popped another round of beers, and Joe and I helped ourselves to another black beauty. Sherry bounced along on the hard console, and every time Joe caught my eye, he gave me a high sign. Finally, he said, "Sherry, why don't you just slide down on Flash's lap. I'm sure he's much more comfortable than that hard seat. You're going to bruise your tailbone."

"You'd like that, wouldn't you?" she said with an edge in her voice, shooting a glare between Joe and me. Her face flashed with anger.

She twisted her shoulders, and I leaned away, thinking she might hit me, but she looped her arm around my shoulders and rearranged her lithe figure on my lap. My face blushed and throbbed like a pulsar, though my coloring went unnoticed in the diffused light inside the cab. Awkward silence descended around us.

But the black beauties soon sprouted words from my mouth. Recalling she was an English major, I tried to channel my sister, and I had little idea what I was babbling about, but Sherry joined right in. I scored a strike when I mentioned *Catcher in the Rye*, which turned out to be her favorite novel. With Joe egging me on from the periphery of my vision, I snaked my arm around her torso, and she leaned her head on my shoulder. I risked kissing her, and she kissed me back. My hand lingered on her breast.

"Why don't you two stretch out behind the seat?" Joe suggested. "I have a mattress back there. It's plenty comfortable."

I stared into her eyes. She returned a look of sleepy complicity, but she said, "Normally, I might, but after what happened to me tonight, I just don't feel right about it."

I nodded and pulled back.

"Hah," Joe spouted, slapping the wheel.

"Not what you expected me to say?" she asked in her edgy tone, turning toward Joe.

"I understand," I whispered.

Joe didn't understand. "I bet Flash can make you feel a whole lot better about everything. Sometimes it's better to forget a bad time by being with someone who really cares about you."

She pointed an aiming eye at Joe. "I know what you're trying to do. I'm not stupid."

"Calm down. I'm just kidding," Joe said, staring ahead at the highway.

"You should use your radio and tell the cops what you're doing. Or give it to me."

Joe grabbed the radio. "We should call in your car while we're at it."

"I have my side of the story," she replied. "And I know who you are." She tipped her chin at his truck registration pinned to the sun visor.

"I could drop you off here."

"Then I'd really have something to tell them."

We froze in place, Sherry and I gazing at Joe, and Joe watching the gray highway and yellow reflectors unfold.

Finally, I said, "Let's forget about it. We're close to Manhattan, and we have plenty of beer and clear weather."

A gust of wind hissed around the rig, belying my comment, though it hardly budged the cab. Soon the prairie gale pounded from both sides, and the cars in front of us swayed to keep in their lanes. I cracked a smile at the timing, and Sherry shook her head.

Joe's jaw muscles bulged as he chewed gum vigorously. He turned and gazed at my hand, and I realized I was tapping a blues shuffle rhythm on the center console, my metallic thumps filling the void between breaths of wind. Bobbing his head in time, Joe dropped his CB handset and took the wheel in both hands, erupting with laughter.

"You took me for a ride, Sherry," he chuckled. "At first I loved you, and then I hated you." He reached for a beer. "But you're all right."

I hung up the handset and popped a can for myself, passing one to Sherry.

"Thanks, I guess," she replied softly, still sprawling on my lap, but her limbs were as stiff as wood. So were mine, but I liked her there anyway.

She studied my eyes like she was searching for a grain of sand. "You did make me feel better." She kissed me hard and leaned away, shifting her position.

Joe's face peered over the crest of her herbal scented hair. He snapped his large wad of gum, shaking his head and grinning like he was right all along. For me, the romance was over, and my fuzzy mind was still bubbling with J. D. Salinger. I asked Sherry if she'd read *Franny and Zooey*. She had. I wished I'd paid more attention to Kathy raving about the stories, but I remembered enough with Sherry's prompting that the cab sounded like a freshman seminar, like I was already priming for the fall semester.

"They made us read *"Bananafish,"* Sherry said with disdain. "Seymour is such a loser."

"He's a veteran. I cut him slack," I replied.

"Make more sense if he committed suicide when he walked into the sea."

"Maybe he'd see a shark," I mused, recalling my last swim in Ventura. "And run back to shore."

"No, the shark should eat him." She clapped her hands.

"I like my ending better."

As we pulled off the exit for Manhattan, my mind drifted ahead to seeing Kathy in Columbus. She might enjoy hearing I discussed Salinger during my black beauty race across Kansas, but I'd leave Sherry out of it. I wondered what my sister would say about my decision to return to New York and Ronnie, but

I could guess. Escaping Binghamton with Rick was the smartest thing I had ever done in her eyes. She would be brimming with advice, practical and impractical. I always listened to my sister even if I seldom followed what she prescribed.

Joe steered the big rig down the dark, empty main street of Manhattan and the narrow side streets to Sherry's front door. She kissed us both in parting and sprinted to the safety of her apartment. As we twisted back to the highway, Joe flipped on his radio and called in Sherry's car, several exits west on the interstate.

"Should have done that to begin with," he said when he hung up the handset. "Should've done my duty."

I had almost forgotten how the night started. "She was hard to read."

"Funny way to put it." Joe reached across the console and patted my shoulder. "You're all right."

"You wonder about her boyfriend out there with the car?"

"They'll check on him." Turning onto the interstate, he pointed his chin at the small door where the box of uppers was hidden, and I flipped it open. "I know everyone out here," he said. "I'll hear the whole story soon enough. Right now, I just want to dump this wheat and get back to my wife."

Handing him a beauty, I dropped one more with a swig of beer, wishing I were that close to Ronnie. A few hours later, we arrived at the grain elevator and pulled into the line of wheat haulers waiting for dawn when the operators open the steel gates.

Chapter 20

Kathy buzzed me in, and I lugged my stuff up to her second floor apartment in a block of four story buildings that could have passed for dormitories, brown brick with small windows and narrow sidewalks crossing a parched lawn stabbed by a few unhealthy saplings. The thin industrial carpet in the hallway was slippery beneath my worn sneakers. The stairway seemed high and the steps many, awakening sweat and a gamey scent from my tired body. It had taken me two days from Kansas City to Columbus with only a few hours of rest last night in a drainage ditch lying between the east and westbound lanes of US40 in Illinois.

My sister gave me a welcoming hug and pointed me toward the shower. She wore a white cotton blouse and blue skirt, not her usual attire. She caught my glance and said, "I have to work tonight, so I got ready early. Always the over achiever."

When I emerged in my last clean T-shirt and underwear but the same dirty jeans, she said, "You'll have to sit in the back corner." She liked having someone accompany her to the steak house because of the cowboy atmosphere. Okay by me, it meant free dinner.

"Where's Jeremy?" I asked. "Ronnie said you might need my help to throw him out."

"That is so like her." Kathy combed back her thick red hair with her fingers. "If anyone was staying with her, she'd probably ask you to do that."

I thought about Bardeen, and Kathy read my expression.

"You know I love Ronnie," she said, "and I hope things work out between you. But maybe you should ask me to throw Bardeen out if he's still hanging around when you get home."

"I can take care of it."

My sister studied my expression. She was a couple years younger than me but several years ahead in college. She thought I should have broken up with Ronnie already, not believing my marriage was worth saving. She was a one strike and you're out person. Over the past several weeks, I found myself edging closer to her position, thinking I should have thrown Bardeen out as Kathy suggested rather than waiting for Ronnie to do it.

"Jeremy's in London," Kathy said. "He's on a T. S. Eliot binge."

We sat down on the couch, and I eyed her canister of weed. She shoved the rolling tray over to me.

"You'd be proud of me," I said. "I spent several hours talking about J. D. Salinger."

"There's hope for you yet. Where was this?"

"Kansas. In a big rig hauling wheat."

She nodded her head as if it made perfect sense. "So, I might get a teaching assistant position for the fall, means a stipend and tuition."

"They should have given you the TA to come here."

"I didn't graduate from an Ivy League college." She shrugged and lit a cigarette. "Did I tell you I'm taking Shakespeare this summer along with Romantic Lit? Anyway, the Shakespeare prof is Justin Rose. Famous. He wants me to work with him."

I imagined all the professors wanted her. At Oswego, she was the toast of the department for her brains as well as her looks. I lit the joint and gibed, "Does he have horses?"

"No," she said with the hint of a smile. "Keith George has the horses. Rose is seventy, but he has power in the department. He can help with the TA."

"Thought you wanted to study Mary Shelley."

"Yeah, Keith isn't happy about it. But I haven't committed." She took the joint. "He usually comes to the restaurant when I work, but he's giving a romantic lit lecture up at Case Western tonight."

As she inhaled, I asked, "Have you heard from Ronnie? I was hoping to call from here."

She set the joint on her ashtray next to her smoldering cigarette. "Yeah, we're all going to the Watkins Glen concert in August. I'm going with Keith, and we're camping together. Your friend David is loaning us tents."

"David camps?" I grinned, trying to reconcile the great outdoors with his slick New York City demeanor.

"He joined the outing club and realized he was the only member. Now he's the president with a storeroom full of tents."

"Sounds like David."

She stubbed out her cigarette. "You need to do me a favor," she implored, her voice serious.

I leaned back on her uncomfortable couch, wondering what was coming.

"Keith is dropping me off at home after the concert."

"That's nice."

"Because it's dad's birthday the next day."

Reading her request, I flicked a match and roasted the end of the roach. Taking a hot hit, I replied, "The last time dad and I talked, he criticized me for leaving Ronnie."

"What did you expect?"

"At least he didn't yell at me about Cambodia."

Kathy smirked, and I recalled the times she stood between my father and me when our arguments about the war escalated, a common scene before I enlisted, with Kathy pressing her hands against my chest and my mother holding my dad from behind as he fumed. I learned to avoid the subject, but my father still brought it up, especially when he was drinking. After my marriage, Ronnie watched our fights in shock, and our visits became less frequent.

"Well, expect an invitation from mom," Kathy said, stretching her arms and neck and signaling it was time to leave.

"I hope I'm working by then," I replied cynically.

"Do it for me, and I'll bring you an extra potato tonight."

After Kathy and I walked a few blocks to the Ranch House, I understood why she wanted backup. Normally independent and sure of herself, her slight figure and wild red hair drew the diners like a beacon. There were few women in the room filled with overweight former football players, already leering as she headed to the kitchen to put on her apron. More a bar than a restaurant, the concrete walls were textured to resemble a log cabin, but the paint had chipped off in sections, looking like a mural of gray clouds over streaky brown smog.

I grabbed a table just beyond the swing of the kitchen door and felt lazy eyes studying my ponytail, taking me back to the lizard bar in El Paso. Although the steakhouse appeared as rough or worse, the heavy diners were less interested in me than their steaks and soft ice cream deserts, more likely to defend their meals than their political beliefs.

The day waitress raced out of the kitchen, pulling on her jacket, and appearing elated she had made it through her shift. Kathy followed close behind with a tray of orders, pausing at my table long enough to hand me a plastic mug of beer.

She made several trips while dodging hands and retaining her cold smile before a huge man at a table near me grunted his disapproval. His red T-shirt strained to cover his bulge as if he had pulled it on several years ago and slowly outgrew it from the inside. He'd need surgery to peel it off. His head was fluted with crevices: a triple neck, a triple chin, and a triple brow. He sat with his wife and two sons who were slightly smaller and younger, all carrying the same fat genes.

"This steak is too tough," he said, jabbing it with his fork. "And it's too rare."

"Yes, sir," my sister smiled. "I'll have the cook take care of it."

After a few minutes, she brought his plate back out, but the man said, "It looks the same. That wasn't long enough."

"Yes sir."

When Kathy came out the next time, the steak was blacker. The guy speared it with his fork. "Still too tough," he glared at her before shooting an amused look at his sons. His wife wore a stony expression, and I guessed she faced his demands every day.

Kathy picked up the plate again and waved for me to follow her. Once inside the kitchen, she grabbed a fork and threw the steak on the tile floor, jumping on the meat several times with her hard-soled shoes. The cook wiped the sweat off his forehead and grinned, "Same asshole, I bet."

I also grinned. My sister could be a pain in the ass, but I loved her.

Taking a deep breath, Kathy turned to me. "Stand behind me when I bring it out. Now you know why I need the TA."

She picked the steak off the floor and threw it on the grill for two quick turns before sliding it back on the plate with a fresh sprig of parsley, leaving the original baked potato. Back at the man's table, she set the plate down and turned it a few degrees. He winked at my sister and eyed me standing behind her before shooting his wife and sons a triumphant gaze. Their steaks were already half eaten. He cut off a hunk of meat and picked it up with his fat fingers, slurping it into his mouth and chewing slowly. He dug into his steak with gusto, and Kathy swung around with a disgusted expression.

"Pig," she said under her breath. No one heard her but me.

Later, she brought me a premium steak, and I wondered if she had tenderized it herself. She also gave me an extra potato as promised, raising grumbles from the nearby tables.

After we returned to the apartment late, I decided to call Ronnie in the morning. One of Kathy's roommates was out, so I squeezed myself and my baggage into the small bedroom stacked with unopened cardboard boxes. The tile floor and the blond wooden veneer of the dresser and closet reminded me of

Ronnie's dorm room back in college. I flopped down on a bed for the first time in weeks, too tired to get up and undress.

I pried my eyes open at first light. With an early start, I should make Binghamton that night. The hour was way too early for Kathy, but she loyally wandered into the kitchen, wanting to make me coffee and see me off.

She caught me checking out her thick yellow and green flannel pajamas with little monkeys perched and hanging from slanted stripes that resembled vines. "Keith has this thing about Darwin," she muttered.

"I thought Darwin was Victorian."

"Not according to Keith's latest paper." She lit a cigarette and began washing out the coffee pot, identical to the one I had in Binghamton, both purchased from my dad's company store.

My phone call woke Ronnie. Her sleepy voice sounded closer than ever, sparking my anticipation. I pictured her lying on her side with the phone to her ear, her hair mussed with sleep, and her skin warm and soft, an invitation to hug. My temperature rose even as I sat on the cold aluminum chair.

"Everything's happening at once," she said. "When will you get here? I'm so excited to see you."

"Probably late, but I might get a lucky ride."

"We got mail. A letter from your new job and a postcard from that Diane woman. She wants you to visit her in Boulder, Colorado. Did you? Your trip sounds like a sexual tour of America," Ronnie gibed, but I could tell she was partly serious.

"She was stuck at a religious retreat with this guy Sam-Raji Wilson."

Kathy turned toward me with a smirk on her face.

"You had to rescue her," Ronnie said conclusively.

"It only took a few hours." I paused, wondering why I was defending myself.

"Forget it," Ronnie replied, taking a deep breath. "Rick called. He's planning another run later in the summer. I told him you're in for a pound. Hope that's okay. Wish he could come sooner; we could use the money."

"Don't worry, I have seven dollars."

"Let's party," she responded in a dry tone. "But I've been so good lately. You'd be proud of how good I've been."

Taken aback by her comment, I replied, "I wish you wouldn't say things like that."

"Don't you want me to be good?" she asked.

I wondered why she asked me that and why she made the statement in the first place. She said the same thing during our Adak phone calls when she was working in the leather shop with the waterbed in the back. I knew what it meant then. Each time she made it sound like a joke, but it implied a flaw about my attitude toward her. Or her perception of me. "I want you to be yourself," I said.

"I know you do," she replied in a warmer tone. "That's one of the reasons I love you. Did Kathy tell you about the Watkins Glen concert? I want it to be our second honeymoon."

"We deserve another honeymoon. Or several."

"One at a time. We'll take them slowly."

When we said our goodbyes, I imagined her hanging up the phone the way she turned off the reading lamp at bedtime with a sensuous gleam in her eyes, pulling me toward the highway the way she drew me under the covers. I wanted to believe our occasional disconnects were minor blemishes in a timeless romance, and I'd wipe them away as soon as I arrived in New York as I had with my previous trips home.

Kathy rinsed out a souvenir Buckeye mug left by a previous tenant and filled it with black coffee for me. She lined up a box of powdered donuts, a bag of Oreos, and package of graham crackers. "Pick your breakfast," she said. "And take the rest for the road."

"How about donuts now, and I'll take the Oreos? I'll pay you back for the food and the phone call."

She waved me off. "I read one of Sam-Raji Wilson's books. Listen to your thoughts because they can deceive you and so on."

"Yeah, I read the cover."

Kathy shot me a bemused look.

"I'm only a freshman," I countered.

"He's really into sex as a central tenet of his teaching, the intersection of the divine and true emotion. A pathway to God."

"Might be why Diane wanted to get out of there," I said sarcastically.

With a disbelieving glance, Kathy lit another cigarette. "You sure have a thing about complex women."

I dunked a powdered donut in my coffee, and Kathy pursed her lips with disgust like she had since we were children. She wrapped her hands around her cup and looked out the window at the identical buildings across the narrow lawn. "Ronnie said something that upset you."

"Just something she used to say when I called her from Adak."

"Undercutting your moment together." Kathy sipped her coffee.

I watched the cigarette smoke disperse in the drafty kitchen.

"Remember your birthday dinner after boot camp?" she continued. "Mom and dad were happy you graduated and made it home safely. But Ronnie said you should have tried harder to get thrown out of the Navy."

"Yeah, so I could celebrate my birthday in the brig."

"Like she can't stand it when things are going okay." Kathy waved her free hand. "But it's not really intentional. I think she's afraid of getting too close. Losing herself."

"About boot camp?"

"Just an example. She couldn't let herself be happy because she would be agreeing you did the right thing by enlisting."

I pushed another crest of donut into my coffee, raising an oil slick spotted with sugar. Kathy was right. Ronnie's habit of bringing up how she was being good, her desire to have children, or reinforcing her political beliefs undercut our moments together. Often her abrupt comments were playful gibes, effectively pushing me away, though she was also protecting herself.

My saturated donut fell to pieces, and I fished it out with a spoon. Kathy followed my rescue efforts, smiling with restraint and waiting for me to respond. I chugged my coffee along with the remaining floaters. "Ronnie mentioned calling you."

"Funny how she worries about me," Kathy mused.

"You mean worrying about you and Dr. Jeremy?"

"Well, she joked about him when she called." Kathy shot me an accusing look. "You thought his showing up here was funny. But it wasn't."

"Sorry about that," I said with a straight face, though I still saw humor in the situation, even if I sympathized with Jeremy.

"Ronnie said she was calling me about borrowing a tent." Kathy shrugged and broke a donut into finger-sized pieces. "But the real reason she called was you."

I tried to read my sister's calm expression to see what was coming.

"She asked if you were really coming home."

"Really coming home?" I repeated. "Well, here I am."

"That's not what she meant."

I waited for Kathy to elaborate, but she nibbled a chunk of donut, eyeing me with her analytical, graduate student intensity. "Was she asking about the metaphysical me?"

"Maybe. She doesn't know what to expect."

"Me neither." I sagged back in my chair. "I want everything to be like it was before the Navy and so does she."

"Does she?"

"She says so." I stood up to pour another cup of coffee. "It can't be exactly like it was, but it's worth trying. Not surprised if we both have second thoughts."

Kathy nodded. "Be nice to her when you get home. You two have been through a lot."

I always expected advice from my sister, but her comment surprised me. "I thought you'd tell me to keep going once I got to Binghamton. Don't pass Go. Don't even stop at the apartment."

"I think that too. But you decided to go back." She brushed the powdered sugar off the table with her napkin. "You know I love Ronnie, but I've never been sure she's right for you."

I cracked a smile. "Sometimes you and I think alike."

"No, you think everything will work out for the best. I expect things to fall apart." She licked her fingers.

Unsure what more to say, I broke her gaze and picked at the crumbs around my plate. "Powdered donuts are so messy."

"Yeah, I bought them for you."

Kathy offered to borrow Keith's car to drop me off on I-71, but the ramp was only two blocks away. After one more cup of coffee, we smoked a joint for the road, and she sent me on my way.

Chapter 21

A maroon Camaro pulled over with a sheen of morning dew steaming off its hood. Nice looking car and fast. As I crawled inside, the driver glanced down at an empty holster propped between the black bucket seats as if the missing handgun would protect him. I wondered where he kept it, but I wasn't alarmed, just my usual aversion around firearms like the smell of decaying meat.

Jonathan's hands shook as he clutched the wheel. His face had the cast of a career drinker with a flushed neck, red lined nose, and thin purple lips. His arms were mapped with dark veins under a veil of tan, blotchy skin, but he was well dressed in western style. He wore a white embroidered shirt, string tie, and blue jeans with a wide leather belt and thick pewter buckle. His hair was oiled and combed back like Jimmy Dean. He told me he hadn't slept last night, and I believed him as I watched him chain smoke Camels and sip Miller High Life to stay awake. He wanted me to take over driving at the next rest area.

The morning grew cloudy and colder, and Jonathan shivered at the wheel. So far, during the course of my trip, I'd avoided rain, but now Jonathan flipped on the windshield wipers to clear a persistent mist, more like the thick fog of the California coast than the heavy rains I expected anywhere near Lake Erie.

After several miles, he broke the silence. "My wife's trying to kill me."

I turned toward him as he waited for his words to sink in.

"I'm sure about it now," he said. "It's the little things. Not warming up my dinner after work and not buying groceries I like." He finished off his Miller and reached for another behind the seat. "I'm going to hide out at my girlfriend's place in Akron. I'll go back down on Monday because I have to work. But I should get out of my wife's place for good."

"Sounds like it," I agreed to make conversation. "If my wife was trying to kill me, I'd get out."

"She's cool about it, though. She won't shoot me. She'll just drive me crazy and make me do something crazy." He paused and glared through the smeared windshield as if she might leap up from the wet pavement.

"Leaving might be the best thing."

"I ain't leaving because she wants me to. I paid for that trailer and everything in it. She don't make shit from her job."

He described his work as a machinist certified by the union and recognized as one of the best around. Watching him, I found it hard to believe he could hold a tool steady. He was sensitive to my doubts.

"I know the devil's got me," he confessed. "I can't stop drinking, and I'd probably die if I did. But I never drink in the morning on workdays, and I always punch the clock on time. You can ask anyone."

"No one should question your personal life," I said philosophically.

"Damn straight."

At the rest area, as I was coming back from the men's room, I saw him take a couple of deep hits from a brown bottle in the trunk. Glimpsing me, he closed the lid. I hardly cared what he drank since I'd be driving, but I wished he'd stash his holster in the trunk, which he failed to do. As soon as I merged back on the interstate, he fell asleep in the passenger seat, periodically cracking his eyes to see if his holster was there like a toddler with an invisible friend.

Left to my own thoughts, I recalled my conversation with Ronnie that morning and how Watkins Glen would be our second honeymoon, a fitting way to end the military period of our lives and its aftermath, however uncertain our future. We'd always referred to Woodstock as our honeymoon, but before we drove down to the concert from Binghamton on a Friday night after work, we hadn't thought of the concert as our honeymoon, just a weekend listening to bands we loved. We took a back route that brought us within six miles of the entrance, where we parked along the road. We had planned to camp, but once we heard the weather reports, we decided to leave my ever-present Boy Scout sleeping bag and blankets in the car.

As a light rain started to fall, we joined the stream of people and passed a musician who was already drenched and standing on the hood of a pickup, oblivious to the water on his polished guitar. When we stepped over the trampled fence and arrived at the large bowl in the hillside, it was filled with wet people and the moist smell of burning weed. We could barely see the stage. The music blared and faded in and out, but we recognized most of the tunes and filled in from memory, singing with people around us. We found ourselves clustered with a dozen new friends, two groups of college chums and another couple, passing joints, bottles of water, and hunks of damp bread. We improvised hand signals under the pounding speakers. One guy sold me a chunk of hashish for ten bucks.

During a break in the music, Ronnie and I announced our recent marriage, inspiring a round of congratulations and wet hugs. The impromptu celebration a few hundred yards from rock and roll royalty felt more significant than the brief Catholic ceremony we had endured for our parents. We passed a hash pipe fashioned from aluminum foil to seal our union. During the evening, small pieces of hash kept falling from our unwieldy pipe, and we began picking up bits of mud, dropping them in the pipe, and lighting them. Every now and then, someone would announce, "I found one," and we'd all lean over for a toke of recovered hash.

Ronnie and I trekked back to the car in our squishy tennis shoes that night and huddled in the back seat under my sleeping bag. The next morning, we put on dry T-shirts and underwear, but our sweatshirts, jeans and jackets were still wet when we hiked back to the music during a brief break in the storm. We found six of our friends from the previous day, but the rest had left. We finally drove home on Sunday evening, both of us shivering, with loose, phlegmatic coughs. Days later, we heard about Jimi Hendrix playing his anthem on Monday morning. But by the time he bent his first notes, I was taking a hot shower at home in preparation for work.

Our honeymoon aura continued for several months until my draft notices began to invade our cocoon like a deadly virus. My low draft lottery number meant we'd enjoy our marriage for less than a year before I was forced to succumb to the draft or enlist. Or flee to Canada or deny the existence of the government as Ronnie advised.

Catching a chill in the Camaro, I turned the heater on low, hoping not to wake Jonathan. He snored fitfully as we approached his turnoff, and I worried about him driving to his girlfriend's place. My concern must have beamed out like an electric shock because he jumped up in his seat and grabbed his holster. His sudden movement surprised me, and I swerved slightly.

"What's going on?" he growled. "Where the Hell are we?"

I tried to calm him. "Just a few miles from Akron. You're almost home."

"What happened while I dozed off?" He snapped his head to the side and back as if he were looking for his wife. He could hardly sit up straight.

"It's been quiet. Nothing to worry about," I said.

"Shit, you say. You don't know what the fuck you're talking about. What do you know?"

Looking over at him with a fixed grin like a cheap Halloween mask, I shrugged my shoulders.

He snarled, "I'm talking to you, hippie. You deaf?"

"I'm here, and I'm pointing your car down the highway. Where do you want to leave me off?"

"Leave you off? What do you mean?"

"Which exit to your girlfriend's house? I'll get out there."

He told me and reached behind the seat for a can of beer.

"Would you like me to drive you to your girlfriend's?" I asked, hoping he would say no, but I had to ask.

"You think I'm drunk, don't you?" he exploded. "Hell, I ain't drunk. I can read a blueprint and hog out aluminum better than you, so I guess I can drive this car. You think I'm drunk?"

I shook my head and stared ahead.

He switched to a calmer tone of voice. "Am I acting drunk?" He drew up his posture and tried to hold his neck steady.

"Maybe you're startled from waking up."

" I shouldn't have yelled at you." He cracked a quick smile. "But you pissed me off. You can understand that, can't you?"

I nodded, counting the odometer clicks.

"Flo will be mad at me if I'm drunk when I get there even if she's drunk as a skunk herself." He twisted the rearview mirror over to his side and straightened his oily hair. He chewed a couple of mints from his pocket and washed them down with a swallow of beer.

I got out at the next exit, and he climbed behind the wheel, appearing somewhat sober after willing himself to alertness. At least he'd be driving residential streets the rest of the way, and Flo could deal with him. Fortunately for me, the morning clouds had given way to sunshine for my run to Binghamton. Better hot and humid than rainstorms.

After a few short rides on I-271 skirting Cleveland, a Baptist minister in a light tan Lincoln Continental Mark VII picked me up on I-90, whispering a brief prayer for my soul. My body was thankful for the air conditioner blasting out of the simulated wood vents. I had stepped from a broiler into a freezer after standing on the hot, steamy asphalt, though Reverend Kirby might describe it as a metaphor of salvation. He offered me a sandwich and shook my hand. He wore a shiny black suit, black patent leather shoes, a gold cross on a golden chain around his neck, and a heavy gold ring with a huge diamond. He wore enough jewelry to put me through college. He had that low, smooth voice and enunciation the clergy share with undertakers. His black hair was freshly cut and oiled in place. I passed on the sandwich.

We cruised over a hundred miles per hour, almost escape velocity, and I averted my eyes from the road, feeling dizzy. Emblazoned on the padded dash was a gold plate with raised letters, reminding all passengers that "JESUS SAVES." Whenever we passed another car, catching it in our airfoil, the Lincoln rocked in a sickening swerve on its soft suspension and kept skimming the concrete with no loss of speed. His manner reminded me of the Rollers back home, and how his shiny suit and god-mobile must be the dream of Alex Roller and his twisted family. They would kiss his white fingers like those of Christ himself. Kirby said he was on his way to Jamestown, which would put me about 200 miles from Binghamton.

We crossed into New York state and turned down Highway 17. The folding hills resonated like family. After touring the spectacular landscapes of the Southwest and California, I had forgotten the beauty I left behind. Unlike the dry hills of the west, the forests here were fertile and rich, bathed that day in a thin mist. Each distant hill was slightly more faded, until the farthest hill was transmuted into sky.

I remembered seeing the volcanoes from Adak on a rare sunny day, Great Sitka to the east with its plume of smoke, Tanaga and Kanaga to the west, two perfect cones, images floating above the mist of the strait. Some days, all I saw were their iced peaks, fading into the blue sky like a cloud or an illusion as if they were memories of the distant past or visions of the future.

And now the layers of New York hills in the distance beckoned like eras of possibility. I recalled walking the ridge of

South Mountain with Ronnie, scanning the distant razorbacks, and I reran the dreams Ronnie and I had once shared, holding each other tightly enough to squeeze the military demons from our minds: finishing college together, living a life of art, music and ideas, and even raising a family. I imagined Ronnie watching the same sky and the hills between us, speeding me toward her.

But once I left the god-mobile, my luck waned with long waits and short rides between small towns. By the time I reached Vestal, a few miles west of Binghamton, it was midnight. Ronnie was already asleep when I called from a pay phone, and she asked me why I couldn't hitch a ride the rest of the way since I'd come so far already. Surprised by her reluctance to pick me up, I said I was anxious to get home, and there were unlikely to be many rides that late. I finally persuaded her to crank up the car.

I sat on my suitcase under a streetlight shining down on a used car dealership. The warm evening had mutated to a heavy mist, coating the polished cars with dew, and soaking my jacket. I shivered and stomped my feet, reviewing my plans for the next week, starting with calling about the job, trying not to dwell on my reunion with Ronnie, and hoping to cool my expectations. We needed time to readjust. I watched the points of light on the hazy parkway slowly separate into glowing twin beams as they approached, straining to detect our old Plymouth before the cars hummed past. Each distant point might be her.

Finally, a red Chevelle bumped over the ramp into the parking lot. Ronnie leapt out, and my blood pressure exploded. We collided together, grasping each other like rescued survivors.

She was slightly thinner, though still as sexy as ever, and seeing her reawakened all my suppressed desire. Her hair was swept under a brown beret, and she wore her black cape with blue jeans tucked into calf-high leather boots. She pushed me back playfully and looked me up and down, cocking her head in appraisal as if she were making sure it was really me. I shook my head at how irresistible she looked, pulling her back for a long kiss. At that moment, I couldn't remember why I had ever left.

She brought me a welcome home present, wrapped in aluminum foil and a bow of thick blue yarn. She urged me to open it right away, and my trembling fingers unpeeled the Allman Brothers' "Eat a Peach." She bounced on her tiptoes and said the album was a preview of the Watkins Glen concert. All I brought her was my remaining cash, $5.35, and a handful of postcards, all I could afford. We'd celebrate for real once I received a paycheck.

In my flush of excitement, I hardly noticed she was driving David's Chevelle, even though she had lurched uncertainly into the parking lot, riding the clutch. Now I understood her reluctance to pick me up in the unfamiliar car and awaken David and Janey to borrow it. She slid into to the passenger seat, wanting me to drive. Leaning uncomfortably over the console and the Hurst shifter, she rested her head on my shoulder. I tried to concentrate on driving David's muscle car. Purring like a large beast, the V-8 leapt into gear as I wheeled onto Vestal Parkway, pointing toward home and our warm bed. Ronnie's kisses and the scent of her skin, brushed with the familiar scent of Oil of Olay, sent my mind speeding ahead of the Chevelle.

As an afterthought, I asked, "Why didn't you take our car? I know you don't like driving a stick."

"I hate driving a stick. Most of the time." She laughed, shaking her head to the side, and raising her eyebrows in her ironic look. Her fingers brushed my thigh. "You should be glad I came out here to get you in the middle of the night."

I leaned down and kissed her forehead. "Sorry the Plymouth's not running."

"I sold it," she said.

The news took a few seconds to sink in. "You sold it? I'll need a car for work. We don't have money to buy a car."

"You didn't leave me much money, remember? I needed the cash, and some dude offered me a hundred dollars. The car was broken down anyway."

"David said he'd help with the car."

"It's not his fault. David's been wonderful. He said the radiator was rusted out, and we'd have to replace it. That's why it kept overheating and leaking. You can borrow his car until we get one." She pushed in the cigarette lighter and pulled a joint out of her bra. "This is from David too. He said you'd understand about the car, but I said you'd just get mad. Guess I was right."

"I'm not mad."

"You're tensing up like you're mad. Pretty soon you'll start yelling."

"Well, I hadn't planned to buy a car. I thought you'd have plenty of money with the last GI check and your paychecks."

"See, you're only back about five minutes, and all you care about is the damn car." She lit the joint and passed it to me. "I thought California would mellow you out."

"This tastes like Rick's dope," I said over my held breath. "Do we have any left?"

"A few ounces. Three, I think."

"That's cool. I can sell them and send Jack the twenty I borrowed."

Ronnie smiled cautiously under the passing streetlights like I was a wild dog she hoped to tame. "I can't believe how wired you are. Take it easy. We're together. We're strong when we're together."

She was right about my mood, but the car shocked me. I took a long hit and thought it over.

"Well, sometimes a car is just a car," I finally replied. I wanted our reunion to work out, even if we still had our differences. I was glad she had brought the number.

She exhaled and replied, "But a dog is always a dog." She went on to tell me Bobo pined for my arrival, and she and the little dog had conspired to keep me prisoner in the apartment for several days until each had their fill. As she described my impending incarceration, I wasn't thinking much about Bobo.

Chapter 22

Ronnie sat with her long, tan legs pretzeled on a kitchen chair, holding the phone away from her ear as if it might bite. She wore a Navy-issue blue denim shirt rolled up at the sleeves and the top buttons undone, revealing peeks of cleavage. She always looked sexy in my shirts, but she'd look great in a canvas sack. "Here he is now," she said, covering the receiver and holding it out to me with a teasing expression. She whispered, "One of your women."

I'd just pushed through the screened back door in the late morning after my double shift. I had no idea who might be calling, someone from all the times I had handed out my phone number.

Sara's voice came through the line. "The boys are at work, but I wanted to talk to you. Hope it's okay. How are things in New York?"

"Working a lot. It's great," I stammered, wishing Ronnie would leave the kitchen, but she grabbed herself a Coke and sat down with an amused expression, propping her head on an elbow.

"For sure," Sara said, forcing a quick laugh. "So, Richard came back from his tour, and we broke up. He was nice about it. I told him I needed space, nothing about Jack."

"You and Richard are separated?" I repeated for Ronnie's benefit since she was trying to listen anyway.

"He said he needed space too, and we can always change our minds later."

"What does Jack say?"

She exhaled like she was smoking a cigarette. "I think he feels more pressure."

"Because of Maine," I suggested.

"This place is all about Maine." She paused. "Not sure what I should do. Thought I'd ask what you think."

"You're asking me if you should go to Maine with Jack?" I glanced at Ronnie who returned a smirk. My hand sweated around the black plastic receiver.

"Well, Seth says I'd be welcome in Maine."

"To live in his uncle's house."

"Without heat." She gave a short laugh. "But Jack hasn't asked me. Not in so many words."

"I'm sure he wants you to go."

"Seth asked me, but Jack hasn't."

"You should trust Jack."

"For sure. I thought you'd say that, but I wanted to get your opinion."

"He probably assumes you're going with him."

"Hope so," she said after a pause. "Seth and Jack are getting out in two weeks, and we're planning to stop in Binghamton. You'll get a call when we're close."

"We'll have a couple joints waiting."

When I hung up the phone, Ronnie eyed me with her head tilted, a half smile forming on her lips. She tapped the tabletop lightly with her fingers. "Why is she asking you about Jack?"

"Sara and I became friends in Ventura," I said, but there was more to it than that. I remembered my awkward offer to Sara when she dropped me off on 101, inviting her to New York if things didn't work out with Richard or Jack. I had corrected myself and said she could visit both Ronnie and me, but my initial reflex emotion lingered between us like the scent of a stubbed-out roach. Her phone call made me wonder if she had similar feelings.

"Friends don't make you blush," Ronnie persisted.

"We talked a lot about our marriages." I turned toward the refrigerator. "I never expected her to call and talk to you."

"She sounds young."

I set a carton of milk on the table and fetched a glass to wash down a slice of cold pizza. I was hungry from work but not hungry enough to cook. "About twenty, I think."

"Is she attractive?"

I grinned, trying to relax. "She's Jack's girlfriend. He always gets the pick of the litter."

Ronnie spun her cigarette pack on the table a few times like she was playing a board game. She glanced up at me and then spun the pack again.

I drank my milk in silence.

Finally, she said, "Letter today from Donna."

That caught me by surprise. "What did she say?"

"You won't like it. She said you acted like an asshole and started an argument in Sedona, and you obviously don't care what happens to me."

"Do you believe her?"

"I don't know why she would say that and write me a letter about it."

"I told you she wasn't very friendly. The guy living there thought I acted okay." I stopped, unwilling to defend myself. I waited for reassurance from Ronnie. My anger rose, and I tried to swallow it down. If the tone of Donna's letter was anything like her attitude in Sedona, I was guilty by association with her ex-husband and our male tendency to neglect our wives. Then I remembered joking with Ronnie about Donna's living situation with her friend Amy and Donna's suppressed desire for Ronnie. "Ha, that's it."

"What do you mean?"

"She wants you to dump me and go with her."

"She did ask me to visit her."

"I knew it."

We both laughed, breaking the tension. Ronnie ended up shaking her head as if to say she mistook Donna's intent, and I saw her gesture as an apology.

She poured more milk in my glass and took a swallow as we cleaned off the table. With the phone call and the letter, my mind raced, so we slowed it down with a fat joint after Ronnie followed me to bed. I had to get some sleep before my night shift. The project was behind schedule, which meant double shifts, overtime, coming home in the early morning or later, and sometimes missing Ronnie before she left for work. I was tired but focused on building up our checking account and paying off our used '63 Ford before I quit for the summer.

After my return from California, we'd fallen into our routine like an old married couple with four decades rather than four years together. No fights about Bardeen, starting a family, or money. We carefully avoided the land mines between us, pretending they didn't exist. Bardeen's name was never mentioned. He was the man who wasn't there, a shadow only I seemed to remember, and I began to wonder if my paranoia, so often diagnosed by Ronnie in the past, was the only thing keeping him alive.

Snuggling under the blanket, Ronnie wound her legs around mine, and we sank together, starving for touch and kneading our bodies into one cell like we'd never allow ourselves to separate again, though I oddly felt like an observer, my body engaged, my mind detached. I knew we were healing, however slowly. Her remedy worked better than medicine.

Jack's phone call from Syracuse came sooner than we expected, just two days before the Watkins Glen concert. He, Sara, and Seth would be swinging down to Binghamton for a quick visit. "Something you should know, Flash," Jack said. His voice strained to project its usual cheer. "Sara's with Seth."

Taken aback, I managed to say, "I never expected that."

"I'm okay with it, telling myself two of my favorite people are together. Could be worse."

"How did that happen?"

"Later. We'll be there in two hours."

As I hung up the phone, Ronnie wore a somber expression. She hadn't heard the gist of the conversation, but she knew Jack's phone call meant visitors, and they'd be hungry. She glanced sadly at our electric can opener, our only appliance other than the percolator. She hated to cook.

"I'll call in some pizzas," I said. "And pick up some Coke."

Her face brightened. "But this place is a mess. We've been packing for the concert."

"They won't care."

"Janey and I were going out for lunch. David was going to babysit."

"They can join us. Martin loves pizza, and he can't hurt the carpet. Bobo will clean it up."

Ronnie flashed a half smile. We often joked about the layers of dirt, grease, and body fluids hiding in the orange shag carpet with its yellow and brown highlights, the ideal color for absorbing pizza droppings, and impossible to clean since it would fall apart.

"Big news. Sara's with Seth."

"Sara must have lost her mind." Ronnie shook her head. "Jack won't be loose for long."

Janey helped us hide as much clutter as we could and redistribute the floor pillows around the wire spool in the living room, which resembled the bong van, only a bit larger. By the time Sara's bug rumbled to a stop in front of our dreary farmhouse apartment, we had three boxes of pizza, a stack of paper plates, and two six packs of cold Coke waiting.

I had expected them to arrive in Seth's Buick, and I hardly recognized Sara's beetle at first under the piles of baggage and rolls of blankets and sleeping bags hanging over the windows. The bug looked like an airport luggage cart artfully tied with manila rope. Jack and Sara leapt out the front doors while Seth unfolded his long limbs from the backseat, where he was wedged between Navy-issue duffle bags. He carefully moved

Jack's guitar away from the door. Hanging from Sara's rearview mirror was the black rubber shrunken head from Seth's Buick.

After a quick series of hugs between me and my friends, Ronnie strode out the front door with a wide smile and approached Jack first, planting a friendly kiss and stepping back to shake hands with Sara and Seth.

"You should see all the stuff we shipped," Jack said when he saw me admiring the pack and stack job. "Quartermaster friend of Seth's sent it all for free. Another Mainard."

"We're everywhere," Seth said wryly, glancing at Sara.

She leaned against him while her eyes followed Ronnie, who took Jack's arm and led him to the front door.

Upstairs, Janey, David, and Martin waited. Ronnie took a joint from David and held it out to Jack. As soon as he secured it in his lips, David flicked his lighter, officially kicking off our lunch party. Martin toddled over to Jack and wrapped his arms around Jack's legs. Passing the joint, Jack lifted the squealing youngster and spun him in the air, already playmates for life. Jack raised him up and down to gurgling laughs until Martin drooled on Jack's forehead. Jack responded with wide eyes and an apish "coo" before rubbing Martin's curly blond head and setting him down on his mother's lap.

Every foot of living room wall supported a back, except for the space reserved for the stereo, spinning through a stack of Stones albums turned down low. Jack recounted their trip thus far as Martin slobbered down hunks of cheese from Janey's pizza. When David started describing our plan for Watkins Glen, I picked up used plates and napkins and headed to the kitchen. Jack followed.

After I stuffed the trash bag, Jack shot me a loose grin.

"I had a date with Valarie," he said. "More than one."

It took a minute to register. "Valarie from the bong van?"

"Yeah, the witch. She's not so bad."

"I thought she was all right even if the witch thing was weird. Not so much her sister."

"For sure. Valarie called the house for you." Jack ran a glass of water from the tap and gulped it down. "Seth and Sara had just dumped their thing on me. Hope you're okay with it."

"You mean Seth and Sara? That's a surprise."

"Me too. I was pissed at first, but I guess it's partly my fault. Didn't know what I wanted." He shrugged. "Still don't. Never had a steady girlfriend before."

I eyed my friend. He handled the situation with grace, but I wondered what he must be feeling under his carefree demeanor. "Still planning to live with them in Maine?"

"Until I get my cabin built." He read my concern and slapped my shoulder, laughing. "We'll be fine. But I meant Valarie. Are you okay with me dating her? She's not a witch anymore."

"Sure, but what about that tattoo on her tongue?"

"I try not to look." Jack raised his eyebrows. "She wants to live on a farm. Spinach and artichokes."

"They don't grow artichokes in Maine."

"For sure. I thought about asking her to come up there, but my life's complicated enough."

I decoded his comment and the glint in his eye to mean Sara might change her mind. "Should be plenty of witches in New England," I replied.

"Yeah, Valarie might fit right in."

Sara appeared in the kitchen with a couple of empty cans. She and Jack shared a quick glance as he passed her on his way back to the living room.

"Jack was telling me about Valarie," I told her.

"You guys and your witches." She shook her head, folding up an empty pizza box and jamming it into the trash. "Nice to have lunch for us."

"Of course. And you met Ronnie in person."

"She's pretty." Sara pulled a cigarette out of her shorts. She wore the same attire I connected with Ventura: tank top, shorts, and sandals. I wondered if she'd freeze in the Maine winters. "Ronnie really hit it off with Jack."

"They met at Logan airport."

Sara gave me a serious look. "There's more than that."

"Between Ronnie and Jack?"

"Not really." She shook her head. "Just a feeling. Like a distance between Ronnie and you." She inhaled deeply. "Like the way I felt with Richard when I knew he wanted to end it."

Seemed odd to compare Richard the gung-ho corpsman with Ronnie the Rebel.

"I think she's looking for a way out." Sara continued, reading my disbelief. "Just saying it because I care about you."

"We're still adjusting." I waved toward the living room where David's sharp voice described Watkins Glen as a Disneyland for hippies. "The concert will be our second honeymoon."

Sara left me with a concerned look and a light stroke on my bare arm, raising a tingle. I followed her into the living room, trying to parse her warning. She didn't know Ronnie that well or me for that matter. But her words carried a faint resonance.

I passed around a box of Mother's ginger snaps and scanned the room, hoping to refresh the party mood. With the stack of albums finished and the turntable spinning hypnotically, everyone had fallen oddly quiet, except for Martin. David and Janey took turns stacking blocks that Martin gleefully swatted down. David caught one in mid-air on a trajectory toward his son's plastic cup.

Seth noodled on my guitar, and we traded a brief grin when I recognized the opening lick of "Ironman," the tune he taught me in Ventura. Sara slid down next to him, leaning her head on his shoulder. Ronnie sat next to Jack, whispering in his ear. Jack looked pleased, but his smile straightened self-consciously when he caught my eye. Ronnie didn't notice. I set the cookies down on the wire spool and restacked the records on the changer before sitting down on the thin carpet.

"Hey, Flash," Jack said. "Congratulations on starting that job!"

I turned toward him. "Got lucky. You know it's the only job I found."

"For sure. A man's gotta work."

"But he's working for the Navy again," Ronnie said to Jack.

"Not really." I shrugged my shoulders. "Helicopter simulator. To teach pilots to fly. Working a little on the Space Shuttle too." My California friends looked impressed, and I already knew David and Janey approved. Parts of my job were cool.

"What you're doing is so far removed from weapons," commented David as he gathered crumbs from Martin's cookie. "You shouldn't think of it as defense. If you were building bombs or missiles, it might be a different story. At least they pay well."

Ronnie agreed with his last statement, adding, "It's amazing how Flash gets these drafting jobs. After we got out of the Navy, he had three offers in the first two weeks. I wanted him to stay on unemployment and take a vacation." She paused and said to me, "And it's not fair you make so much money." She swung her head back to Jack. "I think all workers should make the same salary."

She kissed me on the top of my head to soften her words as she reached over me for the cookies. I loved her as Ronnie the Rebel, and her gibe sounded only half serious, but it carried more weight after my talk with Sara. Usually I dismissed Ronnie's edgy tone, but today it hung in the air like stale smoke. I glimpsed the multi-colored splashes of dried wax on the wire spool, while my friends stared at Ronnie and me with stunned faces like they were watching an awkward scene on television.

David raised his Coke, gently pushing away Martin's grasping fingers. "We should thank the Department of Defense for this fine meal and the great smoke. I'd rather they spent their money on Flash than more bombs for Cambodia."

Jack lifted his Coke can off the wire spool while Ronnie leaned away to give him room. Seth joined him, resting my guitar on his lap.

"Bongs, not bombs," I said.

Seth raised his can high. "I'm for that."

"For sure. I'm a taxpayer," Jack said in a deep Walter Cronkite voice, contrasting with the Goofy image on his T-shirt. "I'm glad my money's going to Flash."

"Me too," David echoed. "I mean your money's going to me. The GI Bill's paying me to sit on my ass and read books."

"And write papers. Or think about writing papers," Janey added.

"Only two incompletes left. Sociology and Geography." He pulled out his stash and started rolling a number on a paper plate. Janey snatched up Martin before his wet fingers reached the pile of weed, and soon he was gnawing the corner of his wooden ABC block.

A fast roller, David sealed the doobie and held it out to me.

I crossed the room and lit the joint, my knees cracking from sitting cross legged. My butt felt numb. Sara and Seth stood and stretched, gazing at one another and then at Jack. Seth still held my guitar in one hand. Jack shrugged as he took the joint from me, checking his watch. "Flash, we better get moving."

"You're welcome to stay," I offered.

"You could go to the concert with us," Ronnie put in.

David eyed me reflectively as if he were counting and rearranging campers in his borrowed tents.

Sara briefly shook her head and glimpsed up at Seth.

"Thanks, but we want to make Maine by morning," Jack replied.

After a few more tokes for the road, Seth leaned my guitar against the wire spool and strode over to me. He shook my hand loosely in his large paw, and as usual I was grateful when he refrained from crushing my fingers like a Coke can. "We all crammed into a motel last night," he said. "Don't want that again."

"For sure," Sara and Jack agreed in unison. Like a choreographed dance, Sara pecked my cheek about the same time Ronnie swept back Jack's blond locks and gave him a quick kiss. He slid away from her, and we traded a brotherly hug.

Ronnie and I followed the Maine contingent down to the street, watching them repack their bodies inside the bug. Jack adjusted the driver seat and checked the mirrors, flicking the shrunken head for good measure. "Offer's still open," he said to me.

"Hope you come," Sara called from the backseat.

I felt awkward with Ronnie standing next to me, but I guessed Jack had also extended his offer to her. "You'll see us soon enough," I finally said.

Chapter 23

Ronnie and I got a late start to Watkins Glen. I'd returned home from my double shift Friday around noon and fell into a deep sleep, my body hibernating in preparation for the weekend. By the time we turned north off Highway 17 that evening, we were already two joints into the Woodstock spirit – our new honeymoon – singing loudly over "Aqualung" roaring from the cheap new eight track deck I had installed the day before, thanks to my overtime checks. I ejected Jethro Tull before it started again and popped in The Band to preview the concert.

David, Janey, and Martin had left earlier in the day and promised to have the camp set up by the time we arrived, marking it with a blue plastic tarp as close to the entry road as possible.

When we reached the racetrack grounds, we spotted several blue tarps before we saw David waving a white sweatshirt to flag us down. He scurried among our friends, borrowing Coleman lanterns to help us set up our pup tent. A vegetable stew simmered in a large, blackened aluminum pot on the edge of the fire, dancing bright in a ring of stones near a pile of split wood. Speeding on crystal, David excitedly offered us some. We declined the lines until morning, but Janey's thick stew, spiced with plenty of onion and wood smoke, was a perfect meal to start our rock and roll weekend.

Our campsite formed a pioneer circle around the glowing fire. David had saved us a space next to his and Janey's tent, where I spied Martin soundly asleep under a pile of blankets with his blue-stockinged feet sticking out. Janey tracked my gaze and threw another small quilt over her son's feet. Kathy sauntered over with a guy who looked only slightly older than us with a low swooping mustache and sideburns under a black cowboy hat with a braided band. He wore a leather vest over his thick, red flannel shirt like any other northeast hippie, but I knew he must be Gordon Keith, the romance professor. Judging by his age, he was another genius like my sister. He casually shook my hand and offered me a small chunk of hashish. I liked him right off.

Kathy introduced the professor around the fire. "We call him Keats," she teased, leaning against him, and wrapping her arms around his waist. He smirked briefly, but I could tell he was taken with her, and aside from the horses Keats owned, I understood better why Dr. Jeremy hadn't stood a chance.

Janey taught us how to pop popcorn over the open fire while bottles of cheap wine, pipes of hashish, and doobies of Colombian weed passed around our circle. We reclined like pagans worshipping the popcorn god. Keats surprised us by bringing out his guitar and playing bluegrass riffs. I was amazed he could play at all, judging from the numbness in my head and fingers. A cold breeze and persistent drizzle finally chased us all into our tents. As I fell off to sleep, I heard laughter and portable stereos in the camps around us, muted by the wind.

Even though the concert wouldn't start until afternoon, I woke up early, ready to go, my body clock scrambled by my work schedule. Janey was up with Martin, who was even more awake than I was. I helped Janey start a fire and coffee, coaxing the wet wood into a hissing flame with a splash of Coleman fuel.

As I gathered sticks around the camping area, Martin trotted behind me, picking up leaves and clumps of pine straw to add to the woodpile. I lifted him up to throw his kindling on the fire, followed by his excited laugh and a clap of his small hands. Our breaths steamed in the chilly air as we labored.

A light rain continued to fall. The campers next door finally offered use of their gas stove since it would be hours before our damp fire yielded any coals.

"We could burn a couple of cars," I suggested when Janey expressed a wish for warmer, dryer weather.

"Good idea. They usually light them up over by the gully." She pointed vaguely into the mist. "Every year we've gone to the Grand Prix, at least two cars burned. I wonder where they get them."

"Maybe they're the losers," I joked.

"They're junkers. People bring them here, just to burn."

I scanned our neighborhood grounds. "That one looks fit for burning," I said, pointing to an old rusted Cadillac, which sat so low on its suspension that its rocker panels rested in the mud. I rubbed my hands briskly as I would over the glowing carcass. Janey eyed me indulgently. "But we couldn't burn a Cadillac," I added. "It's probably protected by the Constitution."

Our attempts at keeping Martin quiet finally broke down. He kept running to each tent and peeking inside until he succeeded in waking everyone up. We appeased our friends with coffee. Ronnie was the last to rise, claiming her usual lethargy, but I could tell she'd been awake for some time.

As we walked to the music stage, Ronnie and I tried to convince our friends that Woodstock was even wetter than the Glen. After the temperature rose to about sixty, and the sun poked through the clouds once or twice, stirring the frothy overcast like a warm, Olympian breath, our story was more believable. At least we were better prepared, dressed in layers with several blankets among us. Expecting a warmer afternoon as if the Grateful Dead and The Allman Brothers would conjure up a heat wave to carry their tunes, I left my heavy jacket back at the tent. Ronnie said I was crazy, but I was glowing with excitement, my mood helped along by David's crystal. Swaggering like a rock star, I carried a hit for later, mist rolling off my face like hot sweat. Ronnie sniffed a small line, but Kathy and Keats declined. Janey never did drugs when she had Martin.

Our small troop merged into the stream of pilgrims, and we soon reached the concert field. Our vantage point was much closer to the stage than we'd been at Woodstock, and since most of the people were camping elsewhere, it was easy to move around the tarps and sheets of plastic piled with blankets and coolers. David produced a yellow tarp from the outing club, and we perched in anticipation, hoping to work our way down front after the music started. My pulse picked up every time someone crossed the stage, though the roadies didn't share my urgency.

Ronnie, David, and I raced at warp two, getting edgy with the wait, but our time dimension flew along with us. We filled the interval with speedy conversation, migrating to literature in deference to Kathy and Keats.

"It's so cool when Ferlinghetti asks Christ to get down off his cross and do something," Ronnie related. "The first time I read him, he blew my mind. He's a real poet. I hated the poetry they made us read it in high school. With Ferlinghetti, I'd found a poet I could relate to."

"Never read him," David admitted.

"*A Coney Island of the Mind* might work in your psycho-geography paper," I suggested. "The neural network of the city as a structural archetype. More like an amusement park than a neural network."

Kathy replied, "You sound more like an English nerd than me."

David jabbed at the moist soil. "We create our living spaces in the shapes we imagine."

"True," Keats said. "And cultures map the universe according to their own mythology." He paused a second and smiled. "That would make it a psycho-astro reading of geography."

"The city as neural universe," I concluded.

"How about the country as neural universe?" suggested Ronnie. "New York City is the intellectual center, and Los Angeles is the entertainment center. Washington's supposed to be the political center, but it's really the asshole."

That quieted the conversation. Finally, Janey commented, "Everyone wants to write your paper, David. Maybe you should just let them." David shot me a sidelong glance as the most obvious volunteer, but I declined and offered to roll another number.

Ronnie swung her head from side to side as if her neural antenna was receiving a transmission. We heard The Band tuning up, and Martin started to squirm. Janey pulled a Sugar

Daddy from her deep pocket, holding it within licking distance of his eager tongue.

The sun began to dry the grass, sending up thin wisps of fog, and the music surrounded us like another natural element. Martin pounded his fists on Janey's shoulder to the beat at first, but then he pressed his hands to his ears and started to cry. She took him back to the camp before The Band finished their set. During the break, we huddled together under our blankets, blocking the persistent wind, and passing the hash pipe. The soundtrack was loud enough that we hardly talked, just nods and expressions like a game of charades until Keats launched his Bob Dylan imitation during a pause. His hilarious drawl on "I Shall Be Released" attracted people from nearby tarps, but Keats graciously declined requests to sing an encore.

Once the Grateful Dead started, the wind picked up, blowing colder and damper, and sending Kathy and Keats back to the warm campfire and the promise of dinner. David, Ronnie, and I clasped the ripped plastic garbage bag around us. The Dead played to a dwindling crowd, and we endured another long break, growing dark while we waited for The Allman Brothers. A light rain started to fall, so I blew another line to make up for my lack of a jacket. David announced that he'd rather listen to the Fillmore East album in the warmth of his chair at home, gathering up the tarp but leaving us the warmest blanket. Ronnie and I held each other close to shut out the wind as we drifted through the sparse crowd to the front of the stage.

Finally, Dicky Betts launched a blaze of blues guitar riffs and lit into "Statesboro Blues," raising my hopes that they'd play the entire Fillmore album.

Ronnie grew restless. "I'm freezing, Flash. Let's go."

"Let's wait until the set's over. We've waited this long." I stood fixed in place. "We came to hear the music." From the stage, I heard Greg Allman announce the next song, but I couldn't discern what it was.

"You can walk me to the tent and come back for the end of the set."

"By the time I got back, they'd be finished. Can't you stay for a few more tunes? 'Stormy Monday' might be next."

"I want to leave now. I'm cold, and everyone else is gone. I can't believe you won't go back with me. I don't know the way."

"It's not that hard to find our camp," I insisted. I described the way back along the main road and wrapped the blanket around her shoulders. "But if you really want me to leave, I will." The Allman's picked up the tempo with "One Way Out," and I started bouncing to the beat.

"No, I'll find the way myself," she responded tensely. "You just stay here and enjoy yourself. I hope you don't freeze."

As I watched her walk away, I had second thoughts about staying. I almost ran after her. But she disappeared into the galaxy of lanterns and cigarette coals, and I found myself swept into the music.

By the time the Allmans stopped after the long encore of "Whipping Post," my toes and fingers were numb from cold. A few scattered groups of revelers stared at the stage, some of them dancing, hoping to conjure up another encore, but I had enough. I walked as fast as I could, trying to plot the shortest distance to our tent. The eerie silence made me stride even faster. Over occasional flickering lanterns, shadows of the tall hardwoods and pines played off the shade of the starless night and extended across the slumped peaks of tents shutting out the storm.

When I entered our small ring, the fire was dead, and the tents were dark. All the way back, I'd been thinking about finding Ronnie warming our double sleeping bag, feigning sleep, and waiting for me. But I felt an odd discomfort, a flu-like turning deep in my stomach, brought on by the cold and the dregs of speed.

As I untied the flap, I heard a rustling inside.

"Is that you, Flash?" Ronnie asked hoarsely.

"Yeah, it's me. God, I'm cold. The concert was wonderful though. Aww, lawd. I feel like I'm dyin'." With my shivering whisper, I hardly sounded like Greg Allman.

A male voice muttered, "Shit."

I unzipped the fly screen, and there he was, lying with Ronnie in our sleeping bag. Stunned, I sat back on my heels and stared into the tent, squinting to draw details from the gloom, but I'd seen enough.

"Come in, Flash," Ronnie implored. "It's cold out there, and you're letting in the freezing air. This is William. He walked me back to the camp because I got lost. I never would have found the way." She quickly added, "We aren't doing anything. He's just keeping me warm."

William, obviously embarrassed by my appearance, raised a stiff hand to shake. I would've had to crawl over his legs to reach it. Instead, I closed the flap in disgust.

"Just give me my jacket," I said, controlling my anger.

"Why don't you come in here with us?" Ronnie asked. "You'll freeze outside."

"Just give me my jacket. Please."

"I can't believe you're pissed because William walked me home. I'm the one who should be angry. You didn't seem to care if I found my way or not."

"The way was easy, and you said you'd be all right." My voice began to rise. "All I want is my jacket."

"I should leave," William offered.

"No, you stay right here," Ronnie replied. "You're not doing anything wrong."

"How can you say he's not doing anything? He should get the fuck out of my tent!"

"Hey," William responded indignantly. "You can't talk to me like that. I was invited."

"You're the one who should fuck off," Ronnie hissed at me. "You'll wake everyone up. I can't believe you're making such a big deal over this. William just walked me home, that's all. And if you want to try and make him leave, you can throw me out first. I can't believe you're starting a fight over this. It's just like you to respond with violence."

She was right. I wanted to fight William. I started to lean back into the tent, but I stopped. My quarrel wasn't with him.

"You never care for anyone but yourself," Ronnie continued.

"You're right. Just give me my coat, and I'll stay out here."

"No way. If you won't come in, you can't have it."

William sighed. "Go ahead and give him his jacket. Maybe he'll go away."

Drive away, I thought. My keys were in my jacket.

"If he wants his jacket, he'll have to come in here with us."

"Forget it." I zipped the fly and began tying the flaps, my fingers stiff, managing only a couple of tight square knots with extra loops. Let them try to untie them.

"Flash, let's not leave it like this. Please come in with us and get out of the cold. I'm worried about you staying out there." Her voice from the depth of the tent sounded muffled.

I gave the strings one last tug and stood up, the icy breeze brushing my cheeks.

When I didn't answer, she called angrily after me. "It's your choice."

I stirred the fire. The coals smoked, but they were too weak to ignite the wet chucks of wood stacked nearby. I found a few smaller sticks, doused them with a cup of Coleman fuel, and lit them with one of my few remaining matches. After an hour of coaxing, blowing, and watching the steam cook from the saturated wood, I had a fire warm enough to feel the heat on my hands. I kept stoking the blaze until I could sit in a camp chair and thaw out my limbs. I turned my chair to direct the heat to alternate parts of my body, rotating myself like a living roast.

I began to imagine how a precisely thrown brand would ignite the nylon of our borrowed tent like a tube of napalm. I should drag William out of the tent and pound him the way I should have when I first returned. I could force them both out, send them off to William's tent, wherever that might be, and keep their jackets. I might keep their clothes. Fanning my anger was easy.

Ronnie wanted to punish me for staying at the concert, but it had to be more than that. She might want a reaction from me, a gesture that I really cared, that I'd fight for her, renew my conviction. I had thought our marriage was mending. Instead, staring at the fire in that moment, I resolved to let our marriage die.

Tossing another split log on the fire, I breathed smoke from the wet pine and tasted the ashes lifting into the thick air. I burned through my pile of wood, each stick wet with memories I could hardly articulate, but I knew they were there: our early days in college, the weekend at Woodstock, the months in Ventura. Igniting more anger than pleasure as if the good times were melting away, my body emptied, no longer cold. I drew strength from the bright coals. Sparks flew up from the heat like stars, creating a new vision. I felt an odd rush of freedom. I knew Ronnie's loss would echo deeply as I set off on my new life, but I detected a sense of relief, even a kernel of happiness in the core of my heart.

I studied the fire all night, only rising to gather more wood and refill the coffee pot. Martin and Janey were the first to wake up. Janey avoided my hunched figure until Martin ran over to throw wet branches on the fire. We watched them hiss and steam, clapping our hands in unison. Clutching her thick blue coat around her, Janey finally joined me, sitting on a camp stool, and raising Martin to her lap. He squirmed until she set him back down, and I perched a fresh pot of coffee to boil on the coals. No one mentioned Ronnie's guest, though Janey kept glancing at the tent. She offered to make breakfast, but I wasn't hungry. We stared at the fire and took turns helping Martin feed the flames. David and then Keats sought the fire's warmth, quietly joining me for a few minutes before returning to their campsites to pack.

Janey and David were lashing their tent and tarps to the roof of the Chevelle when William emerged with Ronnie close behind after several frustrating minutes trying to untie my knot. Ronnie shot me a quick glance before walking over to talk to Janey. I tried to read her look, but it was devoid of expression.

William approached my solitary perch near the fire.

"I'm sorry," he said. He had a sparse goatee and crooked teeth flashing a practiced smile. "If I'd known you were coming back, I wouldn't have stayed."

"My knapsack and jacket were in the tent."

"I'm sorry," he repeated, holding out his hand to shake.

I stood up and clasped his hand tightly, pulling him closer. "Get away from me before I kill you."

He stepped back, stunned by my words. He knew I meant it. I glared after him as he retreated down the access road. Everyone, including Ronnie, had stopped to watch us. I shrugged my shoulders and turned back to the fire.

Kathy emerged from her wet, drooping tent just in time to observe William's exit. "You did the right thing," she said, sitting on a stump by the fire. "She sent you a message you couldn't ignore."

"I didn't do anything."

"It was perfect. No more secrets."

"She could have told me she wanted out." I threw another wet stick on the fire, raising a swarm of sparks.

"It's more subliminal than that," Kathy said as Keats appeared behind her. "Her actions reveal something deeper. Maybe she doesn't understand them herself."

"Sounds kind of literary," Keats said, laying a hand on her shoulder.

"You're right," Kathy replied. "Not the time for this. We can talk tomorrow, Flash. Right now, you need dry clothes."

I nodded, vaguely recalling lunch tomorrow with our parents. I was too cold and wet to consider any deeper meanings. I had another late shift tonight and the drive to Syracuse in the morning. Kathy dropped a quick kiss on the top of my baseball cap as Keats led her back to their campsite.

I poured myself another cup of coffee and got up to retrieve my jacket from the tent. Ronnie met me at the door as I stepped out, both of us silent. Avoiding contact, we began packing the car. Just like the morning after a disaster when everyone tries to act more normal than usual. Before the cleanup and burials begin.

Chapter 24

Ronnie asked Janey to ride back from the Glen with us, obviously worried the fire hadn't consumed all my anger. Ronnie offered to drive in a sympathetic voice as if her driving were significant. I normally drove, but I was too tired to object. Martin and his car seat caught a ride with David in the Chevelle, so I stretched out in the wide backseat of our old Ford and fell asleep under a woolen Navy blanket. My tension and fatigue claimed the last of my energy. I awoke now and then to hear Ronnie and Janey chatting about their art class, the concert, or camping with no mention of William or my all-night vigil. The softness of their voices conveyed their hope that I stay asleep, and I tried not to disappoint. I closed my eyes and willed the time to pass.

Back home, Ronnie and I hardly spoke as we unpacked the car and carried our gear and the leftover food upstairs. We worked efficiently like robots. After I returned from springing Bobo from the kennel, much to the relief of the attendants, I broke the seal of silence and denial between Ronnie and me by asking her to move out.

"You should move out," she countered hotly. Color ascended her neck like steam in a geyser. I felt myself shaking as she continued, "You're the one who wants to break up our marriage." She said everything would have been perfect at the glen if I had crawled into the tent instead of choosing to sit up by the fire.

We slipped into all our older arguments about her desire to go to college and have children, my desire to finish college, how I never gave her enough space, how I thought she wouldn't do the things she did if she loved me, and how she thought if I loved her I'd understand. It was like taking a familiar walk down a harrowing path, through a cemetery with open graves, hearing the screams of the damned, ourselves.

We finally reached the end of the yelling and stood transfixed, facing one another. Ronnie held her hands at her side, gripping the seams of her jeans, breathing heavily, her eyes moist and deep. She looked tired and older, a reflection of how I felt.

"You're so paranoid," Ronnie said in a calmer tone. "Your ideas are so far out. You imagine I love Bardeen more than you, and I'll eventually leave you. It's always about Bardeen. You think I'm trying to fool you into staying with me."

"I didn't say anything about Bardeen. You did."

"But I know you're thinking about him. You're always thinking about him." She paused to pet the dog curled up behind the wire spool. Facing me, she added, "A lot less happened with Bardeen than you think."

"I don't want to know everything that happened."

"Can't you see that by denying the facts, you fill in the details with your imagination?" Her voice changed to her psychoanalytical tone. "Your anger is caused by your stance of denial. You feel inadequate, even though there's no reason for you to feel that way. Bardeen is hardly a threat to your sexuality."

I waved my hands to clear the air. "But what about last night? You can't say that finding you with someone else in our tent was just my imagination. Come on, Ronnie. He even had the gall to come out and want to be my friend."

"He didn't do anything wrong."

"Not alone." I stared at her.

"Your ideas are so twisted. All he did was hold me because I was cold. Neither of us did anything wrong."

"Do you think that's what our friends believe? You invited a strange man into our tent in front of my sister and our friends. They saw him in the morning even if they didn't see him earlier." My anger grew. I recalled Kathy's words, her conclusion that Ronnie made a public display to force me to leave.

"No one would have thought much about it if you hadn't spent the night moping by the fire. That's what everyone saw. Flash, the victim," she said, raising her voice. "You're always so damned noble. You're such a Puritan."

"All the more reason for you to leave."

She flared at me like I was a demon, and I glared back, watching her swell with anger, rising on her toes, her eyes burning deeper into mine.

She leapt at me. She pounded my chest with her fists and pushed against me with all her weight. She kicked my shins. I tried to push her away, but I fell back, tripping on the wire spool. We crashed to the floor together, Ronnie over me, rolling and twisting until I ended up on top. I quickly sat up, but I held her wrists to the floor to keep her from hitting me again. We froze in place.

She gritted her teeth, pulling back her lips. She started to cry, and so did I, but neither of us was yelling anymore. She began to struggle again. Her voice dripped with hatred, spitting out the words, "I can't believe you're doing this to me."

I let go and stood up. I couldn't believe it either. I never thought our fights would go this far. But after all the problems we had tried to work through during our marriage – the military bullshit, the romantic flings, and the lack of money – I wanted closure. I didn't love her any less. But I knew I couldn't love her any longer.

"Okay. I'll leave," I said, once I regained my voice. "I'm sorry."

"No, I'll leave." She stood up from the carpet. "I don't want to live here."

"The rent's paid until the end of the month," I replied even though the rent was unimportant at the time. The thought just popped out.

"I don't care about the rent. I can find a better place."

"Fine, but you should move out soon. I don't want to fight anymore."

"I'll move out now."

"It might take you a week or more to find a place." I stepped back. "If you need longer, that's okay. You can take anything you want. Take the piano, the floor pillows, and the bed if you want it. Take your stereo but leave mine." I paused to catch my breath. "You should leave me the car because I need it for work, but I'll pay you for your half. Take the dog. He's your dog."

She gaped at me, disbelieving, as if this were just one more argument that would subside and be forgotten.

"I'm serious, Ronnie. This is the end for me." I started crying again, but I tried to stop my tears, suddenly ashamed to cry in front of her.

"How can you do this to me?" she asked weakly. She shook and waved her hands, spinning in a circle like she was trying to escape a maze of cobwebs. "You're the one who should move out."

At that, I sighed deeply, agreeing with a nod, unsure what to say.

"Okay. I'll move out," she said. "Anything to get away from you."

I retreated to the bedroom and stared out the window, trying to cool down. I saw a large brown leaf detach from the maple tree and float to the street, beginning to regret my anger. I had no intention of changing my decision, but I decided I should apologize to Ronnie again and make sure she was all right.

When I found her in the kitchen, she was on the phone, her hands shaking, trying to light a cigarette while holding the receiver. Tears rolled down her face, smearing the thin layer of makeup she had worn camping. She was telling her mother how I beat her and how I was throwing her out of the house for no reason.

I stared in disbelief while she described me in terms a prosecutor might use to condemn Charles Manson. Her mother had never liked me anyway, so she was undoubtedly relieved to know I had finally revealed my true self. I could envision her mother on the other end of the phone line, her face so much like Ronnie's but hardened by age and cynicism, biting her tongue to keep from telling Ronnie she told her so.

Her mother's opinion hardly mattered anymore. I left them talking and took Bobo for one last romp on South Mountain before he moved to a better apartment. When we returned, Ronnie was gone. I stripped off the damp clothes I had worn for a day and a half and stepped into the shower to get ready for work and the drive up to Syracuse for my mother's steak and eggs. She had changed my dad's birthday dinner into an early lunch to accommodate my work schedule. I had a few hours before I had to punch the time clock, so I reclined on the orange shag carpet in the spare room and dozed off. My nap in the car had been my only sleep since Friday night. I hardly slept, my thoughts unsettled and the floor too hard for comfort.

After I left for work, my shift passed like an escape, though it was the same dull office and loud factory floor. Working kept my mind off Ronnie, just like it had during the rare times on Adak when I had something interesting to do. That night, we were preparing the simulator for an acceptance test, and it was easy to get caught in the deadline pressure, solving last minute problems and testing changes. The time went fast, powered by frequent cups of black coffee. I refrained from snorting more of David's crystal until I'd gotten more sleep.

Once my shift was over, my body slumped with fatigue, my mind mired in the weekend events and my fight with Ronnie. I thought about cancelling my trip to Syracuse and avoiding an awkward explanation of why Ronnie had not joined me, but I couldn't disappoint my parents. And it was better if I kept moving. Neither Ronnie nor Bobo were there by the time I returned home for a fresh T-shirt, but Ronnie's scent lingered like wilted flowers I'd forgotten to throw out. Smells that once sent my blood racing now dragged my mood even lower. Not pausing to make coffee, I settled for the burned mud at the Texaco near the freeway.

The drive up to Syracuse in the late morning dragged longer than usual, even though my thoughts whipped back and forth like a broken speedometer, my foot heavy on the gas. I should have left the concert with her. I was right to stay for the music. I should have killed William. I should have crawled inside the tent. I should have kept my temper when we got home. I should have taken my knapsack and sleeping bag and slept in the woods. I should have begged her to stay. I was free of her at last. I was devastated.

At each exit, I slowed for speed traps and pressed ahead, alone among the green razorback hills and laboring semis. I wondered where Ronnie had gone that morning. Some weeks, she worked Mondays, her schedule varying week to week according to Bardeen's whim and his middle-aged hormones. She might have hidden out at Janey's until I was safely away, avoiding me until later in the day when I'd be more tired, so we could fight again. I might wake up from my afternoon nap after my trip to Syracuse and find her warm body next to mine, hungry for touch. Or I might come home to the apartment stripped of furniture except for the wax-stained wire spool and the scratched records I had before we met.

My dad met me at the door of my parent's house with my mother's favorite soap opera *As the World Turns* blaring in the background. The theme music was imprinted in my mind like toilet training. Dad had to lean forward to hug me because of his bulk, but he appeared slightly thinner. His day-old beard bristled across his chin like a short steel brush. He always bragged he could jam an electric razor with his beard, but I'd rarely seen him unshaven.

I held out a gift I'd wrapped during my short stop at home, *The Odessa File.* Kathy and I were on a mission to get our parents to read more, and I could count past Christmases and birthdays by scanning the stacks of unopened books on their bookshelf.

"Sorry you had to work," he said with a glint in his eye. "I got the day off because of my birthday."

He wrapped me in another quick hug before leading me inside and dropping the book on the coffee table with a gracious, "Thank you." I realized he hadn't looked for Ronnie nor asked about her. They already knew. The thought puzzled me because not even Kathy knew about my final fight with Ronnie after the glen, and she was unlikely to tell them what happened at the concert.

My sister perched sideways on my mother's brown stuffed chair, raising a limp hand in hello after she marked her place in her book.

"I thought you hated Melville," I called over the TV. I never understood how she could read with the volume so high.

"I'm punishing myself," she explained, "for reading *Gravity's Rainbow* this summer."

"Thought you'd be reading Coleridge or Shelley for your Romance class."

"It's the weekend."

I shook my head and caught my dad's eye, neither of us attempting to decipher her logic. "I'm taking her to Greyhound after lunch," he said, flopping down in his chair and adding, "Your mom's in the kitchen."

"You're watching the soap opera?" I gibed at my dad.

"I'm not really watching," he replied.

When I pushed through the café doors to the kitchen, my mother turned and wiped her hands on her apron. Still an attractive woman despite the years and a few extra pounds, she carried the imprint of Kathy's striking face and thick, red hair even though she wore hers shorter and curled. She pulled me down for an embrace that seemed slightly longer than usual. "I never get the day off," she said. "Hope you're hungry."

"Smells great. I am now."

"Did Ronnie tell you her mother called last night? Your dad refused to talk to her, so I had to. He thinks her parents never liked you."

"He's right about that," I replied, recalling the distressing conversation I overheard between Ronnie and her mother.

"She said you beat Ronnie. I told her she was nuts." My mother stared into my eyes, expressing both sympathy and a hope that she was right.

"We argued," I admitted, "but I never hit her." I felt dizzy.

"Are you okay?" my mother asked.

"Just tired."

"You should be tired," Kathy said, appearing in front of me and opening the cupboard to set the table. She glanced back at my mother, and I hoped we were finished talking about my marriage.

"Your dad stopped drinking," my mom announced as Kathy retrieved a stack of coffee cups.

"He looks good," I replied.

My mother nodded. "You should tell him that."

During lunch, Kathy and I took turns keeping the conversation away from my marriage. She described me helping Martin tend the fire at the campsite, which my mother enjoyed, and I explained the dynamics of flight simulators from the motion system to the loaded cockpit controls, sparking interest from my dad. But both parents continued to follow the TV in the living room, particularly during the loud commercials.

When we finished our eggs and steaks, my mom scurried back to the kitchen and returned with a rectangular chocolate cake with one candle. After our discordant singing, my dad eyed his coffee cup like he was reading the grounds and joked that he should celebrate the rest of his birthday by mowing the lawn.

He held his smile as Kathy served us squares of cake.

He glanced at me and said, "Looks like your friends, the Viet Cong, are winning."

Taken aback, I stared across the table. I knew he was baiting me as usual, but I wished he had not picked this morning to do it. He made it sound like a joke, but that was how our arguments always started.

He added, "They were supposed to stop fighting after the Paris Peace Accord."

"Dad, please," Kathy said.

My mother regarded my dad and me with a pained expression.

"Well, it's true," he smiled. "Our combat troops have left."

"Not the air force," I replied, unable to resist. I recalled my old cynical thought that my marriage, always tainted by the war, might end when the war ended. Now, my prophesy had been fulfilled even though the war still lingered, along with my personal aftermath.

"The Viet Cong have killed a lot of people," he persisted.

"We killed a lot of people. A lot of lives have been destroyed," I said introspectively.

"The Viet Cong will kill more," my dad replied. "Now that we abandoned the people."

I raised my head, feeling my anger breaking its constraints.

Kathy rested her hand on my mother's wrist, trying to calm her.

"Patrick," Kathy said, enunciating my given name in case I had forgotten it. "You told me you didn't believe the Viet Cong were good guys…"

"But at least they're Vietnamese."

"Let me finish. And dad agreed that bombing Cambodia was wrong."

"I didn't say that," he countered. "I agreed Nixon lied about it."

"Please, Dad. You and Patrick are both right about some things. No one wants the war; we can agree on that." Kathy sent me a pleading look.

"Okay. I don't think the Viet Cong are heroes," I said. "But Thieu is corrupt."

My dad glimpsed my mother and turned toward me. "Thieu's a crook. I wouldn't want to live under him."

"The people are getting it from both ends, still suffering," I replied, feeling a dark resonance with my fateful weekend.

Kathy took a deep breath and said, "We all want the war to end."

My mother nodded and went to fetch more coffee from the kitchen. My cup was still partly full, but it seemed lighter as I raised it to my lips. My father watched me and lifted his cup in a toast.

After our years of fighting, this was the first time we ended with a note of reconciliation, other than that moment at the American Legion. Not much but a start, better than the yelling, the slammed doors, and the occasional raised fists.

I sat still, holding my empty cup, and feeling emotionally drained. I might need another pot of coffee for the drive home.

"Wake up," Kathy said to me. "Time for the dishes."

We cleared off the table as our parents settled into their chairs under the blue glow of the TV, sounding even louder like my mom had turned it up another notch.

Tossing me a dish towel in front of the sink, Kathy wore a sympathetic but serious expression, reminding me of our brief talk by the fire yesterday morning at the glen. But she was not ready to start washing. She threw back her shoulders like she was preparing to address a graduate seminar.

"This is how it is," she said, straightening her cigarette pack on the counter, so it paralleled her lighter, both in line with the edge of the sink. "Ronnie loves you, and she wants the security and safety of marriage, but she doesn't want to give up her freedom. She's afraid of losing herself. Freedom by itself would scare her if she didn't have a safe place she could depend on."

I reached for the cigarettes, imagining my sister analyzing the events at the glen for the past twenty-four hours. "You sound like an English major. It all goes back to Gatsby staring at the green light."

"Okay, I deserved that. Are you smoking now?" she asked as I tapped out a Marlboro and gripped it between my fingers. She took a cigarette for herself. My mother let her smoke in the kitchen if she opened the window.

"No. I just play with them," I replied.

"You always think things will work out, that she'll overcome her flights of freedom and realize all she needs is your love." Kathy leaned back and flicked her lighter. Smoke rose and surrounded the low hanging, oval light.

"Guess I deserved that." I spun the cigarette on the counter.

"Don't break it if you're not going to smoke it." She stood up straight. "You're afraid you might go back with her. Don't do it."

I perched the cigarette on my lips.

She continued, "Maybe I shouldn't tell you this, but I heard her talking to Janey about Bardeen. She never stopped seeing him."

"Not surprised. I suspected as much. I sensed his shadow." I lit the cigarette, pulling a deep drag and coughing like I might die on the spot.

"You already knew about Bardeen." Kathy shook her head. "You're a wreck. You're my brother, and I love you, but you're a wreck."

My coughing slowed to a rumble, and I washed it down with coffee.

"You want to go back to her," she said conclusively.

My sister knew me better than anyone, but sometimes she hardly knew me at all.

Chapter 25

When I opened the passenger door of Rick's Ford to welcome him back to New York, two Coke cans rolled out and clanged down the street, pushed by a gusty wind. Midnight the week after Watkins Glen, and Rick was delivering my long-awaited pound. I chased the loose cans a few yards and stomped them with my feet, just flat enough to keep them from blowing away again. Mine were the only lights shining in the neighborhood, but I assumed Grandma Roller was at her post, sleeping about as soundly as a pit bull. Luckily, Bobo wasn't around to bark the cans into submission.

"Gull damn! It's cold. I thought you had summer in August," Rick complained.

"You missed it. We had spring about two weeks ago and summer last week. Bright flowers and bikinis everywhere."

"Fur lined bikinis. Can't imagine exposing bare skin to this wind."

I offered to lug his sea bag, knowing it held my pound of dope. "Not a bad idea. Wolverine fur like our parkas. We should ask Grandma what she thinks." Her door was ajar as we huffed up the stairs.

Still wired from my late shift, I convinced Rick to crack open the brick for a smell and trial smoke. We sat on the orange shag carpet in the living room and spread out some newspapers. I flipped the stereo on low. I was in the mood for The Beatles. The weed burned hot and sticky, reminding me of Rick's earlier trip up north, and we speculated it came from the same Mafia cache.

"You seem awake for the hour," Rick said.

"I did a line of crank before I went in." I pumped my arms like a sprinter. "They love how hard I work, and they want me to stay after the summer and blow off college. No way, but the money's tempting."

Rick shook his finger at me and warned, "Speed kills."

"Been a hard week."

"Give me a snort tomorrow before I set off?"

"Deal." I led him to the kitchen where my refrigerator was well stocked with Coca-Cola in anticipation of his arrival.

Rick sat down at the white metal table with its cracked, red vinyl surface and matching chairs, the only furniture I had left besides the wire spool and the bed after David helped Ronnie move out while I was at work. Bardeen must have bought her a new bed with his discount from the furniture store. Rick eyed the joint as he passed it to me and announced, "Well, this is my last trip."

I shot a surprised glance and he added, "Took Larreau nearly a week to come up with his money, and it was a real hassle getting the score together in the first place, especially when he kept changing his mind about how much he wanted."

While he popped a Coke and sucked down the whole can, I assured him I had the money for my portion. "Ain't worried about your money," he replied. "Your money's nothing compared to what Larreau owes me. At least he gave me enough to cover my cost so far." He belched deeply.

"How much does he owe you?" I asked.

"You don't want to know." He picked up the joint again and added, "Besides, Angela wants me to move to western Kansas, some small town where Bobby has his oil rig."

"She's gone back to Bobby," I summarized. "Seems weird she wants you out there too."

"Nothing weird from her point of view. She wants little Bobby to be around his dad, and she wants me around because she loves me or thinks she does." He passed me the joint. "Maybe I'll go to Boulder, close enough. I heard Martin Marietta's hiring."

"I zipped through Boulder to see Diane."

"Surprised you didn't stay with her," Rick grinned.

With my mouth oiled by speed, I described Diane's rescue and my midnight ride with Joe and his tons of wheat. I wondered if Bobby's rig was anywhere near Joe's modest spread near Hayes. I paused for a deep hit and added, "Got a letter from Diane yesterday. She went to another retreat in Oregon."

"When are you leaving for Oregon? I can give you another ride to Fort Worth. Even Kansas," he joked.

Rick's casual offer evoked the pressure of my current life, sorting through my failed marriage while working double shifts and registering for classes. Hard to believe I dropped everything and hitchhiked to California just two months ago. Not likely I'd head to Oregon now. I cracked a smile, trying to restore my spirit. "Did you talk to Jack?"

"Called him up in Maine to sell him a few pounds, but he didn't have any buyers yet." Rick looked me in the eye. "He said Sara misses you. She wants you to come up to Maine and visit. So does Jack, of course."

"Sara and I became friends while Jack worked at the base," I explained.

Rick wiggled his eyebrows Groucho Marx style and waved the doobie like a cigar, implying a deeper connection.

I shook my head. "She was with Seth when they stopped here." I reached for the joint.

"I didn't get that impression, but you know her better than I do." He winked, pulling a baggie out of his denim shirt. He unrolled a black chunk of hashish and held it like a jewel. "Moroccan. According to Larreau. A present from me to celebrate your separation."

My mood of late droned more like a wake than a celebration, finding it hard to shake the events of the glen and their harsh aftermath, suppressing my emotions. But now, sitting with Rick, the valve released, and blood rushed to my face like I was staring into the open fire. His gift was well meant, and I knew he'd pushed up his schedule to come earlier once I told him over the phone what had happened. I nodded my approval. "Marrakech Express."

"True enough. This is great hash. Sunday morning, Larreau and I watched the sun come up over Cape Cod, and I thought we were watching the red sky of Mars with canals and everything."

"I love extraterrestrial hash." I warmed with enthusiasm.

"Hell, let's do it." Rick produced a pipe from his pocket and popped in a chunk, all in one extended motion, placing the pipe in front of me like an offering. The smoke was strong, but I managed to keep it down, exhaling clear air. Rick flashed a thumbs up and followed my lead.

After the first chunk glowed into ash, Rick asked me more about what had happened with Ronnie. Inspired by the rich smoke, I described my transformation by fire at Watkins Glen, and the events since then. I could tell him anything.

Finally, he said, "Cool down, man. It's over." He squeezed my upper arm. "You're shaking like a wet dog."

"Well, at least I don't have to pick up shit or garbage anymore," I replied. "But I miss the little beggar."

"Hope you mean the dog."

"Right, the dog." I forced a smile. Oddly enough, I began to feel hungry, the smoke overcoming the dregs of speed in my system.

"Have you talked to her since she left?"

"Mundane things like bills and albums. Our biggest contention right now is *4 Way Street*. I say it's mine, but she remembers buying it."

"You bought it on Adak, didn't you?"

"Community property, I guess. Before that, she took all the Jethro Tull albums. As long as she doesn't take my guitar and my party shirt, the one with the red and black stripes."

Rick nodded his head, enunciating his words. "You should get a lawyer, man. First, Jethro Tull, then Crosby, Stills, Nash, and Young, and your favorite T-shirt. Next, it'll be *Sergeant Pepper* and your blue jeans. She'll leave you naked with no music at all."

We stared at each another, our expressions locked in a dare. Rick's eyes twinkled in the yellow light of the failing neon bulb above the stove. Finally, I exploded with a deep laugh, releasing a huge hit I'd inhaled moments before, coughing and searing my lungs, unable to control my roar, and neither could Rick. My eyes watering, I shook so hard I feared blowing off body parts, dispersing my fears in shock waves, and finally diminishing into ripples, until we hardly knew why we started laughing. We gasped for air, and the desperate expressions on our flushed, sweaty faces set off another round of delirium. Forcing my lungs to suck down a series of deep breaths from the open window, I swallowed some Coke and rustled up a dinner of peanut butter and jelly sandwiches.

We sat at the kitchen table talking until the sun tried to rise through the gray overcast, but we gave up on seeing the Martian canals. Rolling one last number from our overnight pile of roaches, we opted for sleep: Rick in the living room on my Boy Scout sleeping bag and me in my marriage bed. I slept soundly for once, hardly stirring until afternoon when I sent Rick on his way with my last line of speed.

After a cup of coffee and another peanut butter and jelly sandwich, I decided to thumb the six miles to campus. I hitched for nostalgia, leaving my car at home, and suppressing a faint desire to keep heading west to Oregon or turn east to Maine. My afternoon was free until I reported for my night shift. I planned to spend a few hours relaxing in the library and hiking through the nature preserve, working on my Ronnie recovery. She had called that morning, rousing me from sleep, to announce another album visit, this time to retrieve Derek and the Dominos. Side Three was marred by candle wax, an artifact of an acid trip during our blissful pre-Bardeen autumn. I wanted to be away when she came to pick it up.

My remedy worked with the help of a thin joint I smoked out behind the Hinman College dormitories near a ring of wild blueberry bushes yielding dark purple handfuls of their tiny, sweet fruit. After gorging myself, I decided to return home for a more substantial meal, and I no sooner stuck out my thumb than a white Chevy swung around the traffic circle and slowed.

The driver was a woman about my age with a pale complexion and an Afro haircut. She smiled pleasantly, her round cheeks showing a blush of makeup under her large framed glasses. She smoked a white filtered cigarette smeared with dark red lipstick and wore a yellow cotton shirt and blue jeans. She looked like an administrator trying to resemble a student, but it turned out she was a junior majoring in business, obviously stoned.

"I'm Joy. Joyce Everett," she slurred. "Glad to meet you and all that. Where are you going?"

"Home. I live off Pennsylvania Ave in Binghamton. You going that way?"

She smiled loosely and pondered a moment. "Sure. I got no place to go. Might as well drive to Binghamton."

"It's not out of your way? No sense going to Binghamton if you don't have to."

"That's what I always say. No sense going to Binghamton. Or staying there either." She shook her head slowly. Every curl stayed in place. "But what am I talking about? I'm the one who stays here even though my friends tell me I should move to California."

I stood there, leaning into the passenger window, unsure if I should get in or not. The door lock was down. "Why don't you move to California?" I asked. I watched her check herself out in the rearview mirror. Her face looked fine to me even if she wore a lot of makeup, her foundation smooth and shiny and her eyelashes dark. Under her eyes, I saw the imprint of party circles hidden by makeup like a pond covered with fresh snow.

"I just got back from California. I almost didn't come back," she said wistfully.

Nodding my head, I replied, "That's funny. I just got back from California in June, and I nearly stayed out there myself."

She had visited friends in San Francisco, near Golden Gate Park. She recalled them gratefully as if she were accepting an award at a ceremonial dinner, idyllic and unreal, like all tales of California seemed to me now, even my own. Finally, when a local bus nearly plowed into her protruding parked car, she asked me to get in. We laughed at our roadside stasis.

"I took two reds," she announced. "My legs feel like rubber, but my head feels great."

"That's cool," I said, pushing my smile up a notch. My head was buzzing with weed, but I never took downers because they made me feel stupid, and I was wary of riding with a downed driver. But it was early Saturday evening, and the traffic was light. "You must be going to a party."

"No, just driving around campus, looking for stray men." She laughed ironically. "But I really hoped something was happening on campus. Not doing much of anything since I got back. I only flew in two weeks ago Thursday, and it feels like a time warp. From fairyland to Binghamton. What a come down. Most of my friends don't know I'm back."

"You're eating reds and driving around town. Pretty risky," I said with true admiration.

"God, I wish I were back in California right now. Instead I'm all dressed up but no place to go. All wasted up and no place to go, I should say." She had this funny little laugh that was more a coda to her statements than a real laugh, like she wanted everything she said to be funny.

"For sure," I said in my Californian lingo. "But you're welcome to stop at my place for a number. I have several flavors of weed, but no downers, sorry," I added in response to her expectant glance.

"Thanks, but I don't know if I should. I have a boyfriend in California."

"That's cool. I'm glad for the ride."

We drove down Vestal Parkway along the Susquehanna River, flashing with early flecks of sunset, making even the tired Washington Street Bridge look mythical, its rusted erector set beams acquiring a rosy shade. The maples and oaks were lush with summer, their limbs hanging heavy with leaves, and turning up Penn Ave, we caught the verdant scent of newly mowed lawns. I thought about rolling a joint and taking it up South Mountain for a view of the sunset through the canopy of trees.

Joy broke our stoned silence. "The trouble with taking reds and driving around all day is it makes me horny. I should be more careful."

I turned to her with surprise like she had just poked me with a branch. Reds were legendary for making women horny and guys sleepy. "Getting stoned always makes you horny," I replied philosophically. "If it didn't feel good, no one would do it." I smiled at my double meaning.

"Well, you need to be more careful too. Two horny people driving around Binghamton together. What will people say?"

"Who cares?" I replied. "We're adults."

"I really should go home," she leaned over and whispered as we pulled in front of my apartment building. I wondered if Grandma was getting an eyeful, but no one was home.

I kissed her carefully, trying to restrain myself like the gentleman I imagined myself to be, until she sucked my tongue deep into her throat and inserted hers in mine. Without her saying anything more, I assumed she'd reconsidered my offer of a joint.

"Let's go upstairs and get high," I said.

She lurched her car into park and followed me cautiously up the stairs. "You're really lucky."

"Sometimes," I smiled.

We never smoked the joint. Within minutes, we were writhing on the floor like we needed each other more than anything else in the world.

The speed of our mutual seduction, which was more like a mutual rape, hardly gave me time to think about what I was doing. But soon afterward, while I still lay on top of her with our clothes loosened only enough for necessity, I realized we were lying in nearly the same location on the ugly carpet that Ronnie and I had shared during our brief wrestling match on that fateful night after Watkins Glen.

The thought of Ronnie gave me a queasy, guilty feeling even though I had no reason to feel that way, and I was glad we hadn't used the bed. I had finally broken my marriage vow, after five years with Ronnie, but I caught the irony. After trying to break my extra-marital maidenhead over thousands of miles of interstate and several unrealized fantasies, I had broken it on my own living room carpet. More importantly, making love to Joy signified I might be breaking free from Ronnie. Even with our separation, I had continued to be attached in subtle ways, still feeling her pull.

"You're really lucky," Joy said softly. She wore a calm expression, blinking her eyes slowly. "I never do anything like this. The last person I slept with was my boyfriend in California. But we weren't getting along toward the end, so it's been over a month since I slept with anyone."

"Been awhile for me too." I kissed her deeply and tasted the ashy flavor of her cigarettes.

"You're really lucky," she repeated. "I can't believe I'd do something like this. You're really something."

"You're really something too."

"Let's get naked," she suggested.

Despite my suppressed guilt, I was eager to accept her offer. I hoped a joint would exorcise my carpet demons.

Before I could respond, I heard a sharp rap on the back door. I leapt up like a thief. The back stairway led from the small parking lot. I glanced at the records leaning against the wall with Derek and the Dominos in front. I had set it apart for Ronnie to pick up.

"I think you should leave," I said in a soft but direct tone. Joy was lying on the floor in disbelief with her jeans down around her ankles and her sweatshirt pushed up.

"I'll go hide in the bathroom," she suggested, standing and pulling up her jeans.

"No, we don't have time," I pleaded. "It's my wife."

"Your wife? You didn't say you were married."

The rapping came again, louder.

"I'm not really married. Not anymore. I'm separated. I just don't want to have a scene," I said urgently. "We're not doing anything wrong, but I don't want to subject you to her. She's my problem to deal with."

"I can't believe this," she said, gritting her teeth as she tugged up her jeans. She cracked a smile, and so did I. We were living a scene from a situation comedy. At least I hadn't asked her to hide under the bed like Diane did to me.

I buckled my jeans and tucked in my shirt. "I'm coming," I called back toward the kitchen. I said to Joy, "I'm really sorry about this. She was supposed to come earlier to pick up some things. I had no idea."

"Forget it." She kissed me on the cheek, and I kissed her quickly on the lips. "Will I see you again?" she asked.

"Sure, you will."

"We'll probably run into each other on campus." She saw I was antsy for her to leave, so she opened the door, and I let her out.

"I'm sure I'll see you on campus," I whispered. "I'm really sorry." I closed the door. She left without our exchanging phone numbers, and I nearly called her back, but the knocking persisted. I ran into the kitchen where I tried to wipe her lipstick off my face with a paper towel. Taking a deep breath, I opened the back door.

"God, Flash. Were you in the head?" David studied me with a sideways grin.

"No, I was taking a nap." I smiled with relief. "Now that I'm up, I should roll a number."

David pulled up a chair at the kitchen table, choosing the guest chair, the one without a rip in the red plastic cushion. I expended my nervous energy by cleaning a small mound of weed and rolling it up in a wheat straw paper. When I licked the glue, I caught the briny scent of sex on my hands, and I wondered if David could smell it too. Just to be safe, I lit the joint before passing it to him.

He asked about Rick's pound, the price for a quarter pound, and what the smoke was like. But he'd known the price for days, ever since Rick had called me. And he knew the dope was the same as before.

His small talk tipped me off. I could always tell when David had something serious on his mind because talked around the subject like a politician, his eyes in a distant, empathetic gaze.

"Ronnie's been asking about you," he said finally. "She's worried about how you're doing. I told her you're doing okay, working a lot of hours, and you weren't going out much." He took a deep hit and passed the number back to me.

It was burning unevenly, so I stopped the run with a dab of spit.

He went on, "She's probably relieved you're staying home, though she won't admit it. I think she worries about you meeting another woman. But she's mostly concerned about how you feel. She hopes you're not depressed."

"I'm fine," I said easily. "I went to the library this afternoon, and I'll be getting out to sell lids to our friends." I waved my hand over the new pound. It seemed strange David was acting as Ronnie's emissary, but I went along with him. "Would she feel better if I cruised the bars?"

He shook his head to dispel my weak attempt at humor. "She still cares about you, Flash. That's why she's asking."

"I still care about her too," I admitted. "I talk to her every day."

"You haven't gone to see her apartment."

"No, and I don't plan on going."

"It wouldn't hurt to go see her."

"Come on, David. You're the one who told me Bardeen's paying her rent and he moved in with her. I have no desire to go see their little love nest. I'm sure Bardeen bought her new furniture and all the little conveniences I never did. I don't need it thrown in my face." I paused to keep my temper, but I felt my color rise anyway.

After Ronnie had moved out earlier in the week, several of my friends were quick to tell me she'd taken Bardeen to parties while I was in California, and she'd told everyone he was much more together than I was, and so on. Grandma Roller joined the chorus, stopping by to enumerate every one of Bardeen's visits, and she even recounted how Ronnie introduced him to the Roller family, which inspired them to pray for me. But their prayers and my friends' sympathetic Bardeen stories gave me little comfort, only strengthened my resolve.

"Sorry," David said. "I didn't mean to upset you. She asked me to talk to you, and I agreed as a favor to her."

I shrugged my shoulders. "I'm not mad at you. I'm just not ready to see her new apartment."

After another toke, he added, "Her relationship with Bardeen isn't the way you think. He didn't move in with her like I thought, and he didn't buy her any furniture. He loaned her money for rent until she finds a roommate, and he gave her a transistor radio as a housewarming gift. That's all."

Pondering the news, I started cleaning another small pile of weed. I pretended not to care. Imagining her shacked up with Bardeen and knowing she went directly from my arms to his had made our breakup easier to handle. I still felt like an amputee, sensing Ronnie as an extension of myself, a part of my body still living only in memory. But I also knew my wounds were beginning to heal. I wanted to avoid reopening them.

Accepting my freshly rolled joint, David said, "Ronnie's not doing very well."

"She'll get over Bardeen," I surmised, trying to keep my distance from the conversation. "Maybe he surprised her by going back to his family, but she'll get over it."

"You don't seem very concerned."

"Of course, I'm concerned. But I can't do anything about it. Bardeen's not my problem anymore." I got up and retrieved two Cokes from the refrigerator. A few cans remained from my Rick stock.

David declined a Coke, but he continued in his serious tone. I had hoped the weed would crack his mood. "Janey and I are going to a marriage counselor," he announced.

"I thought you two had a good marriage," I replied, surprised. They both seemed committed to raising Martin and maintaining a stable home. Ronnie always viewed their life as a model of what our life might be.

"Our marriage has been better since we've moved up here from Long Island, but we almost broke up after I came home from country. Looking back, I wasn't ready to confront a marriage and a baby after a year in Vietnam. "

"Sounds normal to me," I commented, amazed again at David's disclosure. He usually avoided personal topics, especially anything to do with Vietnam. "I can't imagine going from the suck to real life without some difficulty."

"Janey was seeing another man when I was overseas. She told me about him when I came home. I guess she wanted me to know right away, so we could break up then if we were going to. It would have been easier for Martin if he didn't get too attached to me."

He stared at me with glazed eyes, and I realized how hard it was to tell me this. I felt my eyes begin to cloud up.

He continued with effort, "That's why we're going to the marriage counselor. He's helped me come to terms with what happened and how it still affects our relationship."

"If going to the counselor is helping you, that's great."

He picked up the smoldering roach from the ashtray and clipped it into my hemostats. As he fired it up, he added, "You'd like our counselor. He's pretty cool. He's a philosophy professor, and he does counseling part time because he wants to help people. He'll do it for free if you don't have the money to pay him." David gazed at the smoldering doobie. "I even think he gets high, though he can't admit it for professional reasons."

"That's cool." I shook my head. This wasn't the first time David and Janey had encouraged Ronnie and me to patch things up since we became neighbors. They seemed to have a vested interest in keeping us together as if our marriages were built on the same foundation and saving us would help them save themselves.

"Ronnie's been seeing him."

I wasn't surprised. Ronnie the psychology major. I considered his suggestion in another light. "Don't you think it's a little late for us to see a marriage counselor?"

"You only broke up a week ago."

"She should go with Bardeen."

David could tell he was getting nowhere. "Okay," he said, "but you should go see her. It wouldn't hurt anything."

"I'll see her when she comes over to pick up her album."

"She's not coming. Since Bardeen left, she doesn't have access to a car. She'd like you to drop it off." He passed me the roach clip. "I'm betting you want to see her again anyway."

"That's what my sister says."

"She's smarter than both of us," David cracked a grin.

"She thinks so." Sucking a deep hit, I considered Ronnie's request, thinking it not that unreasonable if she was stuck without a car. I was concerned about her even though I wanted to keep my distance. After my evening with Rick and my brief encounter with Joy, I might see Ronnie again without getting pulled back into her orbit. "Okay," I said in my high, hit holding voice. "I'll drop off the album." I exhaled. "But no shrink."

A few minutes later, David strode out the kitchen door, cradling a fresh quarter pound, the same price as before. Listening to his footsteps recede, I decided to take a shower before heading to work. As I passed through the living room, I paused above the pressed shag fibers where I had lain with Joy. The scent of our sex could only improve the orange carpet's ambient aroma of Bobo and rotting pizza droppings. I glimpsed out the window, expecting to see her gone, but her Chevy still hugged the curb with its windows up and foggy.

Trotting down the front stairs to check on her, I knocked on the driver side window. Joy wiped the glass with the sleeve of her blouse and rolled the window partway down. She squinted up at me and buried her face in her hands. "I feel terrible," she said between breaths.

"You don't have to stay out here," I said softly. "Come back upstairs."

"What about your wife?"

"She's gone. She never came. It was someone else."

Joy gave me a tired and distressed look. "Not your wife?"

"I was wrong. I'm sorry."

She took a breath and dabbed her eyes with a soaked tissue. "Lucky again."

"I'm having a lucky day." I extended my arm to help her out the door.

She followed me upstairs and washed her face. She appeared younger without the layers of makeup, her manner subdued. When she noticed cosmetic streaks on her blouse, I loaned her one of my best T-shirts, a full color Mickey Mouse on a gray background. I asked her to wait while I took a quick shower, and she did. We drove two cars to the Argo restaurant downtown, no scenery but cheap and tasty Greek food. Our early dinner was quiet. Both of us were working off our embarrassment, and we awkwardly parted as friends.

Chapter 26

"Let yourself in," Ronnie called from deep in her apartment. It was Saturday night, a week after my conversation with David. I held the tattered Derek and the Dominoes album like a housewarming gift.

Her living room looked like a room in my memory, furnished with familiar objects. The orange crate filled with albums sat next to the two gray cinder blocks, which supported a six-foot long unfinished plank holding the Sears Roebuck portable stereo and its detachable speakers. In the corner was Ronnie's yellow director's chair, and across the room rested two floor pillows, covered with brown and gold squares she had cut from corduroy remnants. I recalled the weekend she had sewn the pillows, a month or so after we rented our apartment, now my apartment. Her electric piano stood next to the stereo.

Leaning against the doorframe, I felt dizzy. I had looped back to a time when the shabby furniture was mine. But I had changed since then, having lived through two weeks of Ronnie withdrawal, and now I saw the apartment as a place where I might have lived if things had worked out differently. The buzz of a small television caught my attention. I hadn't expected to find a TV since Ronnie shared my hatred of encapsulated news and canned laughter. Instinctively, I reached over and turned it off.

"That's okay. You can turn off the TV," she called from the bedroom. "I just borrowed it from Janice to keep me company."

Who was Janice? Maybe she was someone who lived in the building or a code name for Bardeen. Glancing around, I searched for signs of him, strands of his thinning hair on the floor pillows or cheap knickknacks from the furniture store.

Ronnie appeared under the arch leading into the hallway and bedroom dressed only in her bra and white lace, bikini panties. The bra was made of a mesh material that conformed to the shape of her full breasts and revealed the dark circles of her erect nipples. She was always casual about her nudity around me, but now I felt uncomfortable. She held an open bottle of Cover Girl makeup and smeared a stripe on her cheek as she smiled with amusement at my awkward stare.

"Why don't you come in here?" she asked. "Talk to me while I get dressed."

Following her like Bobo, who was absent, I tread quietly, feeling woozy, out of place. Standing in the doorway to her bedroom, I noticed an easel near the window with an incomplete still life of a dried flower arrangement. From its dark tones, I detected Solomon's influence.

Ronnie went on with her cosmetic rituals like no time had passed since the days when we lived together. She chatted about her neighbors in the apartment building like I knew them already. I learned that Janice lived downstairs and had invited both of us to dinner. The invitation was a surprise to me. Ronnie might have told me about it, and I had forgotten, or she had forgotten to tell me. I had not planned on staying longer than a few minutes. I might have stayed too long already. She said another new friend, Michael, was watching Bobo for the evening. She had met Michael at an Earth rally, her latest protest movement. Ronnie thought Michael was gay, which I interpreted to mean he hadn't hit on her yet.

"I'm not going to dinner," I said.

Without responding to my statement, she asked instead what was happening in my life.

I had little news of consequence, except for the incident Wednesday night when Alex Roller, fuming from a loud fight with his wife, punched their garbage can and had to get his hand bandaged in the emergency room at Binghamton General. The episode was distracting enough that Grandma failed to complain about my lack of a garbage can for the first week in memory.

"Why didn't you tell me Rick was coming?" Ronnie asked.

"Thought I did."

"Only after he left." She shot me a playful pout and returned to dabbing her lips with soft pink lipstick.

"He was only here for one day. Not even that. He came Friday night and left on Saturday." I went on to tell her the news about Rick moving to Colorado to be near Angela, and how it sounded like Jack was back with Sara, at least for now. But Ronnie didn't seem interested, which was unusual.

When I paused, she said, "David told you about the marriage counselor. He thinks you should go see him. So do I. We don't have to go together."

"I don't think so. You know I can't stand that psychological stuff, talking about feelings and suppressed childhood emotions. I have nothing against my mother." I pulled my eyes away from her and glanced toward the window. "I'd rather just muddle through life in my own way."

"He thinks it would help you."

"What does David know about it?"

"I'm talking about Dr. Anderson."

I shrugged my shoulders as if to say they were both people who thought they knew what was best for me when I hardly knew myself. Focusing on Ronnie's intent expression, I laughed from the weirdness of the situation like I was watching a science fiction movie: an improbable past extending from my mother and my childhood to a mutated present with my half-dressed wife – my former wife – standing in her new apartment that might have been my apartment.

"You're stoned, aren't you?" she asked. "I heard Rick brought you a pound of weed."

I stared at her in disbelief. Under ordinary circumstances, she might be right, but I had consciously refrained from getting high since last Saturday when I smoked with David. Except for selling him the quarter pound, I hadn't cracked open Rick's loaf. I'd lived the life of a monk, avoiding contact with anyone, and hoping to clear my head for a few days. I felt better than I had since the glen. "Why do you say that? You're the one who turned me on in the first place."

"Because you're always stoned. You think we can talk to each other, but I can't talk to you because you're stoned. You never know what I'm saying." She paused to wipe the corners of her lips and added, "If I'd have known it would turn out like this, I never would have turned you on."

"Are you serious?"

"Just ask anyone."

"David doesn't think I get high too much," I said defensively. "Besides, if I was stoned all the time, I wouldn't be able to work."

"Now, you're getting mad. You're too stoned to talk to me, and you get mad when I try to have a conversation."

"Is this why you wanted me to drop off the album? So you could tell me how fucked up I am? You think I'm too stoned to understand what you're saying." I strained to keep my voice from rising.

She stood up from her makeup stool and dropped her lipstick tissue to the floor. She began to cry, tears smearing her freshly applied mascara. She swept toward me, and I stepped back reflexively, thinking she might hit me. But she hugged me, and I wrapped my arms around her bare back, still holding Derek in my left hand. She felt frail, thinner than I remembered.

Her crying subsided with our contact, and her nearness awakened all my senses. My flesh fit into the shape of her body like we were still part of the same organism, just like we always said we fit together, and my love for her boiled beneath my skin and throbbed in the synapses of my memory. Stroking the back of her head, I held her cheek to my chest. Her foot gently pressed mine. She always said that stepping on my foot should open my mouth like I was a big garbage pail. Drawn by the memory, I leaned down and kissed her, still wary of diving too deeply.

"I'm just trying to save our marriage," she said in a confessional tone. "I want you to see Dr. Anderson, so he can help us save our marriage."

Afraid of what I might say, I did not say anything.

She went on, "Don't you want to save our marriage?"

"I don't know," I said honestly, expecting her to break our embrace.

But she held on. "I understand," she said soothingly. "I know I hurt you when I decided to move out. I shouldn't have left you the way I did."

Hearing her rewritten description of how we broke up, my body stiffened.

She went on, "But you have nothing to worry about now. It's all over with Bardeen. I've been keeping in touch with him because I feel sorry for him. He's like an old friend. You can ask Janice."

I unwound my arms, intending to tell her what I honestly thought about her relationship with Bardeen and the collapse of our marriage, but my words were slow in coming. Letting go of her was the hardest thing I had ever done. My body hung hollow like molted skin. But my past two weeks without her acted like an antidote. Just as I had realized at the glen when I sat outside our tent and watched the sparks of my damp fire merge with the stars, in spite of our continuing physical attraction, we were no longer part of the same organism. The physical attraction was all we had left, embedded in the reflexive memory of our cells. In her way, Ronnie must have known this too.

She abruptly announced she had to make a phone call before we went down to Janice's, and she wanted to get it over with. I never said I was going to Janice's, and I didn't need to ask who she was calling. Not Janice. Sensing my withdrawal, she said, "This will only take a miinute."

I followed her to the living room where she snatched the receiver off the floor, dialed quickly, and spoke in hushed tones to keep me from listening. She tried to keep it short by saying she was late for dinner.

Unsure what I should do, I set the Derek and the Dominoes album down next to all the rest. Many of them seemed like old friends, and when I scanned their titles, fragments of songs and memories sprang to mind. Then back to Derek and "The Key to the Highway."

Leaning back and stretching, with one last glance toward Ronnie, I waved and headed for the door.

She held her hand over the mouthpiece and motioned for me to wait. Her eyes moistened again, but she refrained from saying anything aloud. She would not hang up the phone. I knew my place in her universe had changed minutely, if at all.

As I stepped over the threshold, she whispered under her breath, "What am I going to tell Janice?"

Outside, a dark summer storm threatened with large droplets of rain and deep thunder. So far, it had been a summer of little sunshine, and Binghamton had begun to resemble an ancient city in a rain forest, slowly overgrown with thick vegetation.

I stood next to the curb on State Street and extended my thumb. Tonight had been my first hitchhiking trip since my ride with Joy. Even though my car was running fine, hitchhiking to Ronnie's apartment seemed like the right thing to do, and I was glad to feel the wet air and the uncertainty and promise of my ride back home. Every ride was a new beginning, and tonight I wanted a ride out of the rain, out of the pull of Ronnie's star. One more lucky ride.

About the Author

Terry Tierney is a writer who hails from the Midwest, but has planted roots in the San Francisco Bay Area. After serving in the Seabees, he completed his BA and MA at Binghamton University, and completed a PhD in Victorian Literature at Emory University. He taught college composition and creative writing courses, and survived several Silicon Valley startups as a software engineer. He lives in Oakland with his wife, Michaelyn Burnette, a Librarian from the University of California, their two Persian cats, and their enthusiastic Golden Retriever. Tierney's work has appeared in countless publications. His poetry collection, *The Poet's Garage*, was published in May 2020 by Unsolicited Press. More can be learned at http://terrytierney.com.

About the Press

Unsolicited Press is rebellious much like the city it calls home: Portland, Oregon. Founded in 2012, Unsolicited Press supports emerging and award-winning writers by publishing a variety of literary and experimental books of poetry, creative nonfiction, fiction, and everything in between.

Learn more at unsolicitedpress.com. Find us on Twitter and Instagram.